Passages

Book One: Touch me from Afar

Sandra Wayne

Publisher's Note:

This is a work of fiction. All names, characters, places, and events are the work of the author's imagination.

Any resemblance to real persons, places, or events is coincidental.

Solstice Publishing - www.solsticepublishing.com

Passages: Touch Me from Afar

Sandra Waine

Chapter One

"*Bona sera, signore, parla inglese*?"

"*Si*, signora. How can I help you? Are you checking in?"

The look on the manager's face said it all. The hour was late, near eleven o'clock, and the possibility of erasing that frown from his features seemed impossible. Sam's already frayed nerves shifted into high gear.

"Well, I'm hoping to. I just can't seem to locate a room. I tried several along the plaza. I realize it is very late, but could you possibly help me? Venice is busy with large tourist groups. Or, so I have been told over and over and well…"

"*Signorina*," he interrupted, "I wish I had better news for you. But we find ourselves in the same situation you have previously encountered elsewhere on this night."

"Please, it's *Signora* Arnesen, Samantha Arnesen. Anything you have will be perfect. A closet or even a bench." She swept her hand around the room. "I am not particular given the late hour."

Eyes beseeching, she leaned closer. "I can't go back out there; it is so late. I know it's not your fault. It is entirely my own. But, if nothing truly exists, would you permit me to find a corner and make some calls and check around with other establishments? I will be quiet as a mouse." Clasping hands tightly, her voice quivered. "For you see I am at a desperate point now, *signore*."

Crooking his head slightly, she felt a spark of hope arise. He spun around, hands flailing, speaking rapid Italian to a perky young lad sporting a crisp white and black uniform, who seemed to have appeared from thin air.

As the lad turned and dashed off, the beat of her heart collided with the breath in her lungs. It was deja vu all over again.

"*Signore*, pardon the intrusion. I could not help but overhear the lady's distress and wondered how I could be of help. Allow me to suggest a reasonable solution that should be agreeable to everyone."

Paralyzed, Sam found it difficult to breath. The only part that did move was her lower lip as his midnight blue eyes locked with hers.

"*Signore* Riozi." The handsome stranger addressed the manager. "I can move into the small room I stayed in previously. I know it's vacant. I am only here for the night, so I will give my room to the *signora*. If you agree, I shall return in less than ten minutes for that key and will leave mine."

Her eyes never left his features while that deep, penetrating voice surrounded the air she was trying to breath. She shook her head. Did he just say something else? Immobile, her mind drifted to her ex-husband. Never would he have performed such a gallant act as this, woman in distress or not. He was selfish head to toe.

Unable to avoid it, her eyes raked him from top to bottom. The gray, tailor-made, designer suit was snug around his shoulders. A soft sigh escaped her lips. She housed no doubts that beneath it all was a masterful and strong physique. Sam's imagination took flight as his voice faded off into the distance.

He was standing to close to her. But she could not move away as distant memories came back to haunt her. An ancient call to prayer, the winds rustling the reeds on the banks of a wide river, a camel's grunt.

Then there was silence. A darkness in her mind as reality rose from the past to present. His eyes shone bright, then turned dark. She swayed suddenly toward him.

As her knees buckled, his strong hands were there.

"Are you okay? Here, come and sit. Surely you are exhausted from tonight's ordeal. Rest, while I go and pack. Just give me a few minutes, then you can be comfortable for the night."

A feeling of knowing this handsome stranger made her spine tingle. Did he feel it too or was she just overtired from the train trip earlier today? Perhaps she had pushed it a bit much with jamming a long hike and a cycle into the countryside into her last day in France. Yes, she was convinced. It was just too much. The sooner she was tucked away, the better it would be for all.

Glancing at his retreating back, she felt like a manner-less idiot at not letting him know how much she appreciated his assistance. Indeed, he had come to her rescue. Fumbling in her cross-body bag for a tissue, a wave of anxiety and excitement coursed through her veins still feeling his warm, strong touch.

Signore Riozi had been standing there a few seconds eyeing her skeptically.

"*Signora* Arnesen, here is your key. Would you like Luigi to help with the bag?"

She reached up and took the old-fashioned key, moving it around in her hand. "What floor am I on?"

"*Sette*, room *settantasette.* It's a fine room; you will like it. Fresh sheets are on the bed and linens in the bathroom. If you need anything else just ring the desk."

Just like that he was finished with her. But the hour was very late and she could not blame him for wanting to finish up his night.

"*Mi scusi, signore*, but where is the gentleman that is taking my room? I wanted to thank him appropriately."

"Luigi already met him upstairs and gave him his key. If you request, I will be sure to extend your gratitude when he checks out tomorrow. *Buona notte*."

She rose clutching the key while lifting the bag.

Damn, I am tired, she thought. I can't remember what room he said I am in. Great, I will just wander the halls.

She grinned reviewing the now vacant reception area. Glancing down she chuckled, smiling gingerly at the two sevens on the key.

"Right, got it. Seventh floor, room seventy-seven. Come on, Sam, you can make it."

The bellboy peered out from behind the desk, watching her get onto the single elevator, relieved she was not in need of assistance.

Locating the room, she unlocked the door and entered. Was this for real, she thought, assessing the two lovely large rooms suitable for a couple, or one very handsome man. All the same, it was a bit much for her tastes.

"My gosh," Sam said aloud. "He gave up a suite for me. I must be hallucinating. I need that bed and pillow now."

Throwing the bag up on a chair, she took out her things and wandered to the bathroom marveling at the exquisite marble tiles with sparkling gold everywhere. She stopped, pressing the side of her head against its coolness.

"Sam, you have to get your shit together." She mumbled to no one. Then took the last two steps towards the pedestal sink, washing her face and brushing her teeth.

Then something strong stirred inside her mind.

A voice.

It sounded like his but echoed with another.

Her fingers lifted, touching the mirror, noticing how bright her eyes shown back in the reflection. Yes, her thoughts had wandered back to a different time long ago. A place from the past long ignored. Shaking her head slightly, she picked up all the items, placing them back into the bag.

Climbing into the bed, tugging the fluffy, down comforter beneath her chin, Sam was suddenly afraid to close her eyes.

Would he haunt her again tonight?

The voice with no face attached; the one that sounded so much like the man who had been in here. Heavy lids won out as her brain finally shut down. At last, she slept.

A loud pounding at the door nearly sent it off the hinges making her jump. Biting a hand to hold back a scream, she momentarily sat there staring at it. Quickly glancing at her bag, she wondered if perhaps it was the attendant from the front desk and she had left her credit card in error. Slowly, she got up. Walking over, keeping the dead bolt slid in place, she opened it only as far as the chain allowed.

Two men dressed in dark suits were standing there. Fear raced throughout her body, while mentally chiding herself for being so stupid. She should have just asked who it was before opening at all.

"Yes?"

"Pardon the interruption, madam, but is *Signore* Weaver here? We believed that this is his room. Perhaps we were given the wrong information?"

Sam looked perplexed. "I do not know who that is. Perhaps the front desk could assist?"

Without awaiting a reply, she closed the door and snapped the deadbolt securely.

Was that his name, *Signore* Weaver? Odd, that would not have been a name she'd associate with this guy at all. Something more old European, rich family money and a long heritage. As she slid into bed, her mind conjured up all kinds of mysteries surrounding him.

"Whatever," echoed around the large rooms, "I'll never set eyes on him again. Tomorrow I move on and will leave this behind."

She grinned, squishing the pillow, and settled her weary head down onto its softness. Many hailed Venice as one of the most romantic cities in Italy. Yawning, the smile faded as lids slid down, while she rolled over and drifted off to sleep.

Early the next morning Sam stretched languidly, happy it had been an uneventful rest of night. Rested and refreshed, she was relieved no one else had come knocking. Just as the sun was drifting in through the open shutters, she rose, showered, dressed, and repacked the few items removed last night. Grabbing her bag, she hurried along hoping to find him before he left. She'd made up her mind. She wanted to pay for the difference in the rooms, knowing that was the very least she could do. If he was already gone, she'd ask the clerk to refund his card the difference.

Sliding the key up onto the beautiful mahogany counter, the lobby was quiet. Shrugging when no attendant came out, she swung the tote up to a shoulder and rolled the other bag behind her in the direction of a delicious smell. They would have breakfast staff and someone would be able to help her. Along a narrow lantern lit corridor, she continued, reaching the entrance.

La Calcina's sumptuous breakfast was served overlooking the *Guidecca* Canal. Sam smiled, surveying the beautiful surroundings of this third-generation hotel, restored to its grand splendor of years past. Surveying it further, it was a bit too romantic for her single stay. Setting her bag down, she pressed hands to the windows imagining his face in the reflection back.

"You are up early."

She did not have to even look up to know who it was. Afraid of what she may do this time. Perhaps she'd just melt into a puddle on the floor right at his shiny, Italian leather shoes. Or, continue to appear like an idiot with no command of the English language.

Shaking her head slightly, common sense and her voice returned.

"I'm glad you are still here. I wanted to give you the difference in our rooms. I'm sure yours were a hefty cost compared to where you ended up. If you would be so kind to let me know the amount?"

Heaven please help me, she prayed, having managed to get that all out before his dark gorgeous eyes swallowed her up.

"Was it okay? You don't seem any worse for the wear this morning."

He chuckled.

"It was small," he admitted. A smile spreading across his full lips. "But absolutely suitable."

Sam stepped closer subconsciously placing a hand on his arm feeling the softness of his silk dress shirt.

"Honestly, nice gesture that it was, it does not feel proper paying for less and getting more.

He grinned, eyes boring into her very soul. Her brows drew in, not able to look away as he kept her captive for several seconds.

"I have a different thought on that. I want to make sure you remember what I did. Who I am. So, I'll claim payment in a somewhat offhanded manner. It appears I have a point to prove this morning and only you can help me with it."

She had no idea what the hell he was talking about.

With that, he pulled her into his strong chest, lowered his head and stole a long, sweet kiss. Then turned and walked away.

As she leaned against the dark paneled wall, feeling its coolness with the palms of both hands, Sam watched him leave.

She touched her lips. Yes, they were still warm as a satisfying smile appeared. Sliding her bag under a table, she noticed she was completely alone as the waitress approached.

"*Buon giorno, signora*, coffee, tea?"

"Tea, *grazie*."

After helping herself to the buffet, Sam shot down the last of her tea, paid the bill, and then headed out into the back alley, met by a brilliantly sunny day in Venice. Where to? She had planned on staying here just a day. Keeping that in mind, there was time for one major sightseeing excursion. Then the late train to Milano would be in order.

Knowing exactly where she wanted to go, she approached the *Basilica dei Frari* as excitement coursed through her blood. Loving to get off the beaten path, Sam had read a short online article about the history of this basilica and the strange goings on that had been recorded over the years. Intrigue filled her thoughts.

Stopping to let a small group of school children pass by, she glanced up and spotted him engaged in conversation with the two men. The very same that had visited her room last night. Their new addition was a friar. Her mind reeled. Who was this rogue who had stolen a kiss? Now he seemed draped in further mystery.

Was he here on business or living here? Was she frigging crazy, she pondered, stopping to hide behind Japanese tourists. Invisible to discovery but close enough to eavesdrop, she listened intently to their hushed Italian conversation picking up only a few words.

As they dispersed, the two men accompanied her handsome stranger inside the Basilica. How coincidental it was that they were heading in the same general direction? Lifting the bag, Sam entered, watching them head down the long nave toward the front altar. Strange, she thought, watching them. They were assessing the place. Why? As a pulsating force coursed throughout her body.

As she moved back, bringing them into vision, they disappeared toward the left side of the altar towards a small cluster of confessionals.

Wait a minute, her mind screamed. What exactly do you think you are doing? Would he appreciate you stalking him like this? An internal voice rose strongly up. *Sam, get over yourself.*

Yet as this brain battle was going on, a shiver spooked the hairs on the back of her neck and arms simultaneously. Moving behind a pillar and out of sight, she listened in squashing that pragmatic voice.

Their words were faint but she could make out English and Scottish accents. But, it was just not clear enough to distinguish the full conversation from this distance.

Then it dawned on her. At the *Pensione* he had spoken in perfect American English. Ear turned, she honed in. Yes. Indeed, that was his voice. Placing a packet inside his suit jacket, the men exchanged handshakes as they left heading toward the rear entrance. She stuck her nose out briefly. It was the two from last night. Confirmed.

Then everything turned bizarre.

Out of the corner of an eye, a priest appeared from behind a lovely, hand painted, three-dimensional screen depicting the Resurrection. Patting the handsome stranger's back, they exchanged smiles and entered adjoining confessionals. She moved closer and glanced around nervously. But all she heard were muffled voices. As the priest's door opened, Sam turned looking away as he walked toward the main altar. She stood there, waiting, thinking he was praying, or something. Feeling foolish and awkward, she removed her camera and took a few photos, all the while staying close to that all important confessional door.

Pulling out her cellphone and checking the time, it had been over fifteen minutes since he'd gone in there. Was that unusual? She started to laugh softly into the nave. Maybe he had a lot to atone for. She chuckled harder drawing glances; perhaps he did indeed. Brazenly she walked over and knocked gently on the door.

There was no answer.

An about face was in order and right now. Surely, he must have come out while she was locked in thought or taking pictures and had missed him. Then again, what the hell would she do once she found him? Ask him why he had kissed her?

Strangely enough, a voice inside her head urged her on, to go ahead, open the confessional door. See for herself. Or embarrass them both by interrupting a very private moment. Eyeing the confessional at length, a voice loomed over her shoulder followed quickly by the face of the priest. His eyes pierced her soul and in that instance she truly felt like an idiot. Anxiously, she glanced about for the fastest exit.

"That one is empty, *Signorina.* Go on in. I'll be with you shortly."

Then there it was. The moment of truth. Did she dare do it just to prove some stupid point? Smarter yet would be to shrug it off and leave. This was her chance to flee. He did not know who she was. Oh, fuck it, nearly came out of her opened mouth. Knuckles white, fingers wrapped tightly around the knob, Sam walked in rolling the bag. Then set it down at her feet. Leaning over, she closed the door.

A hint of his cologne remained in the air. How had he come out and she was unaware? She could have sworn her eyes never moved off this confessional for more than a couple of seconds in a row. Minutes passed. Where was the priest? How long had it been? She refrained from taking out her cellphone to check again. That would be rude. Especially if he was opposite waiting for her to speak.

Then the other confessional door creaked. She heard sounds of shuffling and could faintly make out his silhouette.

Voice crackling with nervousness she began.

"Father, I've not done this in fifteen years. I am sure. Where do I even begin? Do you need to know I am divorced, but never married in a Catholic Church? I don't really remember the prayer I'm to use to start all this." She stopped feeling like a fool and gathered her thoughts. "I have to be honest, father. The only reason I am here is to inquire about the man you were speaking with earlier. I know you may not be able to tell me much, but is there anything you can?"

Taking a breath, she wondered why he had not said a word.

"Father?"

A door creaked then it was silent again.

"Anyone?"

Relief washed over her. It must have been a tourist just peering inside then moved along.

"That was close." Opening the door, she stood for a second then rolled the bag out in front of her. Suddenly whispers and stares were all around.

Sam's few minutes of enjoyment at her verbal dialogue with the non-showing priest was short lived. Feeling more than ridiculous, she was glad she had not found him. Really, she had been stalking him. A slight blush cased her cheeks as she smiled to no one except herself. As she glanced around the smaller church, her stomach tightened.

What the hell was going on?

Nudged suddenly by a passing nun, who apologized softly, Sam's apprehension exploded noticing she had twitched her head to one side as if silently showing the right way out. Her hand met the coolness of the large stone pillar, as it penetrated through her skin.

This was not the *Basilica dei Frari*. The women and men speaking in hushed tones all around her were not Italian at all.

They were every bit British.

Stunned, she looked back at the confessional. Was this a dream? Had something happened to her sanity? Was she still at the *Pensione* safe in that nice room? Would her eyes flutter and she was tucked on a sofa having not been able to secure one? Was he a fantasy as well?

Sam pinched the top of her hand, wincing, feeling it acutely along with a tingling apprehension. Had that nod meant something, telling her to move on? But to where? Had the nun meant to do that? Thoughts jumbled together making no damn sense. Nor did the fact that the next person who went to open the same confessional door halted, finding it locked.

Locked? Yes as she watched the same man try one next to it with the same results. Turning, he walked away but not before engaging her in a smile. She was losing it now. First the handsome stranger, the priest, the nun, and now this guy. Fresh air. Yes, she needed to get outside. Eyes brimming with tears at not being able to understand this at all, she tugged the bag along as the whispers increased.

"What?" She bellowed towards a woman staring her. Who turned anxiously and hurried away. Sam closed in quickly on the nearest exit as people moved aside providing a clear channel out. To let the crazy woman out.

Chapter Two

Sliding the handle of the wheeled bag down and securing it from sight, Sam lifted it up and carried it out of the church. Stopping, her eyes gingerly shifted down to the hem of her long dress. Setting her bag on the ground, she hesitantly lifted it up a few inches stunned at what was on her feet. Boots, very gentile, leather boots.

She softly mouthed, “What the fuck…?”

The dress slid from fingertips as a horse drawn carriage halted a few yards away. As if being pulled over by some unknown force, Sam walked over as a door pushed out.

“You look at bit disoriented. Is this an unexpected visit? Perhaps you should come on in and sit. I may be able to help you.”

Silence prevailed. The words would not come as Sam stood rooted for several minutes taking in the street scene. Finally, one of the stranger’s sentences penetrated her confused mind. Only one sentence made it. Is this an unexpected visit? Disbelief shadowed her features. Then in the upheaval, she heard it again.

“Madam.”

Sam reached down and picked up her bag, as a simple gloved hand extended out helping her into the carriage. Sliding a hand over the soft leather, her eyes finally rose to the woman.

Smartly attired, the lady’s eyes seemed kind giving Sam short-lived comfort.

“Nice piece of luggage you have there. Now, where can I give you a lift to?”

The woman banged on the top of the carriage as the horses jolted, moving them forward while pushing Sam further back onto the seat.

"I don't know exactly where I am. I know that sounds strange, but I only just arrived." Trying to calm her frayed nerves, Sam glanced down, opening the small bag in her lap. British pound notes and coins filled it.

"What the hell happened to me?"

The woman reached over, patting her hand. Sam pulled back sharply, fear clear on her white face.

"Love, don't worry. You seemed very flustered. I can help you. Don't try to figure anything out right now. Once we reach the estate, I can help clear some things up for you. For now, just sit back and try to relax."

The rocking motion of the coach was somehow soothing as Sam listened to the hooves hitting the dirt road.

"This is real. I am not in some dream having bumped my head in that *Basilica*." she mumbled. "All because I wanted to know more about... Oh, well. I guess that's just not important now."

"Yes, you should not have followed him. But, I think there is more at work here than we both understand right now. The fact is you did. Now we figure out what's next and how to deal with it. He will need to deal with it."

"He? He is here and you know of whom I am speaking?"

"He sure is, and, Samantha?"

Sam's head swung around facing the woman.

"You know my name?"

"Yes. That and a bit more. Try and stay calm. Answers are not going to come as fast as you want. All the same, it's important to stay rational until you do know more. Don't worry, I'll help you to make sense of this. Now, if you continue to fret, your head will hurt more than it may already. Possibly until you have taken a few more passages. It affects us all in different ways, passing through. Just close your eyes and rest."

"Passing through? Am I dead and this is what it's like?"

She laughed, a soft comforting sound to Sam's ears.

"No, you are quite alive, my dear. More alive than you have been since your existence. Enough. Now let those lids drop."

"Just one more question, please? Well two. Who are you? I recognize you as the nun that bumped me in the *Basilica* back in Italy. But, how are you here?" She paused, reflecting. "Oh, I understand. You came through after that to be here to help. I get it. So, what is his name then?"

"You are an observant one, I must say. Which is quite refreshing compared to whom I sometimes assist. I am Mrs. Hoyt. The main housekeeper for Lord Adam Griffin, the sixth Earl of Ard Aulinn."

"Oh, my, a real Earl. I thought they did away with those titles long ago? Anyway, never mind." Realizing by her attire she was not back in 2015, nor did Mrs. Hoyt acknowledge being the nun. "Where is the estate?"

"You did say two questions, Samantha. But I'll give you one more answer. Then enough for now. It lies outside the village of Chester, near the Welsh border."

Sam smiled, feeling slightly more comfortable and settled back internally acknowledging the housekeeper's firm tone. But then nearly jumped from her seat again.

"But wait! Can't I just go back into the church and transport back to Venice? I know the man after you could not open the confessional door. It was locked. Maybe now it would open?"

Mrs. Hoyt patted her hand. "No, child, you are here for a reason. We have to figure that out before you go anywhere else."

Sam sat back and let the swaying motion of the carriage lull her into a more agreeable state of mind. It was better than another option of freaking out. As it came to an abrupt stop jolting her forward, Mrs. Hoyt's arm prevented her from hitting the seat across.

"Damn, this is not a dream. I am here. Shit."

"I beg your pardon. But, you had better watch your tongue around the men. Hearing it as such may arouse more attention than bargained for. They will think you are a tavern wench speaking such foul language." Mrs. Hoyt's eyes were ablaze. Not with condemnation, rather mirth.

Sam bore no apology. "Are we there?"

"Indeed, we are. Now come along and quietly. Bring your bags and follow closely. We are maneuvering around the rear of the estate in a roundabout manner. This way, I can get you into the room unnoticed."

Shuffling along at a snail's pace, the man appeared by Sam's perusal to sport quite a limp. She had to wonder if it was caused by old age or by battle. Winding up the uneven slippery stone steps, holding a torch, they continued behind until they reached a large, medieval, wooden door. It was cold, damp and housed the smell of piss and mustiness, nearly causing Sam to wretch as they stopped.

The man disappeared as Mrs. Hoyt reached into her heaving bosom, expanding rapidly from the exertion, and produced a large skeleton key. Ironically, it resembled the one Sam had held just hours before at the *Pensione La Calcina.*

She swept aside, whispering, "Get on, woman, now hurry." Sam moved through as the large door creaked shut. "We have to keep our voices very low. Set those bags over near the bed and let's get you into it. We can talk tomorrow. Tonight, you must stay here. Bolt the door after I leave or you may find yourself woken during the night by a lost and lonely drunken soldier."

Glancing about at the simplicity of the room, she had to wonder who stayed here. The blazing fire warmed it into coziness, with softly lit candles producing dancing shadows about the room. The four-poster bed looked inviting enough and comfortable. She could hardly wait to climb in and see if maybe in the morning she would wake up someplace outside of Venice, laughing that she must had drank too much wine the night before and did not remember a thing on her train journey to *Milano*.

"I'll leave you to your thoughts, Samantha. I'll bring your breakfast early. When you hear my raps, open up straight away."

"Sounds fine, Mrs. Hoyt. I assure you I'll be up and about if I even sleep tonight. Would you prefer I call you Mrs. Hoyt or something more formal?"

Mrs. Hoyt laughed softly, eyes amused. "Mrs. H will do. Then you will fit right in as everyone else does. Now, go about your business and do as I have said. There is someplace I must be." Silently she moved from the room checking the handle to make sure Samantha had engaged the sturdy iron lock into place.

"Son of a bitch," Sam whispered, bolting the door then turned abruptly straight into the corner of a dresser with her right hip. For a few seconds it hurt like bloody hell. "Dammit, I really thought this was a dream, but that smarted. Reality check, I guess. Now, what do I wear to bed?"

Her curiosity won over as she pulled open a dresser draw and out a linen nightgown. She changed and was relieved to wash off the day's dirt and make-up from her face using the pitcher and bowl.

Opening the tote, she pulled out face cream and applied it liberally. The room was too warm and dry, but she dared not see if the windows opened. That would entail pulling aside the heavy drapes and could pose a threat. If anyone outside was curious, they may indeed wander up here to investigate. Extinguishing all the candles, firelight washed the room with a soft glow as she burrowed under the blankets, marveling in how soft they were, then drifted off to sleep.

***

Meanwhile, Mrs. Hoyt quietly worked her way back outside through the nearly silent Great Hall. Tonight, there were only a handful of passed out soldiers, who had indulged in too much alcohol. Moving along, listening to snores, she passed through two long corridors before closing and locking a door behind. Now she was back in the main house.

Hand raised, she knocked on his library door then without hesitation, entered.

"What happened? Why were you delayed?" His voice was curt as he glanced at her briefly, acknowledging with his eyes an apology of sorts. She knew something was clearly bothering him.

A hunch formed in her mind. "You seem irritated. Did your day not go as scheduled?"

He shook his head. "It went just as planned." His eyes glazed over, but he was to smart to let her see to much. Regardless she was fully aware something was amiss. He had always been a stubborn lad, so the time of toying with him would be short lived.

"We have an unexpected visitor, my lord. I waited after you rode off on your mount as something delayed me from following straight away."

"Go on."

"A lady came out of the church within minutes of your departure. Standing there dazed and confused."

"Not another transient. Did you get her moving along?"

She watched his face intently. "No, she's here. Came through the church door directly to my carriage and I knew. She's up in the Lancaster Tower Wing. I'll find out more in the morning. I wanted you to know."

"Do you have a name? Where she's headed? What's her reason is for being here?"

"Not much to go on right now. Clearly, she is new. I could tell that straight away. Dressed properly enough though. But one thing stood out clearly. She handled a very expensive bag that does not belong in our era. *Italian* to be sure. From the future."

"Is she?"

"No, she's British and quite comely, I must say. All I've received in advance is her first name. It's Samantha."

Silence permeated the room.

Staring up at the Lancaster Tower Wing, his head moved slightly.

"Find out what you can in the morning. I ride to Shrewsbury for a meeting with the Duke. I may be a day or two. I'll expect more details upon my return."

Hand on the knob, she nodded.

"I will find out what we need to know, Lord Adam. Are you okay?"

He ran his hand through thick hair. "Yes, why do you ask?"

She scrutinized him carefully. "Just making sure." As she waited on a reply.

"Mrs. H, bring her into the house. I don't think that's an appropriate place up there for her."

She smiled softly closing the door. This time it was different. She could feel it. Something electrifying was in the air. With a heightened sense of alertness, she sauntered down toward the kitchens then beyond into her rooms.

This was not the first time a woman had followed him back. But she was always kept tucked away in the Tower until things concluded. Then sent along on her way. Yes, this was getting interesting. She was looking forward to Lord Griffin and Samantha's first face to face meeting here. What had the young buck done now? Moving on, grin spreading with each step, Mrs. H knew the tides had indeed changed. That this time he'd get his just due from that lady tucked away up in the Tower.

Chapter Three

A persistent rapping rattled Sam out of the chair and dashing for the wooden door. Up early and settled into a pretty day dress, she opened it up to a stern look on Mrs. H's face as she rushed in with tray in hand. Sam slid the lock firmly back into place.

"Good morning, Samantha, come and sit. Let's get you fed while we chat. I have a lot of things to take care of today. So, we need to figure out what we can in short order. Then get moving on what's next for you."

"Is he here?"

"You can start by calling him Lord Adam. No, he left at sunrise on business and will be back in a few days."

"Okay. Well, I have a lot of questions. Can you tell me how my clothes changed between the confessional in Venice and that church? Also, how my bags came with me? I checked them this morning and I have everything I had there. But this is strange, I also have a small purse with lots of English currency in it."

"Hm. That is interesting and perplexing. I must admit. I've seen dozens come through over the years. But you have me puzzled Sam. You are different than the others and I need to figure out why. I wonder if your purpose is more complex than what I am familiar with? We may need some outside guidance. Don't you agree?"

Sam looked confused. "You are asking the wrong person, but I understand what you are saying. What others are you referring too?"

"Okay." She grabbed her warm hands. "This may take a bit to digest. All I ask is that you are patient until I am through. Are you ready?"

"Yes, go ahead."

"There are special people who can move between time and space. We are referred to as old souls. We do not question how or why, but we know we have a purpose in being here. You for instance, came with the appropriate clothing. But, also traveled with baggage from your era. That's unusual. It has never happened on my watch before. That makes me wonder if you are going to be able to return at will. I guess we are going to have to wait that one out."

Sam disengaged one hand and put it to her forehead. Closing her eyes, she hoped it would do the trick; when she opened them, she would be back in Italy or even better England. Her true England.

It did not work.

"How much money is in that purse?"

"Not counting the coinage, there is about eleven thousand pounds in notes. That seems like a lot for this time frame. But it means I have plenty to take up a room at the local inn until we get to the bottom of this."

"I'll let his Lordship decide when he returns. Do you have any ties with family history in this period?"

"I don't know, probably. I think we all do. But I don't even know what year we are in."

"Eighteen-hundred and sixty-five. Among your travels in Italy, or before, did you meet anyone that may have said anything to you that made no sense. Perhaps it makes sense now that you are here?"

That brought out a laugh. "I chat with a lot of people along my travels. It helps to pass time since I go alone."

"We may not get too far, Sam. It may take a while for more of the puzzle to unravel. We need to strategize. A story as to why you are here to prevent any unwanted nosing about by gossip mongering locals. How old are you?"

"Forty-four. Mrs. H. I'm no spring chicken."

She smiled. "You look younger than that. His Lordship has eight years on you, if it be of interest." They shared a grin.

"We will keep it simple. You are the spinster daughter of a friend who passed away last year. That is easier than having a husband and children in lieu of the circumstances. This allows free rein of the estate. Just keep yourself clear of the stables and the soldiers. Queen Victoria has a garrison on the border of England and Wales. Often they pass through to water their horses and spend a night or two along their journey to London. His Lordship is well received at Court, so they are welcome here."

"Mrs. H how many of us are there around here?"

"I know of only a handful. For hundreds of year's stories have been handed down. Some say a few of us go back to Egyptian times. Are you familiar, Sam, with ancient Egypt?"

She shook her head, eyes large and bright.

"It was the birthplace of the original Nine Gods of Egypt, Isis being one of them. Surely you've heard of her?"

"Ah, yes, of her I have. But I still do not understand; am I an old soul? Are you?"

"Yes, dear. It seems we have a lot of work to do before we can complete all our earthly tasks and move on for good. Anyway, let me continue. As far as I know, we never work knowingly with each other and rarely discuss where we have been. You need to be very careful. Although the witch trials and tribulations have long passed, there are those that are here to block our progress, trying to affect history in a different way."

"So, I affect history?"

"No, to assist. Often, we are passing documents, providing money, securing a passage or assisting in a recovery. It could be as simple as a nun nudging you, if you know what I mean."

Sam eyed her recalling that nun's habit.

"You need to always remember one important thing. If you affect a historical moment, it will alter your life as well. You and others of historical importance may never exist after that. So be very careful."

Sam shuddered, having not even given that possibility a thought,

"Holy shit. So, it's basically go in, get the job done and get out? How do you know where to transport and when to transport next?"

"That's going to be tricky for you. What year did you come in from? I came through so quick I was not sure."

"Twenty-fifteen."

"You did follow Lord Adam out of Italy after all. I thought you may have." She smiled figuring out a bit more. Deciding that was enough for now, Mrs. H asked one more question. "Did you have family there?"

"An ex-husband, that's it. Both my parents have passed away. I was an only child. Any distant relatives are just that. We have no contact."

"Okay, then I'm going to move you into the main house. Pack up your bags and come with me. I'll have more time this afternoon to show you around the grounds. Until then you are free to roam."

She picked up the serving tray. "Where did you live in England?"

"Exeter. I had a small cottage outside the city and when my mother passed, I retired early to travel. I've been divorced for quite a few years. It's probably stupid to think that I could just hire a carriage, grab up my things and just go, right?"

"Oh, you can do that, dear. But you will be in 1865 and not 2015, so it won't matter."

"This is so frustrating, Mrs. H."

"Come on now, let's get you re-settled. Soon a trip to town will be in order to purchase a suitable wardrobe. The clothes kept in that room were for a few of his Lordship's former mistresses. I doubt you want anything to do with those."

Sam closed the door behind, scowling. So, indeed he was a rogue after all. That explains why he stole that kiss from her and then disappeared. Well, one thing was clear. Under his roof or not, until she figured out why the hell she was here, he'd not lay another finger on her. As they moved down the tower and outside into the courtyard, she had her first real glimpse of the expansive estate.

"Mrs. H, holy... Ah, my goodness. This is not just a home. Hell, a person could go missing for days and no one would be the wiser."

"True it may take some adjusting. But it is yours until we figure things out. Another benefit of staying is that you should not have any trouble avoiding certain people, if that is your desire." She was toying with the lady and enjoying it as much as she had the Master.

Catching that look Sam contemplated what the housekeeper was hiding. It was plain as the nose on her face it was something. As they entered the rear of the house, the eccentric interior reminded her of artwork she'd seen at the Victoria & Albert Museum in London. She'd enjoy staying and exploring centuries of statues, wall hangings and furniture.

A servant took the tray from Mrs. H as they ascended one the staircases, then a second, before she swung down a long wide corridor opening a set of double wide, wooden doors.

"Here you go. I'm sure his Lordship will not mind you in this wing. It's opposite his which are down the other side. Normally only guests are housed here. We don't have any this time of year, so you will have plenty of freedom."

Sam set her bags down mesmerized by how large the rooms were. Quite grander than her humble cottage back in Exeter.

"I don't need this much space. Although it is quite lovely. I would prefer something smaller. So, if you do not mind." Sam turned, speech halted. Mrs. H had already departed and the doors tightly shut.

Okay, so she was on her own now. Quickly, she unpacked and headed out, laughing inwardly, sorely tempted to leave a trail along the hall toward the staircase so she'd know the way back later. Sam was quite sure, walking along all the handsomely painted faces of the current Lord's ancient relatives, that many were in conspiracy smiling down at her. Believing she was totally nuts, she moved on.

Tucked in her small lady's reticule was her Fuji camera and some of the money. With a spring in her step, she suddenly spied a young housemaid moving about.

"Excuse me. How far are we from Chester by foot?"

The perky young maid looked at her with clear anxiety. Sam was quick to realize by that review what it appeared like. She was one of his lordships mistresses gone astray inside the estate. She pursed her lips to hide a smile.

"Oh, miss, pardon me. I walk from town every day. I know it's about two miles each direction. You can leave out the back of the kitchens through the field. Just keep going. You will come right into the greens at Chester. When you return, if you need assistance finding your way back to the tower, let anyone in the kitchen know and they will help you."

"You probably have not been told by Mrs. Hoyt since I just arrived, that I am visiting. I will be staying in the West Wing while I am here. Anyway, thank you for your assistance. Is there any shopping, lady's shops specifically, that you may suggest I visit?"

Sam knew it would be shocking of a true lady of the time to ask a servant for such information, but she did not give a fig right about now.

"Why, yes, my uncle runs a shop there."

"Well, then, that's settled, I shall go pay him a visit. And your name is?"

"Molly, miss."

The servant nodded, curtsied, then abruptly hurried off a bit red in the face.

Oh crap, was she not to have spoken to her at all? No, probably not. Sam knew history like the back of her hand, like who reigned and where, but as for estate etiquette, well, that was a different story. Most of the novels she could recall from her twenties involved men removing women's clothing and clandestine meetings.

She was laughing as she pressed on.

Twenty minutes later she arrived to the lower floor kitchens noticing Mrs. Hoyt was doing paperwork. Others were milling about prepping food, canning vegetables, plucking the feathers off a pheasant as she approached.

"I'm going for a walk into town. Is that okay? I've received instructions on the best route." She kept her voice low.

"Fine. Watch for darkness if you take the field and be back before the sunset."

Nodding, Sam left through the side door and was outside on the path heading to Chester as a sudden quiver ran from shoes to head. Was she alone? Whistling, she spun around and nearly hit the chest of a tall man of the cloth.

"Good day to you, mistress. That's a lively tune you were whistling. It's a shame we never hear more women in our society having such confidence to do it in public."

His comment did not go unnoticed by Sam.

"It appears we are headed in the same direction. Do you mind if I join you?"

"Not at all father, please do. I'd welcome the conversation along the way."

"Are you staying at the Earl's estate?"

"Yes, I am visiting a friend of my mother's, Mrs. Hoyt. I just arrived last night."

"Where are you from?"

"Exeter."

"Did you find your journey here pleasant enough?"

Sam felt it again. A quiver. An important message was passing between them. Was he a contact of some sort? Is that how this works? Get to where you need to be and await instructions; is that what Mrs. H had been alluding too?

"Well, this is me." He held out his large strong hand. "Father Godwin at your service. I think you should come for a visit tomorrow. If you arrive at half-past eleven, we will have plenty of time to chat before I have a later afternoon parish meeting. See you then?"

"Sure, father, I can think of no other who can give me the run-down on the town's goings on than you. To make sure I don't make myself too obvious being new in these parts."

He grinned, nodding, as she extended her hand.

"Samantha Arnesen, father, and thank you. I should like to do that."

Nodding, he disappeared out of sight down the path toward the graveyard and church. Glancing ahead, she saw the green and sighed. It was a lovely, old English village thriving with carriages, horses, people and life. She already felt at home here.

Carswell's Shop housed a large, handsomely decorated, display window with several items of interest lying just inside. Stepping up off the cobbled street, Sam opened the rickety door as a tin bell chimed overhead signaling her arrival.

"Yes, miss, what can I do for you?"

"I was wondering if you may have any day dresses in my size and a riding habit as well that I may see?"

"I believe we do. Come this way. Let's take your measures and see what we can find."

Two hours later, packages loaded on a hired wagon, Sam paid the driver to deliver to the estate as she sauntered through the lovely old medieval town. Dark brown and white Tudor buildings lined each side as Sam appreciated the great beauty of a time that was gentler. No electricity yet, no cellphones or the loud annoying honking of car horns. Yes indeed, this was quite pleasant.

A gentleman and lady came out of a tea shop as Sam thought, well, why not? Sitting alone, it never occurred that it would cause a stir as she sat down at a small table facing the street.

"Tea, mistress?"

"Please. A tray of cakes as well." She smiled to the attendant. How very proper, she thought, sporting a lovely day dress, cute boots, bag, hat and gloves sitting down for a 'spot of tea.' Very English.

Finished, settling the bill and rising, she stepped outside. It quickly became apparent the sun had set. Briskly moving up the hard-packed dirt street, she quickly located the path that headed back through the fields toward the estate. Darkness descended as the glow of gas lights on the property illuminated all the grand buildings.

Slipping through a side door, Sam was out of breath after nearly sprinting up the stairs. Washed up and changed, a quick about face was in order as she headed back down to find the main dining hall. Why was she eating in there if the Lord of the Manor was absent?

Coming down the final flight, she stopped to appreciate the ornate beauty of this level. Tomorrow after visiting with Father Godwin, she'd come back and explore the inside with more thoroughness.

"Mistress, if you do not mind, with the Earl away this evening, Mrs. Hoyt asks me to assist you to a smaller dining area. If you would come this way, please."

Sam startled slightly. Just where had the maid come out of so quickly? Nodding, she followed down a beautiful hall passing lit candelabras gleaming softly against hand carved busts.

"Ah, there you are, Samantha. I hope you don't mind the breakfast room since his Lordship is away. I thought it would be more suitable with just the two of us. Come now, sit so we can be served."

Sam sat down at one of the four place setting.

"Is anyone else joining us?"

"No. It's just the two of us tonight. Sometimes when the Earl's brother is here, or his sister, they like to dine in a less formal atmosphere."

"Thank you for taking care of the shipment of packages. I hope it was no trouble?"

"Not at all dear. I'm happy you found Mr. Carswell's shop. I would guess that all your purchases will be suitable enough for now."

Mrs. H seem to have a well-planned script for all ears that may be near, as Sam hid a smile behind a starched white linen napkin.

"I happened upon Father Godwin along the way to town. He's invited me to visit later tomorrow morning. I hope you did not have plans for me as I readily accepted."

A sharp glance passed between them.

"Absolutely, you will be here for a spell. Making acquaintances will be nice, dear. I hope there will be no gossip about you not being married by your age and all."

Sam giggled, moving her utensils up on the plate as they finished dinner. Rising, taking Mrs. H by the arm, they exited the room,

"Why don't we walk out into the night air before retiring? I do not think it is too chilly." She shut the double wide French doors behind them as they started arm in arm.

"You must be very intuitive tomorrow, Sam, as the good father will have plenty to say, so do pay attention."

"So, he does have something to do with this. I'm seeing a pattern now. First the priest at the *Basilica* in Venice and now Father Godwin." She grinned adding, "I best watch out for those men of the cloth and a good nun or two in following, eh?"

"You hush now, young lady." She laughed softly as well. "Get yourself up to bed and make sure you nod to me on your way out and find me when you return. I just want to know you are back. Unless I hear differently, I fully expect tomorrow night you will dine with the Earl. Best be prepared."

"Woman to woman, Mrs. H, will you give me more details about what type of a man he is? I'd like to be forewarned and forearmed if I can. Remember, I am a modern woman from a modern era."

She patted Sam's arm gingerly.

"Best you discover that yourself so my opinion does not cloud your best judgement of him. Now get yourself along and sleep well."

Sam eyed her skeptically letting it ride for now. It seemed like an eternity before she finally found the correct corridor that led to familiar territory and that soft cozy bed. Lying there with one of the French doors open toward the expansive gardens, she could hear night sounds somewhat similar to her cottage from the future.

The night crickets were chirping a soft repetitive song along with a babbling fountain off in the distance. It reminded her of how much she loved to be outside, free from all and making her own choices. She was indeed a lost soul, or Mrs. H had said an old soul. But she was also a loner and a wanderer.

Then a thought occurred. One thing would remain the same from 2015 to today and that was the farmers market. She'd enjoy going there soon and wandering around aimlessly, getting her feet wet. Meet others. It was nice to not see apartment buildings, sports centers and malls.

As her eyelids finally became too heavy, she heard the sweet song of a lovely songbird out on the balcony nestling inside a weave of ivy. Smiling, that song lulled her into a sound sleep.

Chapter Four

"Father, is all of this for me?"

He chuckled. "Sam, if I may call you Sam? We have this after every Tuesday service, brought in by the lovely ladies of our faith community. Now sit, we have a lot to chat about."

"I think I've figured out some of it. If I may be so bold?"

"Go right ahead. I want to hear all you have to say."

"Passages are used for special people to move something of importance from one location to another. Back in time or ahead. I think it's done at religious sites like the *Basilica* in Venice and the church in Shrewsbury. Is your church part of this as well?"

"I'll answer you all at once. Go on. What else do you think?"

"Well, I came here with all the possessions I had with me back in Venice. Mrs. H says that's unusual. I also have a large sum of money on me in today's currency. I wonder why I came with so much? I had quite a tidy sum stowed away back in 2015."

"Did you bring your purse with you?"

"I did, but I spent a small amount of it yesterday on clothing."

"I want you to take out five thousand pounds and keep the rest in there."

She counted it out, rolled it up and held her hand out toward him.

"Am I here to deliver this to you?"

"Nope. You keep it. I think the best way is trial by fire, so to speak. I'm going to send you on a journey. Are you ready to start?"

Sam was momentarily taken aback. So soon? Then ignored all apprehension forming inside her stomach.

"Okay, I think you are right. Let's get the ball rolling. Yes, I am ready."

"Good. Then the money is for the Iona Abbey. Are you aware of its location?"

"Yes, Scotland, just off the coast. Am I going by a certain route?"

"Indeed, you are. Once there, I want you to wait in the confessional until Father O'Malley comes in. He will speak to you in Gaelic, *Dia Idir Sinn Agus Gach Dochar*, which translated means God between us and all harm."

"That's beautiful. I'll remember that. Do I have any special reply?"

"Yes, *Bealtaine e a rai I gconai*, which means may it always be said. That's it, then you always know who your friend is. If, for some reason, you do not receive that reply, get out. Seek cover and use your wits. An opportunity will always arise providing you with safe cover until you are contacted again. Sam, it's not as easy as it sounds. You are going back in time during the Jacobite uprising. The King's Army is all over the place. If you are stopped, you will need to find a way out. If that happens, there is a secondary passage at *Sithean Mor*, it's…."

"I know it. I've been there. It is the Fairy Mounds."

He smiled. "Yes, you were chosen because you are a smart thinker, have few family ties and are independent in means. If you come back that way you may reappear here in Shrewsbury. Or, someplace close to here. We have no control over that."

"What specifically should I take? Will my wardrobe adjust along the way like it did when I arrived here?"

"The pouch, a dagger or small pistol is always a benefit. Remember you are not there to change history. If you need to delay any pursuer, you must do so with careful thought."

"I understand completely. When do I go?"

"Shortly. Now I need your full attention. This is the most important message I can give. If you end up in a different location than I explained, don't think you are in the wrong country. It means you were rerouted prior to your arrival for a purpose. Normally it is for safety. You still are required to complete your journey to get back. If you do not, you are stuck there until you do. So, it's necessary to find a way. That's why you need to keep that purse private, so if the time or need warrants, you can use it to buy yourself out of any predicament. As we both know, everyone does indeed have their price when it comes to turning a cheek."

"Father, I'm nervous yet excited. Show me where to go and let's do this." Her bravado was rising and she was glad it was squashing the anxiety of what was to come.

"Step into the confessional. But, before you do, are there any last questions?"

She nodded.

"God speed, Sam." With that he closed the door and went about his business inside the church, softly singing Ave Maria.

Thankful that the contents of her bag contained modern day items, Sam sat on the wooden confessional, lifted the dress and fastened a small pistol to one leg and a dagger to the other. Sliding her purse up on her right forearm, she clutched her parasol in her left hand, shoved the door open and stepped out into pouring rain.

Momentarily perplexed, she glanced around the area as rain began to fall dampening her hair. Internally, she was thankful at bringing the parasol along while silently wondering what was next.

She glanced in all directions then looked up at the worn, wooden road sign. Then started the short walk on the Road of the Dead leading toward the Abbey.

The harsh weather and bone chilling wind drove a shiver up her spine as she ditched the parasol, pulling the heavy hood up over her cascading hair. With both hand's free, Sam approached the front entrance with trepidation. Beneath the cloak her breasts were heaving as breathing became labored. Silently, she calmed her frayed nerves and glanced about. Stationed outside was a carriage with four horses. But, where were the soldiers and which side were they on?

The heavy wooden door was slightly open. Silently she slid inside and shook out her hood, but kept it on. Swirling around after hearing voices growing in volume, she watched with increasing trepidation at their quick approach. Shit, she silently thought, it was the King's soldiers. She recalled from past readings of this era they were referred to as the bloody Redcoats. Ruthless cutthroats in his majesty's service.

Suddenly, one was standing at attention before her.

"Oh, I am so happy to see you. I was riding with a small party when my horse lost a shoe. Then to make matters worse, she bolted in this nasty rain. I had no choice but to leave my group to come in here to get dry. They are sending a carriage for me when they get back to our accommodations at *Fhonn Farraig*. I find myself grateful for this respite."

The officer surveyed her top to bottom. "Well, madam, we are at your disposal, of course. In just a few minutes we will conclude our business with the good Father O'Malley. Let me introduce myself, Lieutenant Jarred Banks at your service. We are completing rounds before heading to our encampment. My men have nearly completed our search. If you do wish to engage Father O'Malley, he should be with you shortly."

With a click of his boots, the lieutenant turned and disappeared behind a back door at the rear of the Abbey. She stood by taking a few minutes to gather her thoughts, lower her breathing rate and take in the artistic and historical grandeur of the interior. It was indeed a work of art and a momentary welcomed distraction.

Father O'Malley appeared placing a hand gently upon a shoulder.

"My dear, I heard of your plight. How can I help you?"

"Father, I wonder since I'm here if I may ask you for a quick confession?"

"Of course, dear child. You go ahead in while I'll get my vestibules and be right with you."

Sam went into one of the confessionals and shut the door, quickly lifting her dress. Pulling out the roll of five thousand pounds, she slid it inside the tight bodice of her dress and readjusted the cape. The adjoining door creaked open as he sat in his chair, sliding the small screen over.

"*Dia idir sinn agus gach dochar*."

"*Bealtaine e a ra I gconai*."

She slid the money into his hand which promptly disappeared as he placed the screen back between them. Thoughts of this process came back momentarily; attendance at mass on Sundays was mandatory with her parents.

"Bless me father, for I have sinned."

Suddenly doors swung open on both sides as two soldiers looked towards Sam and the father a bit apologetic.

"Sorry mistress, father. But, the lieutenant beckons you to his carriage. He wishes to extend his services in returning you to your party. He had no idea you were receiving confession. My apologies. Could this wait for another time?"

Rising and nodding to Father O'Malley, Sam knew an alternate plan needed to be put in place as over the soldiers shoulder another man in red was staring at her with something akin to open interest. Her stomach tightened.

"Thank you, father. It appears my confession shall need to be heard another day. Now, soldier, show me the way. I'll not keep your lieutenant waiting any further."

As the carriage door closed and she settled in opposite the commander, she realized this was her golden opportunity to see what she was made of. Adrenalin coursed through her veins, as she had to try and make out the fairy mound with rain streaking her vision off the windows of the coach.

"Are you well, miss?"

"I am, sir, and want to thank you so much for returning me to my group. I also wish to extend my apologies for delaying you. I thought I may take advantage of the good priest and have a confession." She smiled warmly as he returned one of his own. For a split second, something stirred again about that second soldier back inside the church. Had she seen him before? Biting the inside of her mouth, she refocused on this passage.

"Perhaps I did not have that many sins to abolish since I've been on Iona, after all. Such a holy and sacred place."

He chuckled. "It will be a short ride and we will have you back in no time. I thought you may prefer that as well as your friends in having to send someone out in this foul Scottish weather."

"That is very considerate of you." Apprehension churned as she knew it was now or never.

As the carriage swayed she felt a bit nauseous. "Sir," she lifted her gloved hand up to her mouth, briefly shutting her eyes. "Might I impose once again? Could I please be let out, to… well, it's delicate. My stomach is quite upset suddenly. It must have been our picnic earlier on local food brought in from the sea…" She let that trail off, lowering her head slightly.

He banged on the carriage and bellowed, "Halt, stop the coach. The lady needs assistance."

It grinded abruptly as her stomach truly lurched into her throat as she was assisted down.

"If you would but give me two minutes, I will pass over there by that mound and hope to return shortly."

As she walked away, a brisk breeze removed her hood. Not stopping nor caring, she located the largest mound, *Sithean Mor* and moved around the back side. An opening appeared just as she heard voices coming up behind her. It was the Lieutenant and the other soldier getting closer and closer. Quickly stepping in, within a split second she was back in 1865 sitting in the cold interior of Father Godwin's Church of St. James.

Standing, she exited the confessional quite full of vigor with a large smile displayed across her face. The lighting was fair enough with moon beams streaming through the stain glass windows. She reached over and removed a candle, laughing softly.

"Sorry, Lord." she muttered. "I don't know how to even light it."

She placed it back in its holder and felt her way to the side entrance. But, knew the door would be locked with one of those skeleton keys.

She sighed. "I guess I can't send a text to Mrs. H and tell her I will not make dinner. But perhaps I shall make breakfast." Settling into a pew near the front, she curled into a ball. With a satisfied smile and the moonlight streaming down, drifted off into a sound sleep.

Suddenly, someone was shaking her. Really? At this unholy hour?

Faintly, she heard him. "Sam, you are back. Sit up and come to the rectory. We can have tea and then I will bring you to the estate. They must all be wondering where you are by now."

She sat up adjusting her cloak and checked ensuring everything else was where it should be.

"Oh, hello, father, I'm fine. A good night's sleep I had even though your pews are a bit hard. I was warm enough with my cloak."

She rose, smiling at his grin while taking his arm as they left the church. They were sitting inside the warm rectory before he inquired about her journey.

"It went well I can tell. But, you did have to divert?"

Her eyes were ablaze with a voice just as passionate.

"I did, he has it and yes. A plan b was enacted and worked. You were right, I did encounter a small group of soldiers. But all is well. As you can see, here I am."

She grinned tipping back the cup, "But I have to go. I'll walk through the fields. It will give me a chance to digest what just happened. Father, how will I know where and when to go again? I wonder why I did not end up back in Venice."

"Sam, I think you possibly may not be heading back there. If it was the case, you would be there now and not here. Besides, you arrived with all your possessions. There is also one more bit of detail that makes me think you are staying here. For now anyway."

"What's that?"

"I'll let you find out when you get back to the Earl's estate, by which you had better get going now. Mrs. H came herself last night to inquire on you when you did not come back. I did not tell her your passage details, but she was most anxious you were taking one so soon."

"Thank you, father, I'm sure to see you very soon. I appreciate everything you've done for me." She wanted to hug him, but halted, not wanting to overstep any boundaries of propriety.

Quickly leaving, she ran the whole way back. Reaching the rear entrance, she opened it taking the few steps down to the now active kitchens. No one seemed to pay her much attention except Mrs. H.

"Did you enjoy you early morning walk, my dear? Come, I've a tray of tea and crumpets for you in the drawing room. Hurry now, you must be a bit chilled and hungry."

Sam did not dare to try and get two words in edgewise while following along, cape slung over an arm, until they reached the room. Sipping the tea, she took a bite out of a warm, buttery crumpet and sighed. Oh, yes, this was just what was needed. It tasted so delicious.

"We can chat later, dear, but you have a letter that came yesterday from Freedman's Bank in Chester. I thought it may be something urgent for your quick review."

Sam ripped it open as her mouth gaped. It was a request to come into the bank as soon as possible to discuss her draft account balance and possibilities of investing. It matched exactly what was in her account back in Exeter before all this began. Suddenly, her whole world began to tip upside down. Then on top of this detail, his voice once again permeated to her soul.

"Mrs. Hoyt, good morning. You as well, Miss Arnesen. Mrs. H, I wonder if you'd pardon my intrusion and give me a few minutes with our house guest?"

Sam was just tipping back the last of her tea as her hand stopped in mid-stream. His dark eyes locked with hers as a volcanic shiver passed through her frame.

"Miss Arnesen if you are finished, perhaps you'd accompany me so we can engage in a private conversation?"

Chapter Five

It was an eternal walk of what seemed like miles down lengthy corridors as Sam tried to remain calm. To make matters slightly worse, she glanced over and saw that he housed a slight grin on that damn handsome face. Right about then, she wanted nothing more than to just stick her boot out and send him down to the hard, Italian, marble floor.

When they arrived to their destination, he waved her to a chair, helped her sit, then sat opposite. Even though there was distance between them, she could feel the intensity flowing in great strength.

She did not want to look him straight in the eyes right now. Was that even necessary, she thought, suppressing a grin and twisting the top of her day dress into a ball.

"Considering we've known each other for one hundred and fifty years, should I just start with, hey, Sam, what's new?"

She broke out laughing,

"That's a hell of a way to begin our conversation. But, I can tell you, I'm adjusting. Thinking this is really bizarre dream, but I'm going with it for now."

"Mrs. H was a bit put out last night when you were nowhere to be located. She was forced to take action going over to the good father's place to search you out."

"Yeah, well, my cellphone doesn't come in here, so I was in a bit of a pickle, right?"

He laughed. "So, what's your agenda now? Do you want to ride in the *barouche* with me to Chester this morning? I have business at the bank as well. Give us a chance to get caught up, so to speak."

"Yeah, that actually sounds good. I wanted to talk with you about a few things I could use your help with." She rose, placing both hands on the table top for support. "What's good for you?"

"An hour, be out front."

On her way to the rooms, it occurred to her that with all this money at her disposal, she did not need to stay here. Was that part of the design, to find a place of her own? That thought was quickly shrugged off realizing she needed Adam and Mrs. H's guidance until more was revealed.

Then it became clearer.

Changed and back in the large foyer, Sam smiled warmly at the butler as he opened one of the two large wooden doors. Walking out into the warming day, she glanced down feeling positively pretty in her local Victorian attire. Yes, indeed. One would think she was a proper lady.

"Something got your mirth again? Seems like you are about to break into a laugh at any second." He extended a gloved hand toward her assisting her into the *barouche*.

"I kind of feel like that. I have to admit I like the clothes of this period. You know it's funny. When I was a young girl, I loved reading history about this time. It always fascinated me."

He settled beside her as the coach and horses started down the dirt drive.

"It appears all of our backgrounds and interests combine in special ways to assist us in what we do."

"What I find really astounding is how I took care of my first passage. It's also neat how my clothing altered along the way. My British accent was impeccable."

She seemed so amused. Not wanting to burst her bubble so fast, Adam knew he had no other choice. She seemed to be taking it all in stride. He'd never met any soul like her. Was she in shock? He did not think so, but needed to warn her of the ups and downs. What he wondered deep down was how long would she be here? Would she eventually just disappear one day and he'd have no way of knowing where she was, again?

This may be amusing for her, but it was not for him. This was the very reason he had kept mistresses over the years and no long-term relationships.

"Hello? Did I lose you?"

"Just for a second. So, what are your plans now?"

"After the bank, I will know more. I was thinking it may be a better idea to secure my own place. But then again, I don't know how long I'm here. I don't have a clue what's even next. So maybe that's not a great idea. What do you think?"

His brows raised. "Well, are you comfortable with your accommodations in my home so far?"

"Who would not be? It's lovely. To me it's like a true fantasy and it probably is. I wonder what will ensue when the other shoe falls."

"Sam, it will. It has too; it is not all easy. There are many dangers, diversions and, yes, you can throw in a few pleasures too."

"It's just you and I in this carriage with no danger of being overheard. So, I'll be frank. That explains why you have mistresses. I actually get it."

He nearly choked at her bluntness.

"Hey, it's better than even trying to have a long-term relationship and then disappearing all the time and trying to explain to her you are not cheating."

"Okay, from a lady's perspective we'd naturally think you are lying and cheating." But she wanted to say, if you kiss them like you kissed me, we'd hardly care!

"Are you inadvertently asking me if there are any gents like us that I can introduce you too?"

"Nope, not interested just yet. I want to figure things out a lot more than this before I even consider that."

She nudged his shoulder slightly. “How about getting back to my question?”

“About my mistresses?”

“Don’t be an ass, you know what I mean.”

His laughter filled the carriage. “I think you should stay put so we can help you. If you take a place and make friends too fast and then disappear, that may raise the awareness of the local law. If you are here and disappear, we can just say you returned to your home in Exeter or have gone off on your own personal holiday jaunt.”

“That makes sense, but I would like to pay my way and will not take no for an answer. I am a woman of means.”

He crossed his ankles, leaning forward and was met by her very own gloved hand.

“But, Lord Adam, not in the way that was collected previously when you left me in Venice.”

She watched as an arrogant grin appeared on his devilishly handsome face causing her jaw to clench. The air inside the carriage filled with a deafening silence and yes, intimate tension.

“Agreed, why don’t we take care of our banking business and I’ll show you around town before we head back.”

“Sure, that sounds fine. But first I need to know something important. In front of your staff, and in public, how do I actually address you?”

She was right, needing to know what to do to acclimate to 1865.

“Either my lord or Lord Griffin, and I prefer the latter. But when we are alone, Adam will do.”

“Do I curtsey or is that just reserved for higher aristocracy?” He laughed, patting her hand. “Why don’t I let Mrs. H help you out with lady’s etiquette stuff. So I don’t screw it up.”

The carriage pulled to a halt as one of the coachman opened the door and assisted her out. The Earl quickly followed and addressed both men.

"Go have a pint or two. We require about three hours. Meet us at The Red Lion." The coachman nodded as they drove the coach and horses off.

His hand rested at the curve of her back and that slight pressure ripped right through to the other side. They both felt it and knew this was not going to be easy.

"Good morning, Lord Griffin. We were expecting you, so please come this way with your companion." She bristled. Did he always take his mistresses along to the bank? She bit back a snide remark.

"Mr. Jackson, let me introduce you to Lady Samantha Arnesen. She is in possession of a letter from your establishment regarding her accounts. She's a guest at Ard Aulinn, so I hope you do not mind I brought her in with me today without an official appointment."

Yeah, she thought, extending her hand in a firm grip, surprising the banker.

"Lady Arnesen, yes, of course. Let me get you settled with my partner, Mr. Hanlon, straight away. He will be happy to discuss all the options with you."

Seated in a secluded office, she glanced over to Adam in an opposite one. Their eyes met as she smiled. He returned one as her attention then focused on Mr. Hanlon as he came into the room.

"Well, Lady Arnesen, your account is at quite a sizable amount. So, shall we discuss how you may want to invest?"

It took the better part of an hour and a half before they shook hands and she walked out satisfied. Adam met her in the lobby as she placed her hand on his arm and strolled out together. One big perk was that she knew in the future what was big, who built it up that way and how it would turn out for investing. Well, this was a good start in moving back in time.

"You are looking like the falcon that snared the rabbit, madam."

"Feels something like that. Why was the exact amount I had in my bank in Exeter the same as what was transferred here? Any idea on this?"

"That's not something I can explain, Sam. It's just one of the many things that will happen where you will just shake your head and move on."

"I'm obviously going to be sticking around for a while, I'm thinking. Have you noticed all the eyes following us about?"

"Yeah, but the gossipmongers will quiet soon when someone from the bank gets the word out that you are Lady Samantha Arnesen. A guest of the Eleventh Earl of Cheshire. An independent woman of substantial means."

She stopped momentarily as he gazed down upon her beauty.

"Wow, that's pretty cool you can trace your roots that far."

"We actually go back to William the Conqueror. My great ancestor was given extensive land rights and this title, when he served as a general in that army. I can show you his portrait in the ancestry hall at some point."

"I know we all have lineage, after all, there was only one Adam and Eve, right? But, that's impressive, Lord Griffin."

"Very nicely said, Lady Arnesen. Now put your very best aristocratic nose up in the air, for I'm going to take you shopping. We host a ball in a month and if you are still around, you will need a few gowns. What do you say? Are you ready to spend some of that money?"

Together, arm in arm, they entered a very exclusive lady's shop.

Later, her head was so full of muslin this, you must have French lace, oh, Lady Arnesen, you must have ruffles on the sleeves, and hats! Finally, they were finished as she had to admit to being darn hungry.

Strolling back out onto the street, the aroma of fresh bread caused her stomach to react in a most unfashionable way.

"I'll pretend I did not hear that," he chuckled. I have a great idea. Why don't we pick up a hamper so on our way we can picnic? Would you like that?"

"Oh goodness, yes. But, is that proper? No one would think it inappropriate without a chaperone?"

His gaze blazed a heated path right through to her stocking feet as he leaned closer than was proper, that was for sure.

"At our age, we can do what we want. Here or anywhere else."

She blushed as he chuckled, tipping a hat or raising a hand to several whom passed them by. Although a rogue in her eyes, it was clear in this area he was royalty. Grudgingly, she had to admit that the more she was with him the more she enjoyed his company.

"Good day to you both, Mrs. Baker, Mr. Baker. I hope you have been well?"

"Indeed, Lord Griffin. Good to see you again. What can we do for you and your companion?"

There it was again, Sam thought. He must bring his damn mistresses all around town. Morning, noon and night. Irritated, she took over. The hell with etiquette.

"Mrs. Baker, could you please put together a hamper for us? I'd like two of those crusty meat pasties, a wedge of your Cheddar Gorge cheese along with a pair of those delicious looking apple tortes. I think that will do."

Adam stood against the wall glancing out the window letting her have at it. A few minutes later Mrs. Baker brought around a small wicker basket fully stocked.

"Lord Griffin, shall I put this on your ledger?"

Sam wanted to pay but she knew that would cause some unneeded gossip.

"Absolutely and thank you Mrs. Baker."

"Okay, so we need something to drink. Should we secure a bottle of something? I don't know what that would be or where to find it." She was laughing again, softly, leaning precariously close to him as the shopkeeper watched on with a sly grin as they exited the stop.

"Or wine? I don't even know what's proper for this time of day. I've not had my full etiquette lesson yet as you know. But, I will come clean. I never drink during this time of the day. If we do, I am sure I will require a nap in the fields before we go back."

He had no choice but to grin. "Watch yourself woman. Grown men in this day are not supposed to enjoy a lady's company this much in broad daylight. Nor be invited on such short acquaintance to a nap in the field."

She raised a sassy eyebrow at him.

"Fine, stay here. I'll go into that shop and purchase a bottle of wine and two glasses. I will be right back." He opened his mouth to stop her, but too late, she was already scurrying away. He watched her swaying backside enter a different shop wondering how long this would take. Glancing around, the streets were filling up with people and he wanted her quick return so they could get moving along. Looking down, the urge to kick at a stone was strong as the time she was away lengthened.

Then felt a slap on the back. Turning, Adam was greeted by an old friend, Jonas Westman.

"Nice looking basket, old chap, but where's the unwitting snit that you are taking on a picnic?"

"Turn around, she's walking our way now."

Jonas was silent for a second.

"You are just friends, I take it? For I've known you for years and you would never bring any of your mistresses out during daylight hours."

"She's acquainted with Mrs. Hoyt and staying with us for a duration. She needed to come to town. I'm showing her around."

"Including a picnic? I think I should impose and tag along."

"My ass you will and shall get lost just as soon as I introduce you."

"Is that any way to treat a friend? Aren't you still seeing that amazon mistress from… Hell, where exactly is she from?"

"No, she was getting a bit too demanding for my taste, so it was time to bid her *au revoir*."

Both gentlemen turned as she approached with a fancy pouch in hand.

"You were successful, I see."

She smiled giving a swift glance to his friend.

"Lady Samantha Arnesen, let me introduce you to a longtime friend of mine, Lord Jonas Westman. Jonas has an estate down toward Shrewsbury."

She allowed him to take her hand a bit longer than even she knew was proper.

"My pleasure, Lady Arnesen, may I assume you will be at Adam's ball in a few weeks?"

"I am planning on it."

He did not let go of her gloved hand as she smiled warmly up into his golden, brown orbs. She liked him instantly! Was he one of them?

"Let's catch up with a pint soon, eh, Adam? Lady Arnesen, it will be a pleasure to see you again."

She finally had her hand back and had just a second to say, "Thank you, Lord Westman." Over her right shoulder as Adam hastily led her away towards The Red Lion.

The *barouche* and two coachmen were ready as one secured their parcel and the other assisted her inside.

"So, can I ask you a question?"

"About him I presume. I'll tell you right up front he's single and if you think I'm open about mistresses, he's even more so."

His voice was masked well, but she still heard the tenseness in it. "Not that, Lord Griffin. I was wondering if he is one of us like you and I?"

"He is. But you need to be careful. Although we are long standing friends, an ancestor from his past turned out to be a dark horse. There were consequences on both sides."

"This is precisely why you are so important to me. I have a lot to learn between you and Mrs. H. But now, how about a change of subject. Just exactly where are we going for our luncheon? I hope it's near for I really am quite hungry."

"At times you are a bit short on patience, I see. Look, we are already there." Just as he spoke, the door opened. A firm grip on her upper arm kept her from leaping out like a jack-rabbit.

Releasing a disgruntled sigh, she took the coachman's hand, stepped down and politely stepped aside while he got out. Basket and wine in hand, he held the other as she placed her hand over it.

"You were doing good until that appetite of yours got in the way."

"Dang, I'm not about eating like a bird as a lot of women do here. I like my food. Now can we sit and make work of it or not?"

She took a glass of wine from him.

"I'm not sure why I am here, but I am sure it's all your fault. In fact, I am positive about it.

He smiled. "Here's to answers."

He clunked his glass to hers. “Well said. Okay, I know you want to ask, so go ahead.”

“Am I that easy to read? Well, the hell with it then. How many are there around here?”

“Mrs. H, myself, Jonas, Mrs. Baker’s daughter, Anne, and you are all that I’m familiar with directly. But like I said, you never know who else.”

“Aren’t Father Godwin and Father O’Malley?”

“No, the priests, reverends and fathers are protectors of the passages. If you ever are in trouble, make sure to locate a nearby church or abbey.”

They rose, walking a bit further down a well beaten path as the coachmen took care of the picnic items.

“Can you and Mrs. H do a condensed course, spend some time with me? Is that possible? Or, do most just show up here and there muddling along until they figure it out? I don’t suppose there’s a manual, and I am not being sarcastic.”

He matched her smile. “No manual included and yes, we will help you. The sooner the better as I have no idea when you will head out again. I have a feeling it’s going to be soon. You are different, Sam, more so than anyone I’ve come across.”

Even though the men were several yards away, he could not help but notice the effect the wine was having on her. Shit, he did want to kiss her but was a bit worried what could transpire here, out in the open.

“Do you think we can get started when we get back, or am I being a bit too pushy?”

“You are fine, but I cannot tonight. Possibly Mrs. H can. I have plans overnight and will be heading out shortly after we return.”

She immediately assumed that meant a visit to his latest vixen.

“Okay, I see they are all packed up and waiting for us. Shall we?”

As they sat opposite each other in the coach, the invisible barrier went up between them. Just as well, he thought, knowing it was the right thing to do. A bit of separation from the chit was required to avoid any unnecessary feelings, that he clearly wanted to avoid, from arising. Tonight, he'd go and enjoy cards, some booze and a good smoke. Let her think what she wanted.

"You okay? You got a bit quiet."

"Yeah, fine, must be I'm not use to drinking wine in the early part of the day. I did warn you I may need a nap, so I guess I can say I was really not joking." Her eyes transmitted asshole, but her words were sugar coated.

He grinned, letting it go.

The coach halted as she nearly jumped out, but remembered her manners just in time; sitting still until the magical white gloved hand appeared. Once they walked through the main doors, she dislodged her hand from his arm.

"Thanks, Adam. It was an educational day and I appreciate you bending the rules for me to see the banker. I'll go now and find Mrs. H. We've got work to do and I'm ready to get it done."

As she swished off, he smiled, not taking his eyes off until she disappeared down a long hall. Whistling, he headed to his study knowing it was a matter of time before he'd need to kiss her again. Regardless of how much distance he wanted to keep between them.

***

But Sam's thoughts had turned in an entirely different direction. Mrs. H had told her she was an old soul. Was there anyone she could talk to about where she originated from? Here there were no computers and internet, so she could not investigate the mere meaning of being one, which would provide much more detail.

Then a thought occurred to her; the House of Record and Deed must be local considering the size of the village. Perhaps there she would be able to secure more details about her ancestry. Mrs. H would know where she could go.

Moving along the hallways, Sam halted, glancing at the beautiful countryside paintings. Hanging side by side, Adam's distant family members were elegantly encased in gold frames. She had to marvel at how wonderful it must be for him to know who he was and where he came from. She sighed, hearing it echo back as it moved through the long hall.

"What's got you sad, Sam?" She spun around to the approaching Mrs. H.

"Just that I wonder about what you said earlier. You know, my being an old soul. Is there any way I can find out where I came from and just what that means? Is there someone I can talk to about this in more detail? I was thinking about the local hall of records, but now that I think about it, would there be by any chance a local gypsy?"

Mrs. H smiled taking her by the arm as they walked to Sam's rooms.

"There is a woman I know in the next village. She is a Tinker. Her small caravan has been welcomed here on Lord Griffin's land for many generations. They return late summer and early fall just before harvest time and leave before Boxing Day. They are here now. If you want, I can take you to her so there is no mischief. They may try to take advantage of you being a strange lady to this area and all."

"I'd like that. Can we go today or tomorrow? You said she's a Tinker, what is that?"

She laughed. "A Tinker is what we British call a gypsy and I don't actually know where that originated from. Maybe we were trying to make it sound less obtrusive and more romantic. You never know. But anyway, we can go tomorrow. I have things to take care of. Plus, some of your parcels have arrived from your trip today and need to be settled. I've sent a maid up to your rooms; she's awaiting you now. If you want to give her instructions, you are then free to do what it this evening. Lord Griffin advised me he will be out tonight. I can have a tray brought to you if you wish."

"I think I'm good. We had a large picnic on our way back. If I want to eat later, I can always meander to the kitchen and find something, right?"

"As you wish, dear. Now go ahead in and let the maid know where you want your things. Tomorrow we can go and see the Tinker."

Wondering what had brought that on, Mrs. H left her at the doors. Sam helped the maid put things away and then dismissed her. Properly attired in a warmer day dress, Sam headed outside for a stroll through the lovely gardens, enjoying the cooler summer evening.

As she walked along the banks of the winding river, Sam kept aware of her surroundings, memorizing the way back. This time though, she had taken her small flashlight and would only use it if necessary since there was no way to replace the batteries when they wore out.

Faintly off in the distance, she heard voices. From out of the brush a young girl emerged with buttercups woven into one long braid. Reaching, she took Sam's hand like a fairy waif. Sam glanced down into the softest brown eyes, smiling, as the little girl smiled back, speaking softly,

"Come, my mother is expecting you."

Stunned silent, she was led to a caravan brightly painted in green, red and orange. The air was thick with the aroma of smoking meats. A plump woman rose and walked slowly toward her, extended both her hands, clasped Sam's tightly and turned them up glancing down at both palms.

"Come, we have a lot to talk about, Samantha Arnesen of Exeter."

They sat inside one of the caravans as Sam's excitement grew at being inside a true gypsy encampment. The noises of preparing food, cutting wood, kids playing and music moved to the recesses of her mind as the woman began to speak. It was her voice. Familiar, reaching deep inside of her being.

"You are an old soul indeed, Sam, I saw your arrival ahead of time and knew you'd be here today. I see many lives on both your palms, so you have been on this plane for thousands of years." She looked deeply into her eyes and held them for several minutes, neither one pulling away.

"You want to know more about where your soul comes from and how old you are." She released her hands and reached behind her, opened a dark velvet pouch and pulled out a beautiful, clear, crystal ball.

"Here, take this and cup it in your hands. It is heavy. Rest your hands on your lap; it will be more comfortable for you. Now, close your eyes and be very still. Let your mind speak to me slowly and ask me your questions in silence. Be patient while I seek your answers. If things do not make sense right now, soon all will be clear. They will unfold for you at the right time and you will completely understand. Are you ready to begin?"

Sam nodded, eyelids dropping.

"I see you lived before in Italy where water is in abundance. I see bridges, artists and seafood. Yes, I believe it was Venice. I see you before that in Norway or Sweden, it's hard to decipher which it was. I see a family crest of an old design. No faces come to me. Oh, yes, they are. It's a man and a woman, married and she's about to give birth. Twins."

She paused.

"Take heed of a soul that is joined to you but not in a romantic way, although this person loves you. I see a cloak with a hooded figure. Wait, the mist is clearing and I see it is a man and he will be diligent in trying to reach you. He is already in your life or will be soon. Beware. But, know he means no undue harm."

Sam thought that must be Adam.

She rushed in a breath and let it out slowly before continuing.

"I see your handsome tall man who does what you do and he's special as well. Almost like your guardian and your lover, combined. You will not marry him. At least as things are now. You have too much to learn, which will discourage him. Be warned, you may drive him away if you do not tell him what your feelings are.

"I see you moving through many destinations and destinies. When you arrived, I glimpsed the land of the Pharaohs in your life. When you go there, more of your past life will unravel. You may be tempted to hold on to this and stay. You will have choices then.

"I see children in your future, but they are not borne by you. But you will love them as your own." She glanced up at Sam seeing the furrow on her brows and continued.

"You made the choice long ago to take passages and you will need to decide in your future where you wish to stay. I see two men you will love, but somehow the love is different. I do not see who you chose. I see both in your life. Yet I see a third man from your past who still haunts you. You must put him to rest and let him go to truly have happiness and closure."

Sam felt strange; the pulsating energy from the crystal ball raced through her arms and energized her entire being. It prevented her from opening her eyes to see if she was through, not wanting these feelings to stop.

It was magnificent.

"I see your numbers are seven-seven-seven. This dates to ancient Egypt and biblical times. You are indeed a fortunate and blessed soul. I do not see danger by your hand or others in your future as you are protected by this long-lost love. Sam, when you two are reunited, you must make sure you do not lose his protection then or in the rest of your lives. If he stops loving you or does not pass that on to another, it could destroy you."

Sam shuddered as the gypsy's voice penetrated her thoughts.

"Look at me now."

Sam's eyelids fluttered, so empowered, as the crystal nearly rolled from her palms onto the wooden floor. She glanced up at the gypsy.

"I cannot go on. Your spirit is so strong. We will finish this another day when it is right. I will see you again, but it may be a while before this happens. I can't tell you more right now."

Sam handed her the crystal, which she rubbed, wrapped and put in the silk pouch and tucked it right away. They stood, eyes locked.

"I feel so strange now, very different, almost like I'm not even in my body but hovering just outside of it."

"Yes, that may stay with you for just a few minutes or for several days, even weeks. It depends upon how much your spirit is attached to the world beyond. You will know when it leaves you. Just like you will know when he leaves you."

Sam reached inside her reticule pulling out some pounds when her hands stopped her.

"No, a time from now a different form of payment will take place. Until then I cannot accept it."

Sam was clearly dazed walking down the three small wooden steps. Feet finally planted firmly in the grass, she began her walk back hearing the parting comment.

"Sam, when it's time to go to Egypt, just go, and remember you are always protected."

She stopped, but did not turn around. In a complete haze, her boots seemed to know the direction back to the estate. Those words echoed. Her body and mind reacted.

Egypt. The land of the Pharaohs, mysticism, scribes, ancient customs and belly dancers. Glancing down her hands shook, as she moved on, taking the secluded walk back through to her room. Right now, she was glad Adam was not here. She was glad Mrs. H would have a tray sent up to her, but mostly she was glad to have started her true venture. The one that would give her final closure.

Chapter Six

The gypsy woman's remarks remained with her. Some made sense, some did not. She was thankful that no further passages took place as time ticked by. Mrs. H was still smarting about her taking matters in her own hands and going to visit them without her knowledge until after the fact. She promptly chided her for being a bit of a rogue herself. Although Sam had to admit, her own version of what rogue meant leant more toward Lord Griffin than her taking an adventure.

Adam had been conveniently absent. But had heard him a time or two and saw him out in the fields riding with a woman dressed in a very expensive habit. So, had his roaming and mistresses returned? She hardly gave it much thought in lieu of what was ahead of her. Keeping him out of her life right now seemed vital if she was to succeed in discovering more.

He had merely given her a reason to not seek him out. That stolen kiss and their one day out in the town was now quite behind her.

Then it was the weekend before the ball. Her gowns had finally arrived giving a needed diversion. As she opened the large boxes and unwrapped the soft tissue paper, she admired each of them side by side. She grinned, knowing how much she'd enjoy the preparation in getting those on just as much as wearing them.

Leaving them as they sat for the maid to attend, Sam stood at the double-wide French doors overlooking the grounds and smiled, believing a spirit was sharing these rooms with her. The presence of another woman.

"I know you are with me madam. I can smell violets." Slowly she turned around leaning against the railing.

"Go ahead. I give permission. You can shuffle them around when I leave and I nor the maid will be any the wiser."

All she had been able to learn about her strange room partner was from a few of the hesitant, older staff members. She was a woman who liked the soft flowery perfumes of a by-gone era and still enjoyed running her hands along a dress sewed to perfection using the finest silk.

After spending the last few weeks in these rooms and time with Mrs. Hoyt and Father Godwin, today she felt like a walk to town to visit Mrs. Baker.

Resplendent in her day attire, Sam threw a shawl over her shoulders, grabbed her reticule and parasol and headed out. She was getting antsy though now; she wanted to find Adam and insist he let her move into a cottage she'd found abandoned on the property. She was going to offer to pay for renovations and a nice sum for monthly rent. She'd hire someone reliable to help her with these tasks. Now all she had to do was get him to agree. That would, of course, rely on when a moment could be snared from his dalliances.

Just as much as she'd avoided him, he had been doing the same. That was quite clear. But with a plan now in mind, she wanted to move forward. If it took cornering him at the ball, then so be it. It was the perfect solution. Secure and reclusive. But, where the devil had that bloke been?

Shrugging her shoulders, she nodded to the doorman in passing and left out the front entrance. It was nice now she did not feel the need to advise her comings and goings to anyone.

Opening the parasol and heading down the main lane, a smile lit her face as the Baker's daughter, Anne, speaking rather loud, was fast approaching.

"I was just on my way to see you. Are you set on a particular task or just a stroll?"

"Nothing too important. You have that look in your eyes. Do you want to go back to my rooms and have a chat?"

"We need to."

Tingles began in Sam's body. "Good, come on. I take it your parents are fine?"

"Yes, they are. I come with a hello from them both." The butler eyed Sam as he opened the doors and let them both in.

"Is that one of your new dresses from the shop?"

"It is nice. I think he does excellent work. I just got my ball gowns. Do you want to look?" The two exchanged glances as they hit the upper staircase. Their pace increased.

Glancing quickly down both hallways, Sam closed her doors soundly.

"What is going on?"

"Father Godwin thought it may be a good idea for you to come with me on a bit of an adventure. Not quite sure what it is yet. You know how that goes. It involves France and a hat shop, that's about all I know."

"A shopping trip?" Sam smiled. "And you need an experienced shopper because you are too young to make good choices? Oh, I get it." They both shared a laugh. "When do we go?"

"Now. Do what you need. I'm ready. Then we can finish our walk in an entirely different direction."

Sam never left the estate without her pistol, knife, extra ammunition and a small hand bag. Everything else was unnecessary. Suddenly, she halted. A nagging sensation resonated throughout her body as she heard a faint voice inside her head questioning what she was doing. Was it intuition or the spirit sharing her rooms? Heaving the shawl down, she grabbed a small backpack and a hooded cape instead.

"Anything else you think I need?"

"No, let's go. I'm going to try and get you back for your first ball at *Ard Aulinn*. We never know how long any of these trips will take."

Sneaking silently out of the servants' entrance, they chatted quietly through the field. Instead of the familiar left bend toward the church, they went right toward an abandoned rectory long ago left for ruins from the Saxon days.

"I did not even know this was here. Is this on the Earl's property, or are we off it at this juncture?"

"Still on it. They keep this building intact for obvious reasons." She smiled.

"But, there's no confessional. I only see that cellar hole which looks none to inviting."

"Oh, come on. There will be some cobwebs. Pull on your cloak and hood, hold my hand, and follow me."

Stumbling a bit down the few stone steps, the brightness of the day quickly faded into total darkness. Continuing along and up, loud shouts were heard as gunfire rang out. The earth shook with explosions. The dark gave way to light as they climbed the last few steps then halted in disbelief. The streets were in rubble as men in uniforms rushed by them, seemingly unaware of their presence.

Sam watched as a horrified look come over Anne's features which forced her into swift action.

"Get low. Do not under any circumstance let me go. Now run! We need to reach a safer area!"

Crouching, they stumbled over the debris and sped toward a large pile of rubble as bombs continued to explode all around them. Sam's body shook down to the core.

Never had she felt so removed and surreal as she did right this very moment.

Tugging Anne's hand, she pulled her down an alley just as the corner of the stone building was nearly leveled by another bomb. "Quick, this way!"

As the blistering noise started to recede, she turned down a small side street. Then she knew what they were looking for. There it was surrounded by so much wreckage. Staring at the sign hanging on one chain, she read the fading words: *LaBonte Magasin de Chapeau.*

"In here now." She pushed in the door tugging Anne along then secured it. As they moved toward the back of the shop, she saw it.

"Oh, my God! It is a baby in that basket. Sound asleep even through all this noise." Sam crept over and moved the rough, woolen blankets aside, appraising. "It's a boy and a note written in French. It asks us to bring the baby to Nancy. There is a great battle about to begin in Verdun and he needs to get to safety. It's very important to his future."

She handed the note over to Anne who crumpled it into a ball then slipped it inside her dress pocket.

Sam knew she had to take control of this situation. Now.

"You will be the mother, I your lady maid. I am a bit old to have a young one. But, you fit the bill. Look. There are supplies, water, powder milk, cloth diapers and pins. God, am I glad I brought my backpack."

She shoved everything into it, slid off her cloak, draped it over a shoulder and put it back on. Ann suddenly broke out in laughter. Sam glared at her.

"You look like the hunchback of *Notre Dame*."

"Oh, shut up you chit. This is no time to crack jokes." But Sam did smile realizing how hideous she must look. "I don't want to wake the tyke to check his diaper, so let's get him up and going. I can't even begin to see how we are going to get to Nancy. There must be a way already awaiting us and we need to get the heck out of here and find it."

Outside the building Sam glanced frantically for some instinctual direction to come to her. Seconds ticked by when finally her feet started to move. Grasping Anne's arm tightly with one hand, she kept the baby close with the other.

"Shit."

"What? Do you smell horse dung or something?"

This brought Sam out of near panic.

"No, I am looking for some kind of a sign to help us know which direction to take. Hold on, I've something in my reticule that will help. Here is the baby."

Steadying her shaking hand, she removed a circular compass on a key chain.

"What is that?"

"A directional device called a compass. Okay, I have a reading. It is down this street. You hold tight onto him and stay right behind me. Grasp my cloak; if I move too fast I want you to tug it. Don't you dare let go, I mean it!"

Passing quickly by a dilapidated shop front where only the beams remained, Sam glanced down pulling out a bundle. It was a wrapped block of cheese, or smelled like one. Slipping it under her cloak into the side pocket of the backpack, they hurried along never losing pace.

As they moved out of town she took compass readings. Periodically glancing up at the darkening sky praying it would be cloudy as hell tonight. Silently, they crept along keeping parallel to a stream.

"Stop. Hush. I need to listen. But come closer. Let's stay in this brush for a few seconds." A short paused ensued. "I knew it. I can hear voices, but I need to make sure they are French so we need complete silence." Precious moments ticked by as just on the other side of the steam she made out a small band of French soldiers. She threw a stone their direction speaking rapidly.

"*Soldats, nous avons esoin de votre aide*." [Soldiers, we need your help.] That got their attention as two of them waded through the stream and crouched down in her face.

"*Ou devez-vous aller?*" [Where do you need to go?]

"*Nancy*."

"*Venez avec noir*." [Come with us.]

One stood helping Anne and the baby. Miraculously, he had not caused a fuss at all. A lengthy silence followed as they joined the band of men. As the pace quickened, Sam was near begging them to slow down when she saw soft flickers of light up ahead. They were swiftly ushered into a makeshift tent.

"*Notre commandant va vous parler, eu de temps.*" [Our commander will speak with you, shortly.]

Sam nodded as both women simultaneously expelled a deep sigh.

"He's gone to get his commander who will speak with us shortly."

Anne nodded and whispered so softly, Sam had to lean right up to her quivering mouth to hear. The poor girl had clearly never been in anything like this before. Now it was completely clear why Sam was along.

"I think we should feed and change him soon."

"Agree, as soon as we speak with the Commander. Do you, by any chance, speak French?"

"No, I've never been out of England before, Sam. I'm scared as hell."

"Don't worry it appears I do and quite fluently. So, I guess we are all set. I'll tell him what he needs to know."

The flap parted as a rather rugged, tall soldier entered. His presence filling the small tent. Bowing, he removed his hat addressing Sam.

"*Bonsoir, Madame, Je suis Commandant Philippe Petain, vous avez un problem?*" [Good evening, madam. I am Commander Philippe Petain. You have a problem?]

"*Commandant, vous etes un grand soldat que j'ai entendu parler de vous. Ma pupillr est avec le bebe et son pere est moty. Nous cherchons le transport de Nancy.*" [Commander, I have heard that you are a great soldier. My mistress has a baby and his father is either dead or injured. We need transport to Nancy.]

"*Oui, nous avons un hospital, il y a un camion peut vous prendre.*" [Yes. We have a hospital. There is a truck that can take you.]

"*Combien de temps pouvons-nous partir*?" [How long?]

"*Encore trois jours*." [Another three days.] He nodded, secured his hat and left the tent speaking to the soldier posted outside. Believing they were out of danger, at least for the moment, Sam let out a heavy sigh of relief.

"What did he say?"

"In three day's a truck will take us to Nancy where they have a hospital. I do believe, my friend, that is where our little bundle will be left. It's just a hunch, so it is very important that we keep our eyes and ears open and mouths shut while we are here. Especially you. As I don't want them suspicious of your obvious British accent, even though the country's men are here fighting alongside the French."

She slid the cape from her shoulders and took out a small glass baby bottle filled with water. Let out a little and put in the powdery substance. Known in the period as *Mellin*. It looked utterly distasteful. But once she shook the bottle and handed it to Anne, the baby latched on with a bit of a smile. Glancing back and forth to them both.

Did this little boy have any idea what his world held in store? That was hoping they got him to Nancy and it worked out right.

As Anne fed him, Sam disrobed his lower section and put a new diaper on. Secured with pins, she held up the old one wondering what the hell to do with it. She hardly could throw it in the laundry and have it warm and clean in forty-five minutes. Unfortunately, there was a short supply and it was needed.

Knowing the soldier was posted outside, she opened the flap. Unflinchingly, he poised his gun in front of her preventing further movement. It was the shine of his bayonet that mesmerized her for a second.

"*Je besoin de quelque chose dans lequel se laver sa couche.*" (I need something in which to wash diapers.)

The soldier smiled, jerked his head to indicate she was to go back inside than walked off.

A couple of minutes later he produced a large tin can with hot water, placed it inside the tent, lowered the flap and disappeared.

She grinned. "Maybe he thought I'd ask him to wash it." She dunked it inside the pot swishing it around with her hands until it looked clean enough. The rope supporting the tent was a great place to start a laundry line.

"I am so glad you are with me, Sam, I'd not know what to do. You are so smart. No wonder F.G. wanted me to get you."

"F.G., now is it? You make me smile. But, we are a pair, so don't give it another thought. It is very clear we need each other, that's why we were teamed up. Look. He is now sleeping. Why not try and get some rest yourself? I am going to. We have no idea how far we are from the front lines. But, it seems pretty quiet right now."

Having recalled a history lesson long ago about the Battle of Verdun, Sam was not going to tell Anne why she knew they were probably closer to enemy lines than either would like. Hopefully, they would be in Nancy before the bloody battle took place. Their little bundle safely tucked with whomever, and could about face back to jolly old England.

Two days passed and the best they could do was dig holes to relieve themselves, knowing the encampment was busy as hell. At one point, the guard did not stop her as Sam took a chance and peeked out and saw the strangest looking contraption off in the distance. It was not a tank. Or, she had the wrong year in her head. Rather a jalopy with a back bed and canopy.

Inside, she watched Anne who was becoming quite fond of the little guy. What a gem he was hardly fussing at all. He seemed to know it was important to behave. If Sam had known kids could be like that, she may have considered having a few of her own. But as time and divorce took over, she realized her chance to having them had passed.

"One more day Sam. Should we make sure they remember we are still here? It's been nice of them to provide a pot of food every night. "

"If we don't see them come sunrise, I'll ask the guard outside if I can speak with someone. Commandant Petain seemed keen to see us there, though, so I trust him."

She was right. The next morning before sunrise, the flap opened startling them both as their guard motioned them out.

"*Guardez le silence, mesdames.*" (Keep silent, ladies.)

They both nodded yes. Glancing down at the still sleeping baby, Sam was pleased they had him in a fresh diaper and a bottle of milk powder already mixed.

Ushered up and into the jalopy, they both eyed the large red painted cross on both sides. Flap closing, the driver ground the gears as the strange contraption moved forward. Normally, these vehicles were neutral to ambush and bombings. But, perhaps it was not a sure bet and that was why their departure was so early before sunrise.

She wanted desperately to peer out and see how many were accompanying them, but did not dare. They had been so good to them. By the enormous sounds rumbling off the earth beneath the truck's tires, she estimated it was a large ensemble moving on.

Anne rested the baby on her lap while reaching into a side pocket and produced a wrapper.

"That soldier put this in when he helped me up. Look. We have some chocolate."

As if on cue, Sam's gut grumbled. For never had something looked so good. As she ate her piece, she glanced down at her hands. It was hard not to notice they were dry and cracked from cleaning nappies in the hot water. She did not care.

"You have been hogging that little man, but at this point I'm nervous to take him. I think he's adjusted to you so well. Someday if you have kids, you will make a wonderful parent."

"Why did you not have any? Oh, I'm sorry, Sam, I should not pry."

How was she to tell her about divorce? They had that back in 1865. Heck, Henry VIII was a pro at it long before, but it was just not worth discussing at this juncture.

"I was so busy with my life by the time I realized it… well, here I am. A bit too old to begin. I did not want to raise kids and have their friends think I was their grandmother not their mother."

Anne laughed. "Sorry, but that's a really good point."

"I'll make sure you pay for that later."

A bump nearly sent them all to the roof of the truck and back as they steadied. The baby's eyes opened as both waited with baited breath to see if he'd scream bloody hell at being bothered so.

But he smiled.

Unfortunately, that bump caused a tire to puncture as they stopped and were ordered out to wait between the vehicles while it was patched and re-inflated.

Then all hell broke loose as soldiers started yelling. The threesome were thrown to the ground and held there by two other armed men as shots ricochet all around. Suddenly Sam's confidence evaporated. What should they do? Crawl beneath the vehicle? What if they threw a grenade? Should they stay put and be in the line of fire? When a hot, searing sensation pulsated up through her leg. Lifting her dress up slightly, a small pool of blood had formed.

The gunshots finally stopped as they were helped back up by a small band of French soldiers who had reappeared from the brush. Quickly, they were ushered into the back, the others boarded and the transports started moving again.

"Oh, to all that's holy, Sam, you are shot! I see the blood forming on your dress. We need to do something right away. You could be in real danger and I need you!"

Anne's voice was reaching a fever pitch as the baby started to cry and Sam knew she needed to act fast, both for her leg and calming Anne down.

"Stop it, I say. You stop that right now. It's only a scratch." She leaned down ripping the ruffle from her petticoat beneath and tied it around her leg, staunching the flow. "Now you sit still and calm yourself. The baby has been through enough already. He hardly needs hysteria right now. We are on our way, aren't we?"

That worked, harsh as it was. Sam held her hand up halting Anne's apology.

"Nope, don't do it. It's done. We are fine. Learn a lesson from this Anne. You leave your emotions at home. Let's move on. Surely by now he must be hungry. Give him a half feed. We will cap the rest for when we get to our location. Just in case we need to keep our supply running longer."

But the stinging from the wound reminded Sam it required attending. The bullet needed to be removed, leg sanitized to avoid infection. Clenching her jaw, she knew it could not wait any longer. It had to be done.

"I am going to get the bullet out now just to be safe. I have perfume in my reticule which has alcohol to sterilize. Then I'll bandage it back up. The only reason I'm going to do this now is so you can see my process in case you ever need to know. You pay attention and don't go squeamish on me, girl."

It was the tip of the knife going into the wound that made her eyes water. Clenching her teeth, she continued along until it popped out onto the floor of the truck bed. Once the wound was cleaned and bandaged, she wiped the knife, placed it back and lowered her dress.

"You are so brave, Sam."

"Hogwash. It's just a precaution. I'd better hurry. I think we are starting to slow down."

Sam refused to glance up at Anne during the process and finished just in time lowering her dress.

The vehicle had come to a stop and back flap opened and they were assisted outside.

"Nancy?"

"*Oui, Madame, l'hopital est la.*"

"Je vous remercie."

She grabbed Anne's arm and headed. The streets of Nancy were still smoking from last night's bombs. Locals that remained picked through debris searching for what she hoped was pictures or clothing and not deceased family members.

They had to find out who was going to take this baby. As they walked down the steps and into the infirmary, Anne halted. Neither had ever witnessed so many wounded, bleeding soldiers. Cries filled the air as blood streamed on the cold cement floors.

"Get a hold of yourself, there's a nurse coming toward us and she looks like she's about to burst into tears."

As the woman approached she spoke to them in a mix of French and English. "Mon bebe, oh, you bring him safe."

Anne held him out as the woman clutched him so tightly, a squeal emerged from his tiny mouth. Lowering her head, she kissed both his cheeks as tears streamed down her face.

Sam had to know. "*Est-il votre neveu*?" [Is he your nephew?]

"*Non*, no, he is my son. How did you know it was me he belonged to? How to find me?"

Sam cried. Anne cried. The mother cried.

"I did not. We just needed to get someplace safer than Verdun and came here." She knew not to ask or say more. "*Ou est l'eglise*?" [Where is the church?]

"*Deux rues plus loin.*" [Two streets away.]

They hugged as Sam moved on with Anne. "Come on, we need to get the heck out of here before all hell breaks loose. Our work is now done. She told me there is a church two streets down. That has to be our exit point."

"Oh, my goodness. How will I ever be able to get used to not knowing where I am going until I get there? Then respond in horror if I am ever anywhere like this, Sam?"

"You are special, girl. Do not sell yourself short. You were chosen, remember? You need to look beyond all of this and always focus on what needs to be done and go about your work. That's it."

As they walked into the church, glancing around, their arms locked while descending. Both were amazed that the stairs were still intact walking down into the crypt. Torches lit the dank, stone corridor. As they came out the other side, Sam nodded to Anne. They had made it and were back at the ruins on *Ard Aulinn*.

"We did it! Oh, Sam, I wish I could tell F. G. and my parents. I must go; I need to go. I want to see them and my room and… well, eat!"

Sam laughed waving her off. Then headed toward the side entrance of the great estate.

The house was ablaze with light and even though she was in the back, she could hear voices wafting toward her from the front. Oh, my God, she thought. Had so much time passed? It became imperative to get to her room, clean the wound and then locate Adam.

Determination set in. She was going to have that needed conversation tonight and that was that. Period.

Chapter Seven

Into the shadows, she slipped. Hiding a few times to avoid servants until she made it into the bedroom. Gas lamps were lit inside. Her handmaid Abbey was anxiously awaiting her arrival. Pacing, clearly in a tither.

"Lady Samantha! Oh, my goodness. I am so glad to see you. His Lordship had been here three times asking about you."

Sam smiled. "Abbey, I can't explain why I am tardy and a bit messy right now. We have no time to waste. I need to get into the tub. But more than that, I would like you to go and get a few things right away. You must pledge to do it quietly. I need plasters. I had a bit of a spill this afternoon. Nothing too serious. I require it for my leg before I can get dressed."

"Oh, yes, miss. I will be right back. Go ahead and get into the water. It is warm. I had it poured a while ago. When I return, I will help you get dressed. You will be late, but make it."

She was such a cute little thing, Sam thought, as she disrobed, removed the make-shift bandage and slid into the refreshing water. "Ah, this is just what the doctor ordered." Scrubbing vigorously with the thick lavender soap, she rinsed and dried off. The wound looked pink which was a good sign. It would heal properly. Foot resting on the side of the porcelain tub, she poured alcohol over it.

Yup, it stung like bloody hell as she flinched, teeth clenched tightly while finishing the task.

Grabbing the healing balm out of the bag and smothering the area, she slid back onto the fainting chair trying to suppress a grin as Abbey strode in.

Her cheeks were as bright as her eyes.

She was enjoying this!

"How should I wrap your leg, mistress? Oh, that looks horrible. Shall I go get Mrs. Hoyt, or fetch a physician for you? No one saw me. I made sure of it. But, now I am thinking you could use some assistance."

"Heck, no. I can do it. Here, watch me in case you have a child someday and you need to wrap a bandage. There, see, it was so easy. Now where do we begin? I see you have both my gowns pressed and out. Which shall I wear?"

"You want my opinion? Well, they are both so lovely, but I think the soft creamy yellow will look so nice since it is still summer."

"Okay. Let's do it."

A full stream of layers came one after the other: white silk stockings up over her knees secured with garters, cotton drawers, a sleeveless chemise. More ensued. A corset which nearly had her gasping for breath, then petticoats followed at last by the gown.

"My, gosh, Abbey, I'll be in a sweat before I even get down the stairs. Please be a dear and open a window while I put on my slippers. Oh, these are lovely."

As Sam went over to have her hair done up in a swirl, she glanced down at unfamiliar rectangular boxes on her dressing table. "What are these? They are not mine."

"I have no idea, mistress. When I came to wait earlier, they were already here."

Sam opened each side by side then gasped. They housed a set of gorgeous, sparkling jewelry that matched whichever gown she chose.

Sliding her fingers over each piece, she knew it was Adam as her eyes misted.

"Let's get my hair done. Then I'll put on the citrine set."

As Abbey fastened the gorgeous necklace, Sam put in the drop earrings. Both women's eyes met in the mirror.

"Let's do something fun before I go down. Here." Sam turned to Abbey with the other set in her hand. "I want you to put these on so you know you could wear them too. They are not just for rich types like me." She smiled.

"Oh, mistress, I could not… but, oh it's so tempting. If you are sure?" Sam stood and helped turning her toward the mirror, "See? You are just as beautiful, Miss Abbey."

As the box was restocked and placed in the upper draw, Sam grabbed her evening bag. With one last smile toward Abbey, she closed the door. Feeling a bit out of sorts now, she wanted a different entrance than the large grand staircase straight into the path of the aristocrats below.

Slipping down a side entrance and weaving slightly from her stiff leg, Sam finally found the hall leading to the dining room. Beyond was the great ballroom. She had made it. From here she'd find him and hopefully a few other faces she may know. Halting in the shadows, she removed from her clutch a small flask and took a hearty swig of rum. Ironically that did the trick. She screwed the silver cap back on and tucked it neatly back inside.

The moment she entered, a swarm of older dowagers descended all demanding answers. Where did she come from? How long was she staying? Did she come from money? How were she and the Earl acquainted? She smiled, ready to answer with a bold outright lies.

Then she felt his close proximity and scrutiny.

Turning, she weaved through throngs of couples and halted in the middle of the large dance floor.

As if on cue, the orchestra began a Strauss Waltz.

"You are the most beautiful woman in the room."

Her heart hit her throat with a thud, but this was not the time nor the place her inner thoughts reminded.

"That's kind of you to say with so many lovely ladies here. I do have to apologize for being delayed to your festivities tonight, Lord Griffin. But, with all this going on, I'm sure you did not miss me."

Her barb struck.

Looming over his shoulder, a tall brunette eyed her with open and apparent venom. Oh, yes, one of the mistresses was in the house tonight. Sam grinned up into his eyes, but what she truly desired was to give him a good swift kick in a shin.

"Ah, Lord Adam, there is a woman over your shoulders who looks a bit put out that you are engaging me in conversation on this dance floor. I do not think this is such a grand idea if you two are to be acquainted later. That is, to continue dancing with me. But, of course that is just my opinion."

He smiled.

"I can feel her eyes in my back. Or, they are daggers? So, shall we? As my guest in this house, it is my duty to take the first dance with you. She should know protocol by now.

"Oh, I see."

Taking her gloved hand into his, he settled the other on the small of her back. Swirling around faster and faster, Sam finally winced, squeezing his hand for a brief second.

He did not stop, but slowed, "You are hurt. Where?"

"Leg. It is fine, should be fit as a fiddle in a few days."

"We can talk about it later. Would you rather sit or come around the room with me and meet some people?"

"My mind is busy, Lord Griffin, so I do apologize again. For I am not the most suitable partner for you at this moment." Halting at the far side of the room as the music ended, Sam nodded to the brazen brunette then released his grip.

"Lord Griffin, I do think this is your partner. I thank you for taking a spin with me and performing your perfunctory duties. Now you are free to enjoy the evening."

Adam's eyes darkened as their gazes locked. She looked boldly into his. With a slight curtsy and a satisfied grin, she swished off toward a gathered group of lades she was acquainted with from town.

He turned towards her knowing it was coming.

"Leah at this point I'd prefer you not utter a word. She's my house guest. Actually, that it is not entirely true. She is under the guidance of Mrs. Hoyt. They are acquainted. So, let's not make a show of it right now."

He was clearly agitated by what that chit had done. But as he swirled his latest mistress around the room, the sparkle of the gems resting against Sam's soft skin nearly had him missing a step as he contemplated wringing her beautiful neck.

Sam was deeply engaged with two men he knew to be clear rogues and was having a time of it. He housed no doubt she was retaliating. Or was she? As his mind worked, his body responded like a robot out on the dance floor. Did she think of him as just a situation she found herself in? All because of that kiss and what followed?

Ah, hell, he concluded. Let her act up. Right now, he had other things to take care of.

"Really, Adam, this is tedious. You are not even listening to a word I've just said. I'm not that fickle that I don't recognize your eyes wandering to where she is. Am I wasting my time here?"

Lowering his eyes down to the pretty woman, he knew it was time to get rid of this one as well. Damn.

"You know I don't apologize, so don't look for one. If my lifestyle does not agree with you, then I can send for a carriage and have you taken home. It's of no consequence to me, Leah."

"I'm fine right here. I'll let your man know when I want that carriage. But be assured I'm ending it now before you do." He shrugged as the music ended, bowed relinquishing her hand. "Of no consequence, like I said. You do as you will."

***

With the next three rounds under her belt and three different handsome partners, Sam had to admit she was glad when this last jig ended. Followed with the bell ringing for dinner. Her leg was smarting, but it was her own damn fault with that last dance. No one would be the wiser. But, she was in enormous discomfort.

Except for him. He knew.

Settling her hand slightly on his extended arm, she subconsciously touched with the other the beautiful gems encircling her neck. "These are beautiful, are they family heirlooms?"

"Yes, my great-great grandmother. You do them justice." She was being directed into the large dining hall. "I have you sitting opposite me, Jonas will be on your right and his sister, Annabelle, on your left. Just make sure you keep your conversation light." As he pulled her chair out she settled as a finger grazed a right bare shoulder. An uncontrollable shudder passed straight through. His eyes raked her forcing additional discomfort as her eyes followed him until he sat.

Glancing down the long rectangular table, Sam saw his mistress sitting precariously close to a middle-aged soldier dressed in full British regalia. Adam caught her questioning gaze before quickly looking away. Was this how he treated all his women of love interest? Or, was it lust interest? She was not going to be a part of his probably long list. No frigging way, but there was a bit of chemistry existing between them and she was determined to extinguish it right now before falling prey to his insurmountable charms.

It was as if they were already lovers sharing many private thoughts and moments. For they did indeed have this peculiar and special gift in common.

Minutes ticked away as she felt the heat of Adam's gaze sweep over her. A twinge of something unfamiliar weaved through them both as their eyes locked. It was there. Something very tangible.

"I take it your delay was unavoidable, Lady Arnesen, but I am glad you arrived. Let me introduce you to my sister, Annabelle. Annabelle, Lady Samantha Arnesen, from Exeter."

She nodded a hello.

"How long are you here? Do you mind if I use your given name?"

"Of course, you may. I am not sure exactly how long I will stay. I believe it will be of some duration at this point. Lord Griffin has kindly given me free rein while I visit with a close family friend."

"Someone we know?"

Sam was not sure she should say who in this crowd of snobs, glancing at him for guidance. His sly smile said she was on her own, testing her again - the damn bloke!

"No, I'm sure you would not know her. Tell me, Annabelle, wherever did you have your gown made? The workmanship looks positively Parisian."

His foot grazed her right leg as she winced slightly, but still managed to keep her attention on her companion. Vain, the woman was vain, but it had worked. On and on she droned discussing the gown, the custom lace made in the same shop as the Queen, the button fabric - blah, blah, blah - as Sam worked her way through the courses. Thankfully, no one else got a word in edgewise.

As the Earl rose signaling cigars and port for the gents, the ladies left in clusters to the drawing room for coffee, sweets and a full platter of gossip. This was the part she wanted nothing to do with and he knew it.

Great, she thought, as three old crones came her way plastering a smile on her face.

"Lady Samantha, we have a small wager going on. I think the jewels you are wearing are from London, Mrs. Tuttle thinks Paris and Miss Christie thinks they are from America. So, you need to settle this for us. Rarely have the three of us seen gems so beautifully set."

"Actually, they belong to Lord Griffin's family. He lent them to me this evening. I believe they are from his grandmother's side, which is Welsh." She smiled, waving her fan for a few seconds. "They are lovely, aren't they?"

The expression on their faces was priceless.

"If you will please pardon me, ladies, I am a bit parched. I think I'll go in search of refreshment. Can I offer to get something for any of you?"

Moving around the chatter, Sam felt a dire need to bolt. Screaming all the way at the top of her lungs. Thank heavens the butler rang for rejoining in the ballroom. Great, a few more dances and the evening would be over, she realized when suddenly he was there, blocking an exit.

"I insist, my dear, you dance the next with me." It was of course, Jonas,

"I'd be delighted. But not a jig or reel. It would be lovely if it was something a bit gentle, if you will, as this night has taken its toll on me."

Shit, she wished she had not said that. Not wanting to lead this dude on in any way. As a matter of fact, she did not trust him at all, even though Adam's report on him previously only said to be cautious.

As the waltz started, he danced her out on to the floor and swirled them around the room. Heat radiated throughout her leg and it was clear enough was enough. Tempting as it was to just walk off leaving him there, Sam stuck it out. He turned out to be one of those pompous aristocrats, blathering on about something. Exactly what did he do, anyway, when on a passage? Kill someone, steal, just be a jerk? With amusement, she let him just babble on.

"Jonas, mind if I step in?"

"Not at all my friend." As he stepped aside, tipped a finger in a mock salute then sauntered off to sip a scotch off an offered tray.

"I'm actually grateful for your interference this time. Thank you. I'm going to have to sit soon or go back to my rooms and put my leg on a chair cushion."

"Can you hang on a bit longer? I can walk you up as there is something I would like to ask you. I believe this is the last dance. Then the staff will start to usher the guests out."

"I can do that."

"Then wait for me in the foyer toward the side stairwell. It will be closer to your rooms."

Never taking her eyes from him as he thanked people as they left, she sifted between ladies putting on capes and gentlemen their hats. Maneuvering unnoticed until reaching the location he spoke of, an appealing chair beckoned. Slumping down into it, exhausted, it took only minutes before she drifted off into sleep. Then she felt him. Again.

Kneeling, Adam placed hands over hers on a lap covered with yards and yards of silk. He did not want to wake her, but she needed a bed. There was no way he could successfully carry her the country mile it was up to her rooms without that happening.

"Sam," he softly shook her as sleep-filled eyes opened slowly. She smiled, silently rising as he held her hand and they headed up

She opened the doors realizing that Abbey would need to be rung to help her with all the back buttons on the gown.

"I do have something I want to talk to you about, if you have a couple of minutes. First though, would you please undo these? Tonight, I've no patience to wait on Abbey. Surely she is already snugly tucked into bed. Also, I want to give you back both sets of jewels."

Turning, presenting her back, she gave him no time to protest. Chuckling, he started at the top and slowly worked his way down.

"I was thinking tomorrow, if you are up to it, that we'd ride to Wales. I have business to conclude and I think you would benefit from meeting this couple. Is your leg up for it?"

He had finished helping her out of the gown as it fell in a swirl to the floor. Her breathing was shallow. Words way too soft. But, she found the nerve to speak.

"I'd like that. What time?"

"Do you think you'd prefer to ride with an English saddle rather than side saddle, or take the coach instead?"

"To ride, no side saddle. You saw me a while back. I nearly got dragged. I'm not sure I ever want to try that again, lady or not."

"Much safer for us all if you don't." He moved away taking both jewelry boxes. "I already know the rules, Sam, and you are quickly learning them. If what you want to discuss involves my mistresses, then we can save it. She's on her way."

"Adam, that's your business. I'm not in a frame of mind to think about your dalliances and could give a hoot. I've enough on my plate right now. You would prove to be a big distraction if I even let it happen. So, it's best we both forget about that kiss in Venice. I want to talk with you about moving out." She held up her hand. "Before you protest, I need you to hear me. I have a plan that I think would work best for both of us, even Mrs. Hoyt."

"So, you are going to ignore it, are you? How long do you think you can hold out? My guess is that you are stubborn and it may take a while. But, mark my words, the mistress stuff is done. No point. So why don't you tell me about what you want to do tomorrow along our ride. I'll settle for being your friend, for now. Do you think I could start by seeing your leg?"

If the night had not finished her off, his dialogue sure would have. She sat down on the bed in a heap, shoving up her petticoat enough to expose the bandage. It was a bit bloody, but the crinoline had kept it from seeping through to the lovely gown.

He touched it, unwrapped it and held her leg in his hand. "A bullet wound, eh? You packed it with something that looks appropriate and the color is good." He reached to her bedside table and took the other dressings and wrapped it.

"Looks like you had some practice with this." Concern shaded his handsome eyes. "You do know you don't have to do this, right? You are here, nothing will make you go back if you stop taking passages."

How dare he? When she was most vulnerable and at the point of total exhaustion. Especially when his voice turned deep holding true concern and eyes held hers captive.

She touched his shoulder, resting both hands and smiled, "What would I do? Become a woman with no ideals, bored out of my mind? I don't think so. At last I have a purpose. I had no idea I could stop, but I don't want too. Do you? I doubt it."

Rising, he sighed placing hands on his hips, "I know. It was just something I needed to say. I'll see you in the morning. Let's plan on ten o'clock so you can sleep in a bit and have breakfast. Goodnight, Lady Arnesen." His smile was warm and inviting as he slid the backside of a hand against a soft cheek, "Sleep well."

"A good night to you as well, Lord Griffin."

As her doors closed, Sam slid out of the layers and into her nightdress. Lowering the glass lamps, she got into bed and once her head hit the pillow, sleep took over.

Chapter Eight

"A bit of a gimp, I see, but you do look well. Did you get a decent breakfast in you?"

"Yes, to all. Thank you. So, shall we roll?"

He drew in a frown. "Roll? What the hell kind of nonsense are you jabbering about now, woman?"

She chuckled. "Really, Lord Griffin. That's not very gentlemanly, I must say. But, to educate, roll means let's head out. You've been to the future. Surely you must have at one time or another been in an unfavorable area where the slang is entirely different."

His voice was a bit stern. "Sam, you have to watch what you say and when. Not everyone around here understands where I go when I am away for longer periods of time."

"Understood. Would you please give me a hand up? I'm just not that coordinated with all these yards of cloth on."

"Okay, woman, up you go." Sam grabbed the reins in gloved hands, steadying, then clicked her tongue as the mare walked on.

"Where are we headed and how far? Mrs. Hoyt warned me that a storm is brewing off the River Dee and we'd better make haste to make it back before it curls inland and soaks us all."

"So, she's a weatherwoman as well? I wonder more about her every day. Plus, she never seems to age. What magic potions are stored in that cottage of hers?"

Sam laughed as they picked the pace up to a trot. "Okay, so let's get down to business. I've been exploring your grounds and found a cottage that's in need of some repairs. It is solid from thatched roof to stone foundation. I had your groundsman give it a thorough evaluation. So, I would like to propose an offer."

"Go on. There's no stopping you when you get a notion in your head. I'm listening."

"I'd like to fix it up inside and out. I'll pay locally so I won't take up your staff's time. I can pay a fair wage. I'll hire on a maid combined as a housekeeper who I can trust. There I may need Mrs. H or Father G's help. I'll hire a gardener to come once a week to keep the place tidy in case I am off somewhere."

"You've got your mind set on it then?"

"Indeed, I do."

"Why now and what's the rush?"

Their eyes locked, but damn if the real reason was to be revealed.

"Seems logical, don't you think? I may like to have a personal life out from under your roof, so to speak. Especially if I'm to stick around for a spell. I can let Mrs. H know a specified spot at the cottage where we can correspond. Then she will always know what I'm up to."

Their legs touched as he moved closer. "Not liking that, Sam. I know I've not been around, but I've been giving you room to expand your horizons, breath and take it all in."

"That may be partially true, but you've been occupying your time elsewhere. That is your business, not mine. I want to have my own place, Adam." She softened her harsh words with a true grin. "I think it would benefit us both."

"I suppose I have no voice in this, even though I own the grounds and the buildings, right? No, you don't have to answer that. I already know I'm going to agree. So, how soon do you want to start this project? Have you even been inside to see what else is already living in there?"

"If they can get in, they can get out and stay out. I'll make that known fast. I'd already have someone lined up in the village. Two men that need work. One older and one younger and they know how to build."

"Mr. Bruce and his son, I suppose, and if it's them, then you have made a proper choice."

"Good. They are started today. I'm glad we agree. Now let's settle on a monthly rent sum. What do you collect from your other properties around here?"

"Since you are going to take care of repairs and all upkeep how about we say ten pounds a month. I know that does not sound like a lot, but you are going to have your hands full."

She eyed him suspiciously knowing he was already up to something.

"Agreed, Lord Griffin." She reached over extending her right gloved hand. "Do we have an agreement?"

"Aye." He shook her hand. "Now what's next? For sure as this road is dirt you have more on your mind."

"So true. Okay, I'm going to break a rule. How long have you been taking passages?"

He eyed her trying to figure this woman out as her sweet perkiness won over yet again. "Maybe fifteen years. I'm surprised you've barely been here a month and have gone out twice. Makes we wonder what's in place for you. Far as I know, we are out half a dozen times a year."

"Oh, so is there a chief? Someone that sits high on a perch in their castle overseeing all the lands and centuries? I'm not being sarcastic either. How the hell does this work and who manages it?"

"No one knows. That's the big mystery. Fables and myths abound in this part of the country about 'people like us'. There are even children's books written. But, it all still remains as to who and how."

"I'm going to change the subject before it causes us to go all intellectual. I just don't feel like it today. I can tell you after what we did over the last few days, I realize how important it is to appreciate every bit of my life whether I understand it or not."

His brows drew in. "We? You did not work alone?"

"Your turn to break the rules. No, I had someone from here and we worked together."

"Shit, Sam, there must be something I need to know, but I can't figure out what the hell it is yet."

"Two swears in one sentence, Lord Griffin, now you are finally speaking my language." They both laughed.

"I'm glad you are along. It sure makes the ride a lot more pleasant. How's the leg holding up? It must be a bit stiff."

"It's okay. Is that the town we are going to?" She pointed up ahead as the road forked viewing the top of a small spire.

"Indeed, you are going to meet my tenants and good friends. You will like them."

Even as they rode into town, Sam refused to identify the feelings coursing through her. They were out of Chester, away from prying eyes and someplace new. Besides all of that, she was enjoying her time with him. He was easy to be with. Raking him with her eyes as they halted, she slid gingerly off the horse right into his arms and he lowered her slowly to the ground.

Diverting those impetuous emotions, she released but frowned as he seemed reluctant to let her go. Chuckling, he took the reins and tied the horses up in front of the Prancing Pony public house.

"It's safe enough here, but bring your small bag just in case." She unlatched it from the rear of the saddle.

The smell of polished wood and cigar smoke assaulted her senses as soon as they entered. A burly man and rounded woman were quickly on approach as Sam stepped back right into his body.

"Ah, Lord Griffin, you made good time. It is great to see you both." The woman was brazen, shoving him aside quick enough, "Damn, you are still a handsome devil. Come now and give me a big squeeze."

He laughed reaching back for Sam.

"Lady Samantha these are the Hywels, Alwen and Baglen. Alwen has operated the Prancing Pony for our family for nearly forty years."

Enveloped by Alwen right away keeping a firm grip on an arm, Sam was paraded away from the men. "I insist we are on first names. When I am away from the estate, I really like to keep things simple."

Her catlike eyes were sharp and piercing, yet warm and inviting. "Samantha, it is. What's your fancy? A cup of mead, ale or wine?"

In this era, one would not normally drink this early in the day. But, water was hardly stored for more than cooking, bathing and washing clothes. "Ale. It is lovely here. How many rooms do you have upstairs?"

"Ten. We seem to fill them often being in such a good location. We are close to the river and a garrison of British soldiers. They will be here soon enough, though, then we will get busy. I'm glad you two came before that happens. So, dear," she patted a bench seat beside her while she waived a bar maid over, "two pints of ale, Elizabeth, if you would please. So, how long have you been in these parts?"

Sam's stomach tightened staring into the women's green eyes. A picture of not long ago flashed quickly through her brain. Her facial features tightened, leaning close. "I saw you. You were the cloaked woman that left the Labonte Magasin de Chapeau in Verdun."

"Ah, the little hat shop and *la bebe, oui madame*, that was me. You have very sharp eyes."

Sam raised her glass. "To you. If you had not done that..." She let it trail off.

Alwen clinked her glass. "To us all."

"Now, ladies, what are you toasting to already?"

A sharp quiver weaved through Sam before she even glanced up.

"Pardon this interruption. But we met a long time ago in Scotland. On the Isle of Iona. I am sure. If I am mistaken, I apologize."

"Ah, yes. You are correct." She knew who he was. It was the unnamed soldier that was in the church who had stood back watching her a bit to intensely. "I am so sorry. As I recall it was very rainy. I am amiss, soldier, for I do not remember your name."

Every hair was standing at attention on Sam's body.

"Correct, Lady Arnesen, for if I recall I never provided it." He swept his hat off. "Major Victor Savoy."

"Well, let me thank you again for your assistance. It was much appreciated. Tell me. Are you posted here or just passing through?"

Their eyes locked. Sam knew he was one of them, the 'others' she'd heard about. What was his game and where the bloody hell was Adam?

"I am passing through to an appointment and stopped here last night. I saw you and wanted to acknowledge our acquaintance. I hope you pardon my boldness."

Her mind was screaming, what the fuck! But, her smile was sincere. Eyes unreadable. Causing his gaze to become piercingly unrelenting.

"Why, not at all. Have a safe journey, major, and thank you again for your assistance on Iona."

They both knew what she had done in Scotland.

He bowed. "Lady Arnesen, Mistress Hywel, a pleasant day to you both."

Silence prevailed as two sets of eyes watched him leave without a backwards glance. Sam raised her glass swigging down the entire contents. "Alwen, have you seen him here before?"

"No, last night was a first. You know I can't ask. Are you safe? I saw his cold, calculating look and I know he's in passage. You'd better be on your guard. Have you been appraised that both good and bad are at work here?"

Sam shifted on the bench watching them getting closer. Had Adam seen this? She could tell something was not settled with him. But Baglen looked jovial enough. The men sat as talk changed to the arriving storm coming in much earlier than anticipated.

"I've secured two rooms for the night Samantha. The skies are black and the winds howling off the river. Our return back to *Ard Aulinn* will be delayed.",

"And good timing. Indeed it is. For we have elk tonight and fresh rosemary bread. Nothing tastes so grand on a stormy night than a hearty stew. Don't you think?"

"That sounds great, Alwen."

When it was time to light the gas lamps, the innkeepers stood leaving Adam and Sam.

"How's your leg? Do you want to take a short stroll through town before the rains begin? May feel good to stretch a bit."

Nodding, they stood and walked over.

Hanging on a peg at the door was her cloak. Adam took it down and placed it around her shoulders, sliding up the hood. Then gestured her ahead. In silence, they continued along stopping at the church and graveyard.

"Who was he?"

"I wondered if you saw."

"I did. Something did not feel right. I walked Alwen out from behind the bar and saw him engaging you both."

"This is not fair Adam. I want to tell you. Who's to know if I do?"

"Under the circumstances, I think you should. How can I protect you if you don't?"

"But what if I do speak of it, of him and it spirals into something awful for us both?" Stopping, she turned into his arms, eyes locking.

"I have an idea. Come. I want to see if the church is open."

"If you are thinking of involving the priest, I don't believe that to be a good idea."

"No." She opened the door, smiling and moved away from him rather quick for someone with a leg wound. She had her back to him and was doing something as he glanced around the church noticing only two people sitting in prayer.

Smugly, she walked back. What was this beautiful lass up to now?

"Here." She handed him a folded piece of paper ripped out of the back of a hymnal book. As he read it, his face masked over.

"Come." He whispered. "We'd better head back before it gets too foul outside." Once around the rear of the church, he took out a match and burnt the note down. Ashes flowing down onto hallowed earth.

Grabbing her hand, the wind suddenly whipped around them lifting her hood. He moved quickly walking in front of her. They stopped. Suddenly facing him, inches apart, he lifted it back up resting his hands on her shoulders.

"I know him. You are in possible danger. I don't know when or where. But we need to make a pact right now. If you ever find yourself in trouble, real trouble, where you have no way out and have exhausted all your means, I want you to make it somehow to the nearest priest, reverend or father. Write a note. Give it them. It just needs to say 'help' and I will find you. Do you understand?"

She was speechless, partially because he was so close. What had he said? Oh, yes. She had heard him. A note. A priest. Come and get me. But why had he not kissed her? She wanted him to kiss her again and probably again and again and again. What was his delay? Where was her staunch back bone and resolve now?

Reaching up, Sam pulled his mouth down to hers taking fate into her own hands.

He could not resist as their lips met.

Finally.

The intense pleasure was felt down to her toes as somehow the rumble of thunder above reached her thoughts as she pulled back.

"Thank you."

His head moved slightly, eyes briefly closed. "I need you well and safe. What kind of a person would I be since you followed me here, if I did not protect you? And Sam, the next time you kiss me like that, it will end differently. I assure you. You had better keep that in mind."

Her own boldness brought color to her cheeks. How long did she even want to keep him at bay? Keep a protective circle around her heart? Not for much longer, that she knew. This thing between them was inevitable.

"We'd better go now. I hear thunder and it's getting closer and closer. But as for running, I can't do that. I'll walk as fast as possible."

He eyed her, glancing at their surroundings. There was a path from the graveyard that would bring them to the inn.

Sweeping her up into his arms, he chuckled at her reaction. "Nope, keep it to yourself. I am saving us both a good drenching."

Arriving back, Adam set her down opening the door just as the sky exploded.

"Over here you two. I've a nice table near a roaring fire. The food is hot. Would you care for wine or ale?"

Opposite they sat, her cloak hanging on the peg close to their table as Adam replied. "Ale for us both,

Alwen, thank you." She patted his shoulder quickly disappearing toward the kitchen.

"So, what kind of games do they play here? Darts? Cards?"

He laughed. The mood lightened between them. "Darts are played in encampments between soldiers. Cards are played here. It will be much later and you will be long upstairs tucked away when those types of men come in."

"What if I am a natural card shark? Wouldn't you want to have me tweak their ego by sniffing out their weakness and taking some of their money? Maybe it could be a profitable side business, Lord Griffin."

"You and I both would be in big trouble. First, they'd never let a woman sit in on a game. Second, if they were stupid enough to do that, and you won, we'd have to hire protection back to the estate tomorrow to make it safely. Don't forget, we are still in the prime era of highway men, rogues and robbers."

She sighed. It was a dangerous yet exciting time. "Fine. I'll be upstairs. I don't want them getting frisky with me thinking I'm a tavern wench."

His appraisal gave away his thoughts. Sam grinned, cheeks turning a pretty shade of pink. "I can assure you they'd know you are a lady head to toe. But what would, as I have heard out of your mouth before, 'shock the shit out of them,' would be what you have secured inside of your thighs."

She gasped. "What do you know about that?"

"When you showed me your leg, I saw the strappings and figured you were packing something. What are they?"

The blush increased.

"Cat got your tongue, Sam?"

"Stop teasing me right now." She leaned slightly closer as he met her right in the middle, noses inches apart.

"A knife and a pistol. I keep backup bullets in my corset. You did not happen to see those, did you?"

He sat back crossing his arms across his chest, eyes turning a dark blue while a roguish grin made its way across his lips. "Samantha, you watch yourself. I am a man after all."

Tit for tat was what she thought. Raising her spoon, she tasted the stew, moaning softly. "Oh, you have to taste this it is amazing."

The subject was officially changed.

They ate in relative silence as the room filled with smoke and cantankerous voices. Adam knew it was time for her to go.

"You all set?" He rose, taking her cloak while clasping one of her hands leading them over to the front desk. Alwen was ready handing over two sets of keys.

"You two are toward the back so the noise will hardly be heard. If you need anything, Adam can come down."

"Alwen, thank you very much. I will see you in the morning."

As they took the hallway toward the back of the inn and up the rickety stairs, Sam had to let go and move up ahead. At the last door he halted, inserted the key and had the lamps lit before she blinked twice. Parting the drapes a few inches, he peered out.

It was pouring, the wind howling and whistling between the beams. But, inside it was warm, dry and safe. He unlocked the door between their rooms and slid it open a few inches.

She eyed him questioningly.

"Just a precaution. If anything did happen, you lock this side and get downstairs. I'm not trying to frighten you, not that I think I would, I just like to be prepared."

He slipped through the middle door.

"No worries. Tonight I'll sleep with my friends on."

He stopped, smiled then disappeared to his own room.

“Goodnight, Adam.”

“Goodnight, Sam.”

Chapter Nine

There was a knock on the adjoining door. "Would you be decent?"

"That's a matter of opinion, I suppose, if I am or not."

He chuckled shaking his head. "I mean, is it okay for me to come into the room?"

"Yeah." She was struggling to get her dress over her head. It was stuck. His grin grew, stretching across his features. "Need a bit of help, mistress?"

"Shut up. I can't see your face and that may save you a good kick in the shins. Yes, dammit, I need your help."

"There you go," he tugged it down over her petticoats appreciating every inch of this curvy lass. Spinning her around, he began the task of fastening buttons. Standing erect, Sam was trying to contain some unruly curls.

"You know, I like Abbey. But, I must admit you make a fine lady's maid when I'm out on the road."

Brows raised. "You know we are going to have to discuss this eventually."

"What, you being a lady's maid? Is there a secret hiding inside of you, Lord Griffin?"

Laughter echoed around the room. "No, damn that creative mind and mouth. I already feel too familiar with you and not receiving the benefit of sharing your nighttime bed chamber seems wrong."

The brush stopped in mid-air as their eyes locked in the mirror.

Long seconds passed. Finally, composure was restored. But the mark had been made. Her skin burned for want of this man. "I am afraid I don't know where I'll be tomorrow. I don't know where you will be tomorrow. At least like this, I can think about what it could be like. But, if something goes wrong, I don't want to think about what it could have been and will never be because we took things a bit too far."

"See, I look at it the other way. We should do this. Take it for all we are given. Because who knows if I'll ever see you in another lifetime again."

She shook her head in realization that what he said was so damn valid. "I think no matter how strong I am, I will not be able to resist what's between us. Unfortunately, I am just not ready yet. I feel like I need to find the key to a hidden door first. Am I making sense?"

"In a way, yes. But at least you acknowledge this exists between us."

She laughed. "I never doubted that at all. If you had not kissed me like that in Venice, I'd not be here right now, Lord Griffin. It is indeed entirely your fault."

He conceded, knowing there was much more at work here than a kiss. "You ready to have a bite and leave? We need to get back before the afternoon. I have somewhere to go."

"A passage?"

"Yes. I will be gone a few days."

"You know upfront where and when? Why do I not get advanced notice like this? Do they not know where to send the memos?"

He shook his head giving up. "To coin a phrase from your era, because you are a newbie."

She shut her door as they walked down the hallway. "Oh, stop it Anyway, how many centuries have you been in?"

"Too many to count."

"Do you have a favorite so to speak? Where you like being more than any other?"

"Here. This really is home."

"So, do I. But I admit I liked Scotland in the 1700's. I did not like France during the Great War." Stopping abruptly on the rickety stairs, he grabbed her just in time before knocking her down them.

"We'd better keep this kind of conversation to more private locations now, Sam."

"I got a bit carried away. Sorry about that. I'll zip it. Oh, look, there's that soldier. Still here. That's ironic, isn't it? He gives me the creeps. I just don't trust him at all."

As they approached, he nodded. "Lady Arnesen, nice to see you and Lord Griffin this morning. I take it you passed the night here while the storm surged outside."

Adam stepped in front of her defensively. "We did and are on our way. A good day to you, major." As Alwen rushed up to grab Sam's arm, the two men exchanged long, hard looks.

"That bloke gives the hairs on my arms quite a ride."

Sam laughed. "That's one way to put it. But I'm going to forget about him for now. As they say, forewarned is forearmed."

"You'll do just fine, mistress. But if you ever need anything and are out on the road, especially to the north, you make sure you trust anyone you encounter that is a true Norse."

Sam found that extremely strange since she'd not been anywhere near Norway, Sweden, Iceland, or the real north countries. Shivering slightly, she recalled a similar message from the tinker.

"I've got a nice breakfast for you both. Now sit and I will bring tea."

She shifted gears so fast, Sam had to stop and digest it as Adam slid in opposite. "When I'm back, I'm going to take you out to shoot and teach you a few things. I want to make sure you are fully equipped to outmaneuver the likes of him."

"Well, hello again to you too." She leaned closer. "Did I tell you that back in my time, long ago, I learned how to shoot a shot-gun from my adoptive dad and my heritage is Norwegian. Arnesen derives from the eagle. I am an amazing predator and hunter."

He could not help but smile at this intelligent and sassy woman. "All the same, I want to test your prowess and see how I can help you. I have a feeling that at some point you will be tested beyond your knowledge. I want to give to you an edge. It may save your life someday."

Thank heavens Alwen arrived with two heaping plates of eggs, sausage and toast. For she was tempted to fire back how she had survived on her own all these years. Hundreds, so to speak.

"Here you go, my lovelies. Eat up. The day has dawned bright and clear and you should have a pleasant enough ride back."

Sam was keenly aware of how close that Savoy was to their table. She made sure they kept the conversation a bit on the menial side until bidding their hosts good-bye and were mounted on their horses outside.

"How often have you gone back to 2015?"

"Three times. Sometimes finishing business is required. Then there are times where once is enough."

"I feel like I'm not done in Scotland for some reason."

He shrugged. "That could be. Time will tell. Shall we pick up the pace a bit? Is your leg up to it?

"It is. I think these two deserve a good run. Let's have at it."

After nearly two hours he finally slowed to a trot. "Can you stay close to the estate while I am gone unless you are called away? I'd feel more comfortable if you would consider it."

"I am planning on spending a lot of time at the cottage, driving the Bruce's crazy with renovations. Other than a few trips into the village and spending time with Father G, I will keep my adventures local."

"If you see him looming about, feel free to shoot him between those unruly brows. I'm the lord in these parts. No one would question if you did."

She laughed. "I don't think he's stupid enough to come and pay me a visit."

"Perhaps not. But all the same, keep those friends of yours on you no matter where you go."

"I can assure you other than when I sleep in my bed here, they are always on me."

The stable hand was awaiting them as they turned up the lane behind the estate. They dismounted and went around the side terrace and entered his study. When inside, she headed toward the door. But he halted her.

"Sam." he hesitated as their eyes locked, his filled with an unasked question.

"I don't know what it is yet. So, I can't tell you and that's honest. It's just a feeling that has come over me. If it's something you need to know about, I'll pass it along."

Then added as an afterthought, "Safe travels, Adam."

She closed the door behind her heading at a clipped pace to the rooms. Something of great importance was there as she pushed open the door closing it with the back of a boot. Leaning up against a perfume decanter it sat. Reaching for the paper, she turned it over eyeing the royal red waxed seal.

"Lady Arnesen, I need you to come to Norway. Seek passage to Northern Scotland. From there the journey will be clearer. Go to the ruins on Adam's property as soon as possible. Your instinct will provide more detail."

She turned the hand note over then back again, but there was no signature. Looking at the seal, she realized it was from the House of Olaf II Haraldsson.

Oh, my, she thought, recalling recent discovery of her true family lineage. This was a forewarning of the time-period she would be travelling to. Sometime in the first century.

Who had left this?

Damn, her heart was racing!

"Oh, my gosh. I'm off to the dark ages."

Her grin spread and voice quickened. "This just gets better and better." Quickly she threw some dressings, balm and extra base layers into her bag.

With hand on hips, Sam stood back evaluating everything. A quick bath, new bandage and change of clothes were in order. It was late summer here, but as she was travelling north, cold weather clothes would be a necessity. Hastily, she rang for Abbey, began removing her gun and knife setting them under one pillow while preparing to leave right away.

"Yes, mistress." Abbey stood just insider her door.

"Oh, good. Please bring me a kettle of hot water. I need to refresh and change and then I'll be heading out. When you come back, I will have a letter for you to give to Lord Griffin. Make sure you hand it to only him. It is critical he receives it straight away. There will be another to deliver by early light to Mr. Bruce in the village. "

The maid closed the door and rushed off returning minutes later with three other servants all carrying large pots. The tub was quickly filled to half and it was enough for a fast bath and wash of hair.

"Abbey, you are a godsend. I'll dry off while you hand me my clothes. The letter for Lord Griffin and Mr. Bruce are over there on my dresser. Take them both. If you would run down his Lordship's now, I want to ensure he receives it before I go, please."

"Yes, mistress, I'll be quick. I know you are in a hurry."

Sam put the necessities back in place. Reached into the dresser and removed extra bullets and slipped them into one boot. Partially dressed, she sat and awaited Abbey's return to finish the buttons. Glancing around the room, she decided to bring her small Vera backpack and put in tissues and a few other things just in case.

"Mistress, he was in his study. I handed it to him. But did not wait. I returned straight away."

"Wonderful, remind me when I get back to take you to town. We should go shopping for a new dress. Also, I wanted to run something by you. Would you be interested in coming to come work for me at my new cottage when it's livable?"

"Oh, mistress, what? You are leaving us? Oh, of course. The letter to Mr. Bruce. It is about renovations, correct?"

"Yes, I am letting a cottage on the grounds and Mr. Bruce and his son will be updating it. If I am gone a while, I'd like to have someone keep him on track. Do you think you may be interested in doing this for me? We can revisit this again when I return. I spoke with Mrs. H already and she is leaving this to us to decide."

"I would! What do you need me to do beside give him the letter while you are away?"

"Just go over and check his progress. I've written up a short list of things he's to work on first, which matches what I put in his letter. It is over there. Just be my eyes and ears while I am away, okay?"

"I will, mistress, and thank you."

"Excellent. Then it is agreed. When I get back, we go shopping. Will you also let Mrs. H know I had to go out?"

"I will, anything else?"

"No, you can go. Thank you, Abbey."

Stepping out the back entrance, Sam lifted the hood on her cloak and walked on. Missing Adam by mere minutes.

***

The sky was lit with stars as the full moon guided her steps toward the ruins. Somehow this time was different, she could feel it. Walking down the stone steps, Sam, felt prickling alertness as she began the descend up the other side. Immediately, she was propelled onto a horse, quickly grabbed the reins tightly to avoid falling off and beneath their pounding hooves.

Fast approaching was a league of Anglo-Saxon soldiers. Glancing, while the stead ran at a break neck speed, their uniforms appeared to be under the rein of King Athelstan. Damn! Glancing over her shoulder once more, she caught sight of none other than Major Victor Savoy.

Arrows were flying as the mare raced, barely keeping ahead of the charging group. Loud voices were getting closer and closer as fear and adrenaline intermixed. Their voices rising one above the other. Yeah, it was Savoy. Demanding she halt in the name of the king.

A wry smile creased her lips.

Like hell she would!

That's when a piercing pain racked her shoulder nearly knocking her off the mount. Placing a hand there, a warm stickiness seeped into the glove.

"Oh, mother of God. Not again! Really? What the fuck was that?"

Thoughts streamed through her brain faster than could be processed. Realizing the best course of action would be to dismount, Sam pulled the reins tightly, rearing off to hide in the thick forest. The bleeding needed to be staunched. Jumping to the ground and slapping the mare's ass, she and the animal disappeared in separate directions into its denseness.

Slowly moving further in, she listened acutely for their approach. An arm, out of nowhere, reached out. Grabbed her roughly, strongly, then slapped a hand across her mouth.

In vain she tried to bite it.

"Shut up, woman, I am trying to help you! "He hissed. "The way I see it you have two choices. Scream and they will find you, in which case as I will move away unnoticed. Or, you can trust me. Do you want to leave your fate in their hands, madam, or in mine?"

She nodded her head.

"Wise choice. Now, I'm going to remove it."

Turning around as his other arm held her body tight against his, she tried to gain freedom. His grip was iron tight wrapped around her.

"I am shot, you ass. I need you to let me go so I can check if it passed through and get a bandage on right away."

"Let me look," He could see the blood forming on her under garment. "It has passed right through." She stood hands on hip ready to wage a dark war with this man who was apparently here to help her.

"How the hell did you know which shoulder? I did not tell."

"Because I shot you with an arrow, lass."

Her face blanched. "You what! For heaven's sake, why did you do that?"

"I needed to get your attention. Now, keep yourself calm. I know what I'm doing. I am here to assist you."

Laughter burst out. "Oh, really? How nice of you to shoot me then offer assistance. That's just grand of you. What else are you planning? Mind telling me up front so I can be more prepared?"

He weaved the bandage over her shoulder and ripped off a piece stuffing it under the wound.

His silence pissed her off. “How about we start with a name. Who are you?”

“Gunner Gudrun at your service, mistress.”

This was just uncomprehensive. Why he’d shoot her to help her out of a chase from those soldiers? Hovering on her lips were a large stream of vulgarities. “And you know who I am?”

“I do. Now, if you don’t mind, I’m sure by now they’ve caught up with your mare and are doubling back. My stead is back a bit so we need to move on and get him.”

Walking beside his tall, robust frame, her mind did wander taking quick glances at his clothing. For sure he was a manly man as she caught sight of his horse just up ahead. He was enormous! As if she was as light as a feather, the stranger lifted her up setting her before him, then mounted taking up the reins. His large frame enveloped her body, making her feel quite small, all of a sudden.

“Where do we go?”

“Northern Scotland. There’s a village where a woman will help us. She’s a Beaton. Then we move on to Stavenger.”

“Norway? That’s in Norway. How the hell are we going to do that?”

“I needed you injured to enable us entry into this village. It is highly protected. With you a Scotswoman and requiring the services of the healer, they will allow us in.”

“But won’t they stop us because you are from an invading territory? Is not that too dangerous?”

“I can speak with a Scottish brogue, so they won’t have any idea. Besides, my clothes are just servants as to not raise suspicions. I go by the name of Shamus Dougall and have our papers secured if needed. You, mistress, are Lady Elles of Kincard. A long standing family in the Highlands. We were put on by those damn Saxons, who are short on any dignity, the bloody heathens.”

"You speak well, but better curtail using words like dignity. I doubt in this time servants speak like that. Right? I suppose if I look in my bag, I will see my own papers?"

There was no comment as his warm breath permeated threw the layers of clothing. Brows drawing in, Sam had to wonder why he was affecting her so strongly.

"How long before we get there? I would really like to know that damn band of unsavory cutthroats will not get their hands on me this night."

"I was warned your tongue could be foul."

She lowered her head, glad for the darkness as she felt the heat on her inflamed face. "I apologize I offended you. I will curtail my vocalization of what is really the truth."

He chuckled. "Spirited too. Nothing wrong with a spirited woman."

"Anyway, how long before we get there?"

"About five hours of riding. Are you feeling well enough? I tried to give you a clean wound. But if you start to feel feverish, we will stop and I'll clean it out."

"I think we'd better muddle on and leave it. Then the guards at the village won't think we are up to something."

"That's your choice. But, you need to make sure to tell me if it gets worse. I hear you have quite a stubborn streak in you."

"I won't ask who fed you all these lies. So, is Kenneth II still King?"

"Yes, although his health recedes."

"Oh, my goodness," she said out into the dark night, "I'm in the year 995. The Dark Ages."

"Mistress, women don't speak out like you did earlier, or now. They stay behind their men well out of sight doing women's work. It's going to be hard for you to not be verbal when you see village life in this time, but you must. Remember we have a higher purpose."

"You said what I see for village life in this time. I surmise you are on a passage as well?" Answers were needed and time was of the essence.

"Yes, to guide and assist. No further discussion. I will not disclose what is burning to be asked."

She smiled, unwittingly leaning back into his strong chest and felt protected and safe.

"Get some rest now, mistress, you will need it."

She had to get the last word in before sleep closed in.

"That's an interesting word."

"What is?"

"Mistress. Some men use it in a polite way. Some to hide their inability to commit."

Her eyes closed as his arms tightened around. A thought suddenly sprang to life. Was he the other one the tinker had spoken of?

Body sagging, breathing quieter, he knew although it was dark, that she rested a bit easier. Pulling her closer to ensure she did not fall, he lifted a hand up tugging on his beard. All the warnings about her had been accurate.

Chapter Ten

"Mistress, rise and look awake. We are fast on approach to the village perimeter and are under observation."

Moaning, Sam's eyes did not fully open. The burning in her shoulder increased, forcing her back into unconsciousness. Placing his cheek to her forehead, he quickly slowed the stead. She was burning hot.

"Damn."

Two armed clansmen stepped out of the woods, halting progress. "Identify yourself."

"The name's Dougall with Lady Elles of the Clan Kincaid." He held her and the reins with his left hand while reaching under his cloak for his packet of papers.

Swords were drawn in a flash.

"Easy there, Dougall." One of them moved forward slightly and halted, clearly recognizing a man of their own. "What ails her?"

"Shot by a band of Saxons, led by that bastard Savoy."

Both men eyed each other briefly.

"We need a warm place I can lay her. I need to look more closely at the wound. She has the fever in her." He threw down the pouch as it landed at their boots. Once reviewed, it was handed back up to him.

"Do you have papers for her as well?"

"Aye, on her. If you want me to set her down, I can provide them."

"Of no matter. Go ahead slowly."

As Gunner kicked the sides of the mount and moved on toward the castle, he glanced around knowing this settlement would eventually become the thriving City of Aberdeen.

Even in her sleep she moaned, as concern became etched on his bearded face. As they entered the inner courtyard, they were detained a second time.

"Stop there and wait."

He pressed his mouth to her ear. "If you can hear me, we are inside. I hope to have help soon." She pressed a hand against his chest. She had heard.

One of the men returned, followed by a small, heavy set woman. Her hair and hands flailed madly in every conceivable direction.

"Come along and follow me." As she gave Sam the once over. "Oh my, she's a lady. No dragging your muddy boots, now get on with it!"

Gunner smiled. Yes, this was the woman they were hoping to find. The great Beaton.

"Put her on that bedding. Now hurry, take the cloak off and turn your back. I need to ask you questions while I work."

Instantly he did as bid.

"Oh, bless her, but praise all that's holy. You got here just in time. I will mend the devil's work. Go. Get yourself some bread and wine in the hall. I'm sure the Laird will want a few words before you come back here to your mistress."

Glancing cautiously around, Gunner strode up the stone stairs, weaving his way back toward the Great Hall. The second he sat, a wench sauntered over settling a foamy mug of ale and plate of meat before him. Her grin said it all as he provided one right back.

Under apparent observation, he dug into the food not stopping until the plate was empty. Pushing it away, crossing his ankles and leaning back, he watched as a gangly youth approached.

"The Laird will see you now, follow me."

With few exterior windows and thick wax candles lit, the room still appeared to dark for him.

“So, Shamus Dougall, how is it that you are here with the lass? What happened and where?”

“She is my charge. I was transporting her to Kierloch when an attempt was made by a band of Saxon soldiers to detain us.” He stopped, leaning cocky to one side smiling. “I managed to get us on our way, but not before the lass was hit.”

“Kierloch, you say? She’s Mistress Elles of Kincaid?”

“That she is.”

“Kincaid once assisted my very own wife at a time of need. ‘Twas before we were wed years ago. I am foul in not extending my hand to you. Rupert Donald of the Clan Donald and Chief Laird of Castle Druim.”

The two shook hands. “I will extend our full hospitality while she recovers. I assure you that the Beaton will heal her. She performs incredible deeds.”

Gunner nodded. “I’m sure in this case I can say we appreciate your assistance. I was in a bit of fear for the mistress, as she took a fever. I’ll go back to see if I can gain access. Your Beaton looked hell bent on keeping me out while she worked her magic.”

He chuckled. “We don’t know if she’s a witch, but her healing powers and knowledge of the herbs are amazing.”

Nodding, closing the creaky wooden door behind him, Gunner circled back down to the Beaton’s room. Hand poised on the latch, it suddenly swung open causing him to start.

“She’s high in fever and has lost blood. It’s up to her now and the good Lord above.”

She rushed passed as he glanced watching her hastily retreating form. Was she leaving Lady Elles alone with him? Returning? What a strange little woman she was. Roughly tugging on the closest chair and pulling it over to the makeshift bed, he glanced down at her face, dewy with fever. Gently he took a small hand in his large, calloused one.

"I'm here." Was all he said. Feeling a tinge of remorse that he had to do such a thing to get them into this village.

Thirty-one hours passed. Still he did not leave her side except for private matters. In between, she weaved between gibberish, talking about a man named Adam and cycling. That did bring a smile to his face. Once he was placed at a very important place in time. In 1960's Europe during one Tour de France. A time of peace and love.

It had indeed been the golden age of psychedelic images, wild parties and some interesting music. All the while, he was glad he had finished his tasks and had left with all brain cells miraculously still working.

As he lit more candles, she stirred at last. Quickly, he went over sitting down. "So, was it worth it?" she whispered. "Shooting me with that arrow or whatever it was."

He clasped her hand tightly. "Indeed, it was. For the woman that is attending you is the very woman we seek."

"Well, she'd better be damn important," she hesitated a bit breathless, "Shamus Dougall."

"Quiet up now, lass and rest. Do you want anything? You've been lost to us for a few days."

"Yes, I am parched and hungry."

He rose and took his own platter off a rickety table and brought it over as she gingerly sat up. "I won't have you feeding me, I may choke." She grinned, no longer mad at this handsome rugged stranger. Yes, he indeed did have charm lurking beneath the surface of that strong body and wild beard.

Darn, if he wasn't even more alluring with the heavy Scottish accent and kilt. A question did burn, but not one she dared to ask. Was there anything else in the way of garments under it?

"Point well taken. Here eat. I'll go up to the hall and let the Laird know you are awake. He's been asking about you daily."

"Do we 'know' him?"

"Aye, I do. But only as I have the history of Castle Druim and his clansmen. He does not know who I am, mistress. But beware. Long ago your father assisted his wife before they were wed. That's why he's extended his hospitality to us."

"Shit, do you know what my father did? He's bound to engage me in conversation and I have no idea."

"The Laird assisted her and her lady in waiting when they were hindered by a group of unruly drunken men at an inn in Blackburn. It is a distance away from here. But you could always say your father did not regale of his earlier tales with your mother present and be done with it."

"This is not good, Shamus. We need to get on our way. I have an idea. I will feign my weakness longer than it affects me. So how are we going to get the woman to go with us? Maybe she's content now."

"She has no choice. But that task falls on you. Get to know her and find the right time to tell her we are here to take her home. Whether she wants to go or not."

She sighed. "I suppose you have already secured us passage and a ship's journey it will be."

"It's all arranged. But, take notice. We have only five days. By that time, you must have her ready for departure. Any further recuperation can be done on board. It is a Viking vessel."

She slid the platter toward him as he picked it up and set it on the table, turning back. "I will…" his voice trailed off as he saw she was tucked back in and already fast asleep.

Moving about the castle in complete freedom, Shamus took care of what he needed to do. Lady Elles, on the other hand, felt cooped up in the alchemy chamber and wanted out. Some fresh air and yes, she wanted to get going.

Finally, after nearly three days an opportunity presented itself.

"Mistress, I don't even know your proper name so I can thank you. My strength improves daily." Lady Elles stood to be assisted in dressing.

The Beaton, hands on plump, rounded hips stared into her eyes for several long seconds. "Mistress Elles of Kincaid, I know why you are here."

Apprehension sprouted as she placed the shift back over her head and the Healer buttoned it up. "In fever, you spoke in a foreign tongue. Don't worry, Lady Elles, I am packed. Let your burly man know. Be forewarned, we are going to have a hard time getting out of here. It is well guarded around the entire area, inside and out, tight as a cork in a jug."

"Perhaps your knowledge can guide us. Is there a weakness? A tunnel? Something that can help achieve success?"

"There is. But you two will need to trust me. I won't speak about it, even though we are safe enough here to discuss it without being heard. There are not any vents for our voices to pass along or keyholes to peep through." She smiled.

"I don't know how that will go over with my companion." Turning towards him as he came down the stone steps.

"Mistress, you are up. Is that a good decision?"

"Is the door closed above?"

"It is." He eyed the two women warily. "Why?"

She gathered him in as they spoke in whispers. When finished, the Beaton added, "Mistress, the Laird will want to at least meet you so you can extend a proper thank you for his generosity and kindness. I suggest you come up tonight for the meal?"

"That's appropriate. I agree."

"Now, come, fresh air is needed. You." She pointed a finger at Shamus. "Make yourself busy until then. Perhaps take a wash?"

He eyed her sternly, flashing a warning at the excitement lurking beneath the surface of her tone. "Healer, you are different. Even I can see that. Keep those emotions under control or they will know something is amiss."

Both women watched him leave. Disappearing up the stone steps and through the door. The Beaton gave one more look over her shoulder once outside to make sure he had indeed gone about his own business as Lady Elles's voice brought her back to the present.

"This garden holds wonderful healing properties. I've not seen some of these plants where I came from."

She smiled. "My name is Gerda, it sounds better than Beaton or Healer."

"Are we being watched?"

"No, I've been here too long for anyone to care much when I leave the Keep."

"You must miss your home and family a great deal." Lady Elles touched her arm.

"Aye, mistress I do." Her eyes welled up as she quickly shook her head, warding the somber mood off. "I've never even thought about escape. It always seemed so hopeless. What I don't understand is why you two? Who sent you?"

"I can't tell you. Even if I knew. Rest assured we will get you out. I promise."

"Okay, well come along. The sun has set so we had best go inside and prepare. I will route you by his table. Do you know what to say?"

"Yes, I am ready."

As they maneuvered through the populated Great Hall, a heavy Scottish brogue halted their progress, "Ah, Mistress Elles, it must be. At last we meet!"

Cool accessing eyes swept over her as he bowed slightly. She nodded. "I am glad for a bit of fresh air finally. Your Beaton has worked amazing healing skills on me. I am very thankful for such hospitality lent toward myself and my charge, Dougall."

He patted the chair beside him. "Here, you do look a bit tired. The Beaton told me you had lost a fair amount of blood. Come and have a bit of wine and meat with me."

He stood, pulling out a chair as Lady Elles walked around the long wooden table. Every step came with scrutinizing stares from all around the candlelit room.

Gerda nodded. "Laird, I need to get these herbs set properly. I will take a platter with me this night." He watched as the Beaton disappeared from the great hall.

Sipping the wine cautiously, with a stomach nearly empty, Lady Elles stayed on high alert. "I heard of your ordeal with that blackard, Savoy. An ugly sort under the protection of the King's rein."

She grimaced, nodding. "I agree completely. He is a foul Norseman hiding under that imperial soldier creed of his."

"Fear not. When the time is right, we will take care of our friend from the North."

He meant Norway, for many had come to this area of Scotland plundering and then hiding, taking to the highways and being funded by some organization of rogue soldiers called the Imperials.

"Let us not speak of him for now, mistress." As he patted her hand she feigned a yawn.

"Oh dear me, I do apologize. But, if I may be so forward. I believe my own good father mentioned assisting your dear wife once. Will I have the privilege of meeting her?"

"No. She is in Perth with her sister who's expecting their fifth child. I will not see her back for quite some time.

But you are right. Your father did do her a service. I do believe it was at the Inn at Buckthorn, if I recall the story."

She peered into his eyes never flinching. "I beg your pardon. But, I believe it was the Inn at Blackburn that she and her lady's maid were assisted, if I recall correctly."

He relaxed immediately. "Yes, dear, I do believe you are right. So, do not laugh. For an old man, I am becoming and with that my memory fades."

An old man, my ass, she thought. His eyes were clear, strong and bright and his strength noteworthy against the tightness of his cloth shirt.

She rose. "I'm sorry I am of little company and conversation tonight. Perhaps another day will find me a bit livelier. I would beg your pardon so I can have a rest."

He pulled her chair further back. "Why of course. Make sure the Beaton looks you over. If you feel more rested tomorrow, I shall have you moved to a more suitable room." She smiled, moving away toward the spiral stone stairs back down to the alchemy.

As she slowly walked down them, she saw Gunner and the Beaton deep in conversation.

"What are you two plotting? I must have my say in it. Now give me what you are discussing."

They both swung around having not heard her arrive. "Damn, lass, you must not do that again. You move to silently!"

"So?"

"Here, put your cloak on. Dougall is going to close our exit and then double back to the forest and meet us down at the beach." Close to the burning fire in the hearth, her foot pressed down on a floor stone. A small chamber door slid open. "I found this months ago. It goes down to the beach. Unfortunately, I never located a latch to know how it closes. So, if anyone came in while I investigated, they'd realize what I was about and sound the alarm. I wanted to keep it private. I walked it just the other night. A day prior to your arrival."

"But wait, didn't Rupert have this keep built? Surely he must know about this passage."

"Aye, he did have it built. But, this room and two above were already here when a battle was fought and he took it from the Norseman. He should not even know of its existence."

"How long will it take us to get to the beach?"

"I can only measure it by my candle, about two fingers wide." She pointed to Gunner. "His journey will be a bit further. I've already outlined a route that should get him outside the castle and to the woods unseen."

"That part is not guarded, Gerda? This place is like a fortress. Even I noticed the men in the woods at different locations when we were out in the garden today."

She smiled. "You both make a good pair, I daresay. He asked me the same thing before you came down from supper."

Lady Elles grew stern. "Enough of that. It is imperative we all make it to the beach. Shamus, when do we go?"

He pulled the cloak over her shoulders and spun her around fastening the clasp under her chin. "How about now, mistress?"

Nodding, she let Gerda go first. Each lit a torch that the Beaton had procured early that day. Down the cramped, cold, dark passageway they went. The light was their shining star as the heavy door closed behind them. Rats scurried blinded by the flames shadowing off the stones. It seemed like minutes turned to hours before she could see over Gerda's head the cloudy night sky.

"Stop." She whispered. "Give me your torch. We need them extinguished before exiting the passage. There can be no chances taken that guards posted above will see them."

"Oh, mistress, you are clever, for I had not thought of that. But what about signaling the boat?"

Lady Elles laughed softly putting both out in the sand. "Hush, I hear someone just outside the cave. You stay back. I'm going to investigate."

Lifting her gown, she removed her revolver.

There he was. She squinted her eyes to be sure. Yes! It was the outline of Savoy! Slouching down, she caught him by surprise and kicked the boots out from beneath as he hit the deck. Quickly, she leaned over with the butt of the gun and gave him a good enough slug to keep him down for the count until they were safe away.

"Come out. Watch out for this ass. Hurry!"

"Oh, mistress!"

Lady Elles grabbed her arm rather roughly, tugging her along down the path. "Now, did Dougall advise where we wait?"

"Yes, down there. At the crop of large rocks. The longboat will be coming in now so we can board. His orders were explicit. He told me not to tell you until we were this far."

"Go on."

"He said, if he did not show up when the sun fully sets into darkness, at the boats arrival, we were to sail without him. Under no circumstances are we to wait."

She felt a prickle of anticipation at those words, as in the now growing darkness she took Gerda by the arm. They moved along the beach toward the approaching longboat. It was very difficult for her to grasp how time was read without an actual watch. This was a very weird experience and one that taught her she needed to learn more about it at some point in her future.

As the boat came in, guided by the gently rolling surf, the oars were raised by the men. Standing on a large rock, she grabbed the tossed rope, giving it a needed tug and winced at the pain in both her shoulder and leg. At last, it was partially up onto the beach.

"Evening, mistress, I see our cargo. Where is your companion? It was advised there would be three." His heavy Norse accent was simultaneously threatening and stimulating.

"He should be here within minutes."

He jumped out of the longboat, lifted Gerda up and placed her in as she was helped further back.

"Mistress." She turned looking up at the cliff as loud voices and unfamiliar noises could be heard. She stiffened. He had been discovered!

"We must go. Take my hand and get in so I can shove off!" Clasping it, he pulled her quickly on board. Sitting in the bow she suddenly realized something needed to be done. They could not leave without him. She would not allow it.

"Can you shove the boat off but we wait a few yards off shore?"

He pushed the boat, jumped in and sat taking up an oar while they hovered momentarily. Then, nodded to the other men as they began rowing out toward the ship.

"Wait! Please, stop! Let him swim out to us!"

Longbows and crossbows were ricocheting off the boat, whizzing into the water as he dove in and began to swim.

"Mistress! We are jeopardizing our mission and the lives of us all if we remain here any longer!"

Watching his progress, emotions bordering on hysteria, Sam leaned over nearly falling into the swells of the water.

"I know. But he is almost here! Look! If you don't wait a second longer, I will jump in!"

His gaze warned her, as he noticed Gunner was just about to grab the front of the boat.

"A few seconds more is all you have!"

Reaching the longboat at last, Lady Elles, with the assistance of another man, pulled Gunner up and in.

"You had specific orders not to wait for me!"

"And you are grateful I don't listen to orders. I knew you could make it, Gunner, so perhaps a word of thanks we did!"

He nodded to the men taking up an oar, as they were safely out of the bay. She glanced over nearly being eaten alive by the darkness of his eyes.

As they approached the ship, she grabbed the netting and started climbing up.

"Gudrun, is it appropriate for you to have your hands on my bottom half? I don't recall asking you to help me up the riggings."

He grinned into the moonlight. "Just trying to help, mistress, with your injury and all."

"That's BS and you know it."

"I'll not reprimand you on use of that. For I wager no one else that may have heard would understand what that means."

It was her turn to grin as she lifted a leg and was pulled over the railing. With everyone on board, the anchor was lifted and sails hoisted. Never had she seen such a swagger as the one being done by the approaching Captain.

"Gudrun, *du gamle J'vel*!" [Gudrun, you bastard.]

He turned to her, a broad grin on his handsome features.

"Mistress Arnesen, you will need to block your ears when this man speaks. He's already referred to me as a bastard. Let me introduce you to Captain Knutren. Captain, Mistress Samantha Arnesen and Mistress Gerda."

He bowed smiling gallantly. "Ladies, our pleasure to have you aboard. You will find your shared room is tidy, but, quite comfortable for your journey. Mistress Gerda, you will be home soon. But first you need to see to the birth of a special baby."

She grinned, knowing It had been in her palm reading.

He extended his arm, “Shall I show you your cabin?”

Sam hovered back, a strange look on her face.

“You were Lady Elles back there. On our journey to Norway, you will hold the same name you were born with in England.”

As she started to mouth what the fuck, he stood with hands on hips towering over her. “If you continue to use such language, I will have no choice but to kiss you.” He turned, laughing boldly over his shoulder and joined the men on deck.

“But wait.”

“Shit.” He mouthed out loud, then stopped. It was the tone of her voice. Soft and inviting. The temptation was too much to know what she would ask. Turning, he walked back.

Chapter Eleven

"If we already know what she's going to do and she's keen on it, why can't I return now?"

He leaned close to her and, for a split second, her heart stopped as she thought he was going to kiss her.

"Mistress, you still have other business here, that's why."

He saw her bright eyes become brighter and the flush on her cheeks and smiled, raising a brow, then leaned in and did just that. He met with no resistance at all.

"Don't tell me there's another. I won't believe you for a minute."

She stomped her foot on top of his boot as he grinned. "Did you even give me a chance to tell you there was? I did not realize I had to fill you in on my personal life. The Captain was right. You are a bastard!"

Somehow, he had steered her from above to below deck and they were at her door. Opening it, Gerda was already lying down with a huge smile on her face. Why should she not? She was going home. Sam apparently was not and needed to get away from this obnoxious man.

Turning, he was still there, smug as all hell as she kicked at the door, slamming it shut in his face. His laughter resonated through the thick wood infuriating her further.

"What did he do, mistress? Your face is bright as the noonday sun!"

"Stop it, Gerda, he's an ass."

"Your reaction says something entirely different."

"*Det er dritt*." (It's crap, I say.")

Gerda threw her quite a belly laugh. "That's crap you say? Since when do you speak Norwegian?"

Sam stopped moving up onto her berth. “I’m really not sure. Can I tell you a truth since we are bound together on this ship? I’m thinking when we are through, our paths will never cross again?”

Gerda nodded crossing hands over her chest when there was a loud rap at their door.

“Who is it?”

“Mistresses, I have a tray for you, open up.”

It was a young lad, a deck hand trying to carry successfully a silver tray holding a feast. Gerda jumped up and took it. “Relay to your Captain our gratitude, lad.” She closed the door setting it on a rickety table and glanced at her to continue.

“My real name is Arnesen, Samantha Arnesen and it’s ironic that I’m headed to where my name originates from. I’ve never been there before.”

“You will discover quite a bit on this trip. If I had my spearmint leaves, I could make you a tea and read them. But I don’t have any on me. I left behind everything.”

“Tea?”

“I can do things that show me what has not come to pass using tea leaves. There are other means too. But I must be cautious. If discovered. I could be labeled names and improperly imprisoned

“Like witchcraft and sorcery?”

“Keep your voice down. Let’s not mention that again. I am not one of those. But I have unique gifts as well.”

“Sorry, I did not mean to offend you Gerda. Were you truly trapped in Aberdeen? Did you never have a chance to escape?”

“Once. We were invaded by my own people. They locked me away in the Keep when that happened. When the Norse were driven away, I knew all my hopes were lost. I have to say, the Laird and his people always treat me with respect, though.”

"Did you ever have any doings with that Savoy person?"

"The one you knocked out at the cave? Yes. That man made my hairs rise, he is a leering bastard to say the least. I prayed to Thor asking him to come from the sea and swallow him up. He was in the village once and tried to detain me. But, one of the Laird's men was with me and persuaded him that would not be such a good plan." She grinned. "There was a confrontation. Savoy ended up with a knife wound to the face. He was alone, so he was forced to allow us to move along our way. But, I wonder if he's like a demon reappearing to take revenge on some lost soul."

Sam shuddered wondering the same thing. An immediate change of subject was in order. "Do you have family back in Norway?"

"Aye, I do. Lots of them if they are still alive. We live in a small village near *Stavenger*. As soon as I help with the births, I will go to them. It will be wonderful to be back in my home country."

"Do you happen to know how to read palms?"

She grinned, sitting beside her, taking the right one and studying it. Her brows furrowed. "Mistress, have you been married and released from that marriage?"

Sam smiled. "Yes, a while ago. What else do you see?"

"Two other men. One I think you know, or maybe you know them by now. Both are handsome, strong and quite persistent in their interest in you. But they are from different times. Oh, you are in for quite a ride! But, I also see another woman who has given you advice. You must heed what she has said."

She pulled her hand away. "Shall we have some wine? I don't know about you, but I want to eat and then sleep. Maybe in the morning the captain will let us up on deck." She stuffed a piece of meat in. "Oh, you have to try this. It is delicious. I wonder what it is?"

"It's actually not meat but salted fish. Smoked then pulled off the bone. It's very traditional in Norway."

"Well, it's good. So, you had better help yourself to some before I devour it all."

As they finished, Sam took the water from the wooden bowl and washed her face. She was not going to put on any night cream until candles were out. This woman was already a bit astute, two men, great. Now confirmed by a Tinker and a Beaton.

As her head hit the pillow and Gerda blew out the candles, she was lulled to sleep by the rocking and pitching motion of the ship. "I'm happy for you, Gerda, sleep well."

"Mistress, I'm happy for you as well. For when your choice is made, you will be very high in spirits."

Sam rolled over and closed her eyes not wanting to think about either of them right now. She was exhausted. A leg and shoulder still smarted and her heart was torn between one left behind and one here. Yes, a good night's sleep was in order.

When the day dawned bright, Sam rose, glancing out the small porthole. As she stretched, Gerda was nowhere to be found. Quickly cleaning up, she grabbed the cloak and headed topside.

On deck, she saw the captain, Gunner and the second mate who had the helm in hand. She took her time walking toward them as her sea legs were waking up themselves. As she started to pitch, Gunner was there taking her arm. "Good to see you up and about mistress. You've been asleep for forty-eight hours."

"Are you kidding me?"

"No, we were going to wake you to eat, but left you alone. You should have some food and wine and let Gerda, or, the ship's surgeon check your wound and put on new bandages."

"Oh, my goodness. I'm up here six seconds and you are bossing me about already! Can you give me a chance to catch a breath?" She tried to tug her arm away but his hand held fast with that annoyingly handsome grin on his face, again. Damn him! He was all those things Gerda said and more!

"See you are feeling better and you've found your tongue. What's gotten into you today?"

"Maybe the feeling that everyone else seems to know what the hell I am still doing here. That may have something to do with it."

He leaned in. "You can swear all you want in front of me, but keep your voice low. Others don't need to know what you are about." Glancing around, it was clear the deckhands were close enough to have overheard the tirade.

"Yeah, dressed like a lady, but the mouth of a tramp."

She laughed. "Well I must have woken on the wrong side of the berth, that's all."

He would not release her hand. "Apology accepted." He stared at her boldly, eyes daring her to spew off another round.

"Fine." was all she muttered as they moved along and stood next to the captain.

"You are looking better, mistress, the sea air must agree with you."

"I think so too as well as the good food and wine. How long will it take us to make land in *Stavanger*?"

"We should make port tomorrow midday."

"Your ship is beautiful. It has been a long, long time since I have been on one so fine." She took Gunner by the hand unexpectedly, "Would you take me around so I can see more? Gerda, care to join us?"

An obvious slow smile lit her face as she shook her head.

"What was that for?"

"Who knows, she's a mischievous sort, that Gerda. You seem right of foot on board."

"Yes, I've been on a few over the years."

"So where do you live? Where do you hang your longbow when the day's work is really done?"

He pulled her toward him, holding both her arms.

"A day's sail from the main port. You would not be interested."

"Do you have a ship of your own?"

"I do. It is anchored off shore."

"Will I get home from where we are headed?"

He shrugged his shoulders, noncommittal, leaning back against the port side rail. "What if you are not to go back? That you are to be here for quite a long time? I sense you are leaving behind someone you care about."

"Damn it, I don't even know where the heck I belong to know if I should have a relationship with anyone." Her voice had turned annoyed. Why could no one just tell her and be done with it? "This may be the only time I apologize. So here it is. Sorry. I appreciate your help. Not the fact you shot me. But, I will leave that one be for now."

An apparent nerve had been struck.

"Come on, Gerda is waving us down. It must be time to eat. With food in your mouth, that language can be curtailed."

She jabbed his ribs knowing he was fooling around, but was right. The less she said right now the better. As they ate, good ole Gerda chatted away about her homeland. The fish, market, her mum that had passed away, father still alive, brothers, all seven of them and two sisters. Yes, before they had all finished, even the captain was smiling having not uttered a word himself.

"Mistress, we should look at that bandage now. The ships surgeon has given me fresh ones to apply."

As she followed her down to their cabin, Sam, glanced back grateful Gunner had moved on with the captain and had not seen her do it. What was this all about? Did she have leave to have a relationship with him? In truth, he had been born centuries before Adam.

"Samantha Arnesen!" She hissed out into the cabin.

"What is that you say, mistress?"

"Nothing. Just spurting out loud. It's nothing."

"There, that new bandage should be suitable for the next few days. I am so excited. Tomorrow I will set foot on my home soil again!"

Sam laughed caught up in her excitement. "I know it. Once the duties are taken care of with the birthing, you will be reunited with your family."

"I was forward, mistress. I asked the Captain to have a plate brought to us tonight. I did not feel like small chatter. I hope you don't mind."

"Not at all. You know you can call me Samantha or Sam. It is just us down here."

"No, I cannot. If I get comfortable doing that and it happens in public, there will be a lot of explanations expected. None of which can be answered."

"I understand."

Staring out the porthole, she was thinking about Gunner as Gerda worked about the room humming away. She never even heard the knock at the door or plate being set down on the table. Finally, the aroma reached her nostrils. Glancing down, her eyes raised back out to the glistening water watching the light of day fade over the ocean. It was beautiful. Yes, she could not deny it. Her heart was stirring.

Directly above, Gunner stood with one booted foot up on the cross rail, while he swigged down the rest of the ale, glancing out over the water. Those stirrings reached topside to him.

Chapter Twelve

"Who are those men?" Gunner had a solid grin planted on his face. "Those are from the House of Arne, they are here to give us safe passage to Randaberg."

"Where the hell is that?" she was close to him, his ear down to her mouth. "Where the mother is about to give birth."

"Did you say *Arne*? I know my real parents' name derived from that." She held him back with a strong grip, surprising him for one so petite.

"Yes?"

"Did you hear me?"

"I did. Now come along with no more questions, do you understand? They just have to wait."

Cantankerous slaps followed strong handshakes as Gunner spoke in hushed tones to the large band of guards. To Sam, they did not look welcoming at all. It fit a historical picture she'd viewed from previous studies.

She knew them to be a mixed breed without scruples. Pagans and savages who pillage, plunder and rape leaving a swathe of fear and dread behind. A shudder passed through her as she was hoisted onto a large gelding. Gerda on the other hand, seemed to enjoy a burly man's touch on her as she flirted with him shamelessly. Sam was all too amused at how comfortable she looked in their present company. In any event, they were safe.

Holding tight to the rope, they galloped off at a rapid pace as she wondered how long before she simply fell off. Gerda seemed right at home on hers. Which Sam found amusing.

Gunner was ahead as suddenly two of the men came up, one asking a question. Or, perhaps by the way they were looking at each other, she was their discussion and no question had been asked. Keeping her eyes forward, Sam attempted to ignore them.

"You English?" She stared at her inquisitor for a few seconds. "No, my last name is Arnesen." His companion spoke. "What village?"

Damn, now she was in trouble. Was the village her ancestors hailed from even in existence yet? "It was burned when I was small. I do not know the name. I was taken to another land. This is my first time back."

Shit! Would that work? She glanced straight ahead not wanting to engage in any further conversation. Her mind beseeched Gunner back to her side, right this very second. But, it did not work

"She," he pointed ahead to Gerda, "we knew when she was young. Are you friends?"

Too many questions were being asked. "Yes."

His thigh brushed up against hers. Although he nodded as if in apology while his eyes were keen at taking her in. This was enough. She felt completely ill at ease. Finally, at her persistent silence, they moved up as a small village came into sight.

But, something was amiss.

Gunner, turned and came back.

"You stay with these two men over there under cover. Keep quiet. Mounts stable and absolutely no speaking."

Gerda came close. Horses side by side as the two men raised shields and weapons. A distant whistling came from behind as cold fear gripped Sam.

"Gerda," she barely got out, "stay close to me no matter what happens. If I tell you to get down, do it fast and keep low. I can't protect you if you wander off." She seemed to hear her but what worried Sam was how her eyes had glazed over.

Sam shook her arm roughly. "Get a grip, woman, I need you to have your wits about you."

Suddenly, the guard to her left fell, arrow piercing right through his back and protruded out the front. Gerda was on the verge of screaming as Sam quickly reached over and placed a hand over her mouth. Gerda nodded she was okay. Sliding down off her mount, landing with a thud on the rough gravel, she whispered. "Get down, now."

Pulling on her leg, forcing her to slide off, they crouched as both horses pranced nervously. Crawling on their bellies, the other guard followed them toward the brush. "Stay close to me," he pointed to Gerda. Then glanced at Sam. "You are not so important."

She understood while clutching the coldness of the knife just as two men jumped out of nowhere, seized the guard and were inches from slitting his throat as Sam threw the blade hard as possible, hoping for the best.

Backwards he fell, embedding it further, eyes closing as he passed out. Right about now, she cared less if he was dead or not. By her quick action, the other man had time to draw his sword, killing the other attacker.

He nodded. "Stay here. Pull your knife out of him and prepare. Guard the Beaton with your life." Both women watched him scour the area searching for more of them.

Sam turned the man onto his stomach, put a boot on his back trying to pull it out, but slipped, falling onto him. He did not move as horrified, she put a knee on his back and pulled it. The gross sound nearly caused her to vomit. Using the grass, she wiped it and stood to a petrified look on Gerda's face.

"Are you hurt? Is that his blood?"

Sam glanced down and shook. Had she killed him? He had not moved at all. A lot of blood had soaked her and the ground under him. She had to know. Reaching down, she placed a shaking finger against the hollow of his neck to check for a pulse. It was there but very faint.

Someone was approaching fast as she spun around, poised, knife raised ready to strike again. Her motion was brutally stopped by an iron grip.

"Woman, are you injured? Where is the other man?"

"He's there." she pointed. Just as he made his way back to them. "The other one was pierced by an arrow."

He shook her roughly. "Dammit! Answer me. Are you hurt?"

"No. No I am not. He is though. Do we just leave him here?"

"He tried to kill you, mistress. What would you do now? Bandage him, leave him off in the next village so he could stalk and kill you?"

"No, but he is still alive, although barely."

Gunner was pissed off, speaking briskly. "Gerda, is there something you can quickly do? The rest of the men have checked the village. It was pillaged by the Normans. They must have been part of it and are still close by. We need to divert. Do something now. They will be back here shortly."

She pulled up some moss and spit on it several times, placing it on the wound under his shirt. She took her elk skin horn filled with water and placed it beside him. "It is in his hands now if he lives or dies."

Sam picked up her cloak from the grass and threw it over her body just as the men reappeared. They all stood near and glanced down at one of their own dead. Conversations took place but neither women could hear. Once concluded, Gunner approached.

"Let me get you onto your mount." She put a leg up and took the rope. He was watching her closely now knowing she had never been in a situation like this. "I'll ride with you both."

Sam nodded, but remained quiet. As they moved on and darkness took over the day, it started to rain. He reached over and pulled the hood up over her head and handed over a piece of dried fish. Taking it, she clicked her heels into the mare's side and moved up next to Gerda. "Are you doing okay?"

"Mistress, I'm more worried about you. I've seen plenty of savagery in my time. But I don't think you have seen the likes of what occurred today."

She handed her the fish. "I'll be okay. I'm adjusting my thinking that he was alive when we left. If any bit of magic will heal him, it will be what you did. I'm going to keep that thought because I may never know."

"Better that you are long gone if he does live and heals. No man would want to be knowing he was bested by a woman." She smiled, patting Sam's hand. "You are a lethal weapon with that, mistress."

"It is a benefit to carry certain items of comfort Gerda." Sam nodded to her slowing the mount as Gunner caught up. "You are not hungry. But still need your strength."

"I can smell his blood on me, Gunner. I can't eat right now. How much longer before we get there?"

"Daylight. Do you want to ride with me? I'll tie your horse to mine so you can rest."

"Of course not. Then I'd appear weak."

She smiled as they exchanged a long look.

"They won't say it, mistress, but they think you are a warrior from the House of Arne and have the blood of the Goddess Freyja coursing through your veins."

"Frey what?"

"Freyja. The Goddess of love, fertility and battle. I'd say that about sums you up."

Thank heavens it was dark, for she was sure her face was flamed again. "Funny I did not know that. I am more familiar with Thor, Forseti and Hoenir."

He chuckled catching himself. "Hoenir, the Silent God? Mistress that's priceless."

"Glad I could lend a bit of humor to this dark night." Ironically, they were both smiling as the soldier from earlier rode up beside her.

Sam locked eyes with him.

"You fought well, Arnesen."

Nodding, she did not reply as he clicked his heels and continued up ahead. Now, at least in this group of men, she'd be left to her own devices and was safe.

Gunner took out his skin and drank of wine, handing it to her. She took a large gulp, swallowed then took a second before handing it back.

"It will warm your insides in this dankness."

"I don't suppose there is a hot shower waiting for me when I get there?"

"You don't quit, do you? A true picture of you is forming in my mind."

"Do you think we could disperse with the formalities in lieu of what we've been through? Do you think it would be permissible to call me Samantha?"

"It took you long enough to ask."

She gave up at that point and just shut up. As they rode through the night and the sky was returning to daylight, she saw the village and Keep. "What is that?"

"Where hopefully we won't be long. It's Castle Berghus. Just a note here. You need to pay attention to not being alone in halls, rooms or grounds. Either I am with you or Gerda. I can say the men from this area are ruthless and would not hesitate to take you in broad daylight in front of their wives."

She nodded appreciating his frank candor. As they dismounted, the group dispersed as Gunner took her by the arm, motioning Gerda to move up ahead of them. Apparently, she already knew where they needed to go.

In the great hall, Gerda halted taking Sam by the arm. “We need to go up there. Don’t let go of me. Now come along. Time is ticking away.”

Turning to speak to Gunner, Sam stopped as a wench with heaving cleavage launched herself into his arms and planted a hearty kiss on his lips. Quick enough she had tugged him into a secluded location. Jealousy, strong and undeniable, sprang to the surface as Gerda dragged her up the remaining stone steps onto the second landing.

Bastard, she thought! How dare he? But then again, what the hell was she thinking, anyway? If this was what men who take passages do, then she’d think long and hard about having any kind of relationship with Adam if she ever got back there again.

“Mistress, why are you making this so hard for me? We need to hurry!”

“Gerda I’m sorry. Where do we go?”

“Into a bedroom to help with birthing. Asta does not even know she’s having twins. But I do. I saw it in the leaves. We must be quick about getting into her rooms.”

She swung a large door open to a rush of ladies in waiting coming over to halt her progress.

“Stop, I am Gerda the Healer. Listen to me so we can help Mistress Gud. I need a large kettle of hot water, a knife, clean linen and some silk twine. Now, please go and get what I have asked!”

People started hustling from the room as she slid her cloak to the side and rolled up her sleeves, sitting down beside the Mistress Gud.

“There, there, I will help you. How much pain are you in?”

She was sweating as Sam took a cloth, wiping a brow. “Who are you?”

"I am Mistress Samantha here to help Gerda." She placed a hand under her shoulders and lifted. "Here, take a sip of some wine."

Sam was afraid to take her cloak off for fear the woman would see all the blood. That just did not seem like a good idea since she was about to give birth. As the ladies started coming back with the necessities, one came over and tapped Sam on the shoulder.

"Mistress, Master Gudrun asked me to give you this. He instructed me to wait while you changed and to take your dress with me." Sam turned expecting to see the wench from downstairs that had accosted him. Suddenly relieved it was not. Great, she thought, it was probably one of hers, though. Regardless, she stepped back behind the barrier and hastily removed it, rolling it into a tight ball, then came out and handed it over.

She whispered. "You take that and burn it without talk, am I clear?" Her voice commanded complete authority as the maid nodded and hurried from the room to do exactly that.

"Mistress, wash your hands. I need you to take the white cloth and fold it into fours and have it ready. I am going to lift her up and I want you to put the knife beneath her spine, halfway down."

Sam nodded working quickly.

"Mistress Gud, are you ready to start pushing?" She nodded, clenching teeth as the pains increased. "I'm ready. I have instructed a servant to wait outside the door for news to take to my husband." As the moans increased in earnest, her delicate hands clutching tightly at the bedding. "Tell me when…" Her voice quivered in pain.

"Push. Yes, harder. One more mistress, I can see the head! Oh. It's a red-haired girl." She handed her over to Sam as she cleaned and wrapped her snugly.

"But wait, there is another on the way!" Gerda's excitement radiated around the room. "Push, my lady, push again!"

The squeal of a second arrival brought Sam closer, ready to take the newborn.

"It's a boy! You have a handsome son, and a comely girl." Gerda handed him to Sam as she quickly had the twins nestled side by side in a basket.

"Oh, Mistress, they are indeed beautiful and listen to them talking to each other. They will always be close. Do you have names for them yet?" Sam knew she was rambling on. But, since she had no children of her own, seeing this process was amazing.

"We had not thought of two, but the boy is going to rule someday. So, his name is Olaf II Haraldsson. I think his sister should have the great name of Gerda."

"Oh, how lovely of you to do that. I am honored."

Listening to them, Sam crept over to the door and opened it. "Go and tell the King he has a fine, healthy son and daughter, Olaf and Gerda." Closing the door, it dawned on her why she was here.

Her head began to spin slightly, mouth going dry. When she had paid for her family ancestry, she recalled seeing this name. Asta Arnesen Gudbrandsdatter. This was a long distant relative. Her ancient family.

Creeping over toward one darkened corner, she wept. Finally, as the tears diminished, she wiped away the rest and found a true smile emerging from inside as it ended up on her lips. This would be a time she'd remember all the rest of her days.

There was a soft knock on the door as the King came in. Proud as a peacock, love shone brightly in his eyes as he quickly moved over to his wife's side. Gerda had placed both children in their mother's arms, as he reached down gently touching both with a fingertip.

“We must go.” Closing the door, Gerda, took her by the arm and squeezed it. “I heard you crying. Are you okay, mistress?”

“Yes, it was the first time I’d seen a child born, let alone two. Gerda, you are indeed a miracle worker. That was beyond words.”

“Thank you. I will stay on a few days to help them. Then I will leave to join my family in the village. You will be leaving sooner, I believe.” As she moved off suddenly.

Feeling him before he even arrived, Sam glanced up as he approached with a servant in tow.

“I’ll take you to your room where there is food and wine. Gerda, go with the servant and she will show you where to sleep this night.”

“Wait.” Sam spoke. Turning towards Gerda’s arms. “I will think of you often, Healer.”

“And I of you, mistress.” Quickly Gerda was around the hall, out of sight.

“This way, Samantha.”

He opened the heavy wooden door stepping aside to let her pass. “I see you got changed in time.”

“Thanks for taking care of it. I hope you did not remove it from that wench you were locked with and left her standing someplace cold.”

“A bit jealous?”

“Nope, not at all.” She went quiet, but the urge to hurl something harmful at his head was absurdly strong.

"I’m going to be sharing your room tonight. There is a rough crowd down there celebrating the King and Queen’s new additions. So, I want to prevent any issues with delaying our departure tomorrow.”

She spun around, furious, staring him down, but was instead met with his hard, muscled chest.

“Calm down. I will sleep on the floor in front of the hearth. It is only one night.” She closed her eyes to will her heart from pounding as his hands moved slightly down to the curve of her waist.

"Are you afraid to look at me?"

If he had said look at me, she would have bristled, but instead he was daring her and she was no coward.

As she raised her eyes to him, her toes lifted and met his lips. The braided rope belt fell to the floor as he hoisted the shift over her head and stopped at the ties crossing over her heaving bosom.

He took her lips again. Not so gentle this time as she weaved her arms up around his neck and grabbed his long, unruly hair. If he shaved the beard and cut the hair, would he be truly handsome as imagined?

"Samantha, if you were just the wench downstairs I'd not hesitate to have you on your back right now. But, you are not. We've been through a lot. Here tonight is not where I want it to begin for us."

He lowered her to the bed. She turned and eyed it. Yes, she internally thought, it would serve them both.

"So why don't you just go and do that, with that wench down there. Get it out of your system and then return. You can knock and I'll let you in."

He grinned expecting a retort of such. "Because I am protecting you and she is more than likely already entwined with another. Possibly two."

She scuffed up the dirt on the floor with one shoe. "All right, then come over and sleep here. There is plenty of room for us both. I promise you I will not try and seduce you in the same manner that you use. Especially during the lateness of the night."

She slid under the furs, laid back on her side of the straw mattress, closed her eyes and was asleep in minutes.

He chuckled, settling down opposite following her lead and was also asleep in short order.

Chapter Thirteen

Oh, this dream was delightful, she thought, resting under his chin. Then, an exploration began while weaving an errant hand beneath his tunic to feel the heat of his skin. He was a chiseled being, as gentle fingers cruised over the hard plains and valleys of his chest. As her hand moved slightly lower, she felt the hairs, sighing, as suddenly her body was swung swiftly backside with his lips possessing such searing passion, it forced her toes to curl.

She wove her hands up under his thick long hair, clasped them behind his neck, noticing a crevice. His hand cupped a breast long before it had peaked, hurting against the rough shift she was wearing. When his lips left hers and he leaned up on elbows, his deep raspy voice penetrated her sleep induced brain.

"That's a hell of a way to wake a man up, mistress." Her eyes shot open, cheeks inflamed. But where could she go with him holding her down like this. So, she smiled, which threw him off guard. He truly had expected a knee to the groin. One eyebrow cocked as a crooked grin appeared on his handsome face.

"What, no fighting? No slugging or throwing me to the dirt floor?"

Instead, she wiggled, knowing that caused him much more discomfort.

"Samantha, I'd take you here, right now and you know it. Don't fool with me. Besides, it is nearly first light. As much as we would both enjoy our tryst, we need to head out of here before the King and Queen want to see you. I'm sure sooner or later they will have more questions. We cannot stick around to answer them."

She looked put out that he was making so much sense. But, he had not budged an inch.

"You had better let me up then. So, we can prepare to exit before any of that can take place."

He slid off her and sat on the side of the bed glancing toward the now brightening sky. "Yeah, we have to go. Can you be ready in a couple of minutes?"

"Yes." She rose throwing the tunic over her head and picked up the rope, tying it. "That's it. I can put my hair up on our way out." Sliding the cloak on, she glanced about the room. "Let's go."

They crept down the stairs and through the hall. Moving slowly against one far wall, he surveyed the scene. Everyone was sleeping. Slowly, they continued along taking the safest exit. Once outside, he lifted the hood, reminding her instantly of another man at another time.

"We just need to go to the Chapel. It's a short walk. Stay close and be quick with your steps."

Nearly jogging to keep up with his long strides, they arrived outside the lovely, old, stone chapel. Halting to glance up at the beautiful workmanship of the stain glass windows, he tugged her inside.

"No confessional?"

He grinned. "No, they did it face to face in this era. Those came a few centuries later."

"How do we get out then?" As if in a trance, Sam glanced about at the cold, stark beauty. She turned toward the altar as a soft, golden beam encased it.

"Go, we don't have all day!"

She moved into it, walking down a long tunnel brightly lit with torches.

"Well." she said out loud noticing he was not behind her. "This is very different."

Up ahead, the paths forked. As she walked by the path to the right, she halted and looked back.

"Hmm." she said continuing. "Maybe he was staying or his beam took him a different route." Shrugging, she continued along the path to the right.

The announcement was loud and clear.

"Mind the platform. The train to Exeter is now approaching the platform."

Exeter. Momentarily dazed and confused, Sam watched the train approached. The doors opened and she got on, found a vacant seat and fell onto it. Pressing her forehead against the cold glass, the countryside passed quickly and she knew it well. The train stopped as she rose and got off.

"Holy shit, am I really back?" She mouthed rather loudly.

Up ahead parked exactly as remembered was her red Spark. Sitting in the car, a grin formed while turning the car key. She tested the wiper blades. Even though it was not raining.

One of her favorite songs, Karma Chameleon, blared from satellite radio. Which quickly brought her mind back to the present.

Clicking in the seatbelt, Sam shifted through the gears, depressed the button so the sunroof opened and burned some serious rubber out of the parking lot. The attendant smiled, waving to her. She knew him! It was Dave. Damn, what the hell had been going on? Did someone throw a mind-altering drug into her lunch drink? While she tried not to think about it, or anyone for that matter, she was pulling into her driveway.

Lifting the wreath on the back door, she took out the spare key, unlocked it and walked in. A loud sigh escaped as she moved through the utility room removing her Sperry Topsiders. Her Pinarelli road bike was straight ahead, leaning against a wall. It was indeed like a long-lost lover. Oh, if this was real or not, she was going to take a ride. Throwing her clothes right there, she changed and was out on the road in five minutes.

Glancing down at her speedometer, she knew exactly what route to take. Pedaling down a lovely, English, country lane, one she knew so well, Sam released a hoot that sent a bouquet of pheasant scampering from the brush as she sped by.

Weeks, had she been gone weeks or longer? The date on her Garmin said it was 16 September and she had left for Venice in May!

She spewed out loudly, “Oh, Mother of God. I was gone almost four months? Could that be?” Glancing up at the puffy clouds, Sam noticed they were beginning to turn into angry storm faces. “I’d better get my ass in gear and head back. That’s not a pretty looking sight at all.”

She pulled the bike up on the porch and brought it back into the utility room. But, did not put it away, “You and me, my friend, tomorrow. I sure am glad to see you again.”

That night she was restless, tossing and turning endlessly, it seemed, for no apparent reason at all. Here, she was safe from the likes of Gunner, Savoy and even Adam. If they were even real. Fluffing the pillow and turning a cheek, she glanced out the open window watching the storm come straight for her. All she could think about, as sleep claimed her body and mind, was Dorothy in Kansas.

Birds were singing, had she not heard the same song at Adam’s estate? She opened one eye slowly to check, and then the other, a smile on her face. Nope, the harsh storm winds had passed and this morning she was indeed inside her cottage in Exeter.

Three days of riding ensued which had her spirits soaring high as she tucked the bike in the closet. Dripping sweat, she started walking up the stairs peeling cycling clothes, bit by bit, until she was naked at the top then started a bath.

Sliding in with a sigh, Sam settled back, head resting on a pillow, and closed her eyes. This was heaven. These were the two things she missed being anywhere but in this century. A bath and bike. If she was stationary in the latter part of the 1800's when bikes were invented, it would have suited her a bit more. But alas, this was a nice treat!

"You really should lock your doors, you know, although I have to admit I was looking forward to finding you at the end of the clothes trail."

She reached for her gun, pointed it at Adam, then lowered it slightly as the movement spewed water all over the tiled floor. Her lower jaw dropped as she put the gun back behind the pink fluff and reached for a large towel, standing.

"This makes me wonder more and more who you really are because you found me."

"When you did not come back, I had to."

"Did you ever think maybe I needed a bit of time alone?"

She watched his eyes rake her over. Slowly taking in her wet, reckless curls then finally reaching her toes. She let the towel slip, putting on the robe and tugged the straps tightly keeping it shut.

"I really wanted to make sure you are okay and my cellphone in 1865 is not as savvy as yours in 2015."

"Very funny." She walked over having pulled the plug on the bath and stood within fingers reach of him. "I'm well, as you see. So, do you want to tell me how you can come here if you are not on a purpose?"

He leaned against the door jam. "Well, Sam, it's like this." His finger found its way to that tie, eyes steady with hers. "I have liberties that not everyone else does. So, I took one and came thinking you may be here. If you were not, I was going to head to Norway."

The tie was undone. "Do you know all my moves? Honestly, were you aware of me before we even met in

Venice? Did you have anything to do with it not being by chance?"

She felt that one roaming finger touch her right hip.

"Yes, to all three."

His left hand moved up her curvy waist as she leaned toward him. The robe slid away into a heap on the floor.

"That's not fair." Her voice was hoarse.

"Then make it fair."

She unbuttoned his shirt, closing her eyes as she stood on tip toes and kissed him. His shirt went to join her robe as she pressed her breasts into his chest. His breath into her mouth was warm and rushed, then she stopped and leaned back.

"Gunner was you."

"Yes."

"You were with me in Aberdeen and on the ship and you slept with me at the castle."

His warm lips caressed the curve of her neck lowering his mouth down and sucking on a puckered breast.

"Yes."

She left her body then, not just by the power of his touch but by the power of his love. She slid his belt off as his jeans followed.

"Glad I took my shoes off downstairs so I could creep up on you."

"Why did you not tell me?" They were head to toe naked.

"Because how well would it go over if I told you I had to shoot you to get you to help me?"

She managed a small smile.

"So how did you know it was me?"

"The notch in the back of your neck."

He leaned down and positively possessed her mouth lifting her up as her legs wound around his powerful hips. "And your kiss. No man has ever kissed me like you do."

He found her bed and slid them both onto its downy softness.

"But you let Gunner kiss you when you have feelings for me."

"But as him, you let a wench in the hall kiss you when you have feelings for me."

He smoothed her hair back brushing her cheek with the back of his hand.

"She caught me by surprise. In short order, I disengaged her and went in search of a dress for you."

Her hands slid over his hips, his ass as she rose slightly pulling his lips back to hers. She did not care about what he did or she did. When or where and under what name. Gunner there, Adam here.

"Sam."

"Stop all this talk now, Adam…"

His finger found her moistness and swirled around, as her body slightly arched. Reaching down and enclosing his enlarged manhood, she stroked him, running her finger over his tip, causing a shudder to stream through them both.

In a swift motion, he opened her thighs up more as she brought them high up his back. He entered her, moving slowly in and out as her nails dug into his back. Their momentum increased so fast she released him to clutch the pillow, moaning into his mouth.

He leaned down, clasping her hands in his as he forcefully plunged, until their release came in such a rush, that emotions so strong rocked right from her loins into his.

He cupped her chin with two fingers, lifting her mouth up taking more of her sweetness.

"You are small. I must be too heavy on you." He started to lift but a strong grasp stopped him.

"No, stay right where you are."

He lowered back moving to his side. She did not want any conversation; the need to digest all of this, all of him, more important. Staring into his eyes, a soft smile would not be denied.

"So, are you ready to come back with me?"

"Well, not quite yet. How much time do we have?"

"A couple of days, why?"

"Because here, it's just you and me. There is no Savoy, no demands and finally no wenches and mistresses."

He had no choice but to grin at all of that. "Sam, why don't you bring the things you want with you on our return?"

"How am I going to get my bike and other items back and not be reviewed as a bit odd ?"

"Yeah, well, the bike won't work. Plus, our roads are not conducive to having those thin tires. Leave it here. You can come back when necessary. The important thing is knowing when it's time to go. If you do not, then there may not be another opportunity. Unless, someone comes to intervene."

"Can you always see where I am?"

"Yes. It seems I can. I do not have such an option with others."

She was confused, not understanding what he was saying. He leaned down, kissing her lips softly then pulled back knowing there was more.

"Then how come I can't see you?"

He laughed. "Well I am here right now, woman, but when I go, you will be able to."

"If you needed me to save you, how would I know where and when to get to you?"

That caught his fancy. "I suppose. But I can't see you coming to my aid, but you never know." He pinched a nipple as she pushed him onto his back. "Well, maybe you will want me to come to your aid.” She slid warm kisses down over his stomach, then lower still.

“Sam.”

“Just relax, Adam, I promise you won’t need anyone to save you now.”

Chapter Fourteen

For two days and nights, they spent all their time together. But when duty called it was time to go.

"Sam pack up what you want. We head out this morning. I have to get back before tonight."

"I'm ready now if you want. Should I get my keys or are we walking? The closest church is about twenty minutes away on foot."

His hand curved over her butt, appreciating every single inch he now knew so well.

"Keys. Yes, we will go back the same way you came in. I'm really surprised you did not get towed having your car there that long."

"You think it's invisible, like our passages? Maybe I should call up a cab and leave it here? Yeah, I'm going to do that it. It won't delay our departure but a few extra minutes. Here, ring this number and tell them to send one. I'll just take a walk through and make sure everything else it taken care of."

Placing them up on the hook, she checked all the windows and doors. He was outside waiting with the few things she was taking in a small backpack when the gravel under tires indicated the cab was pulling in.

They both got in as she spoke to the driver.

"Exeter Station, please."

He nodded and sped off getting them there in less than twenty minutes. Paying the man, Adam grabbed the backpack from the trunk.

"You use this for hiking? It looks like it could tell a lot of stories."

She got their tickets as they waited for the train. She glanced up at the electronic sign and back at him.

"If it could talk, I'd have to kill it. Besides, the other one I have back at your estate is one I'd like to keep around. This one could be handy with some of the places I've been going of late. The next train is in four minutes."

"Would it tell me about all the past romances?"

She gave him a sour look. Had she told him about the ugly divorce?

"Did I tell you I was married before? Perhaps it was not you. It was Mrs. H., damn, I can't remember now."

"No, it must have been Mrs. H. Is it a subject off topic for further inquiry?"

"Hey, it's over. He was a cheater and a liar and I was too busy with my career to give a damn until it got nasty. So really, it was my fault. I could have paid more attention to what was happening. I don't think I cared enough. Makes me sound cold and callous, I know."

"Sam, you are none of that crap, so let that be. It takes two to tango. If you insist on taking any blame at all, make it no more than fifty percent."

She smiled. "This, Lord Adam, will be our horse and carriage."

The train arrived as they boarded and sat and he looked up at the train map on the inside of their car.

"We are off at the next stop. So, how long ago was it?"

"It was finalized earlier this past winter. When we met in Venice. I had just quit my job and decided to run wild and travel. Just find the girl I pushed aside a long time ago and rekindle that relationship."

"You found her, that's for sure, or I think you did." He put an arm around her shoulder and squeezed, leaning down to an ear. "You know the saying, right? His loss my gain."

She smiled snuggling with him as the automated voice announced the next station. Side by side they exited the train as he pushed open a stairwell and they climbed up a secluded set of steps and were now back at the ruins of Ard Aulinn.

"Stop." He grabbed her arm. "Tell me what you feel this very second."

Her face was lifted toward the warm sun as she inhaled the fresh air.

"Peaceful, I feel very peaceful." They continued along toward the estate.

"So, when you are on a passage and you know there is something you must do, like kiss a wench or kill a person, you just settle it within yourself and get it done, right?"

"Right. But where are you headed with this?" Skepticism was written all over his face.

"Well, I did two things you do not know about on my last passage."

He did not miss a step. "How can that be? You were not out of my sight for more than a few minutes in total. What is it?"

"Savoy. He was waiting for us at the exit of the cave. I slugged him with the butt of my gun. I'm not so sure he was alive. I think so, but hell I don't know. The other one is I know that the Queen is an ancestor of mine."

"That's a tall order of events especially for Savoy. He's going to hunt you down for sure, Sam. We need to take extra precautions right away. As for the visit, did she know your name?"

She shook her head. "Gerda promised not to mention me by last name. Simply introduced me as Mistress Samantha. The King did though, does that count for anything?"

"Technically, no, because he is not an Arnesen. The queen is. You are fine. We need to find out why Savoy pursues you. He's going to be mighty pissed off, especially if he has a lump to keep reminding him."

He held the back door open as they walked down the hall, into his study and up the winding stairs to her rooms.

"I want you to move into my rooms." He held up his hand as if he knew a protest was to follow. But what was odd to Sam was how he towered over her right now. Weird. He had never been like that. Dominating. He had always treated her like an equal.

"Listen, there are several reasons. More staff are on that side. I can keep track of you and I think it's time you carry something a bit bigger than that dagger. I know your accuracy. But some of the people you come across are burly and stronger than you."

She was not buying any of it. He skirted around the true reason. For now, she'd let it go.

"Maybe I should go ahead in time and spend a few days in the company of the Special Services? Perhaps a few days with the Royal Navy's elite force would do the trick?"

He raised an eyebrow. "Yeah, not likely. You'd enjoy yourself way too much. But I do know a devil of a rogue from Ireland that would be up for that job in a heartbeat once his gaze rested on you."

She smiled raising both brows. "Is he as handsome and tall as you? Perhaps we should get in touch with him?"

"Woman, you need to remember whose touch you prefer above all else and quit thinking you can flirt with all the good-looking blokes you are going to encounter."

"Well, considering the last bloke was you, posing as another, I guess I'm pretty safe, aren't I?"

He laughed. "Enough, you win. This time, anyway."

They had reached her rooms as he closed the doors behind them.

"Pack up what you don't want Abbey to see and let her move the rest. It will give the chit something to take care of. If you do it now, I'll help you. I don't think you even know where my rooms are, right?"

She laughed, shaking her head.

"No, I don't have any idea in this huge place. So how many are there here anyway? Rooms I mean."

He was at one set of large windows glancing out over the gardens.

"Adam?"

He turned. "Thirty-two."

She walked over surveying outside, but found nothing amiss.

"What's up?"

"It is fine. I was just gathering wool. You ready?"

That was bullshit and she knew it. Something had drawn his attention. Handing him the larger bag, she pulled the small roller.

"All set."

As they left her wing and entered the center halls, she walked along the family portraits and glanced at them one at a time. This was one place warranting a return visit. It took nearly fifteen minutes before they halted at his doors. Opening, she stepped around going in.

"Oh, this is nice."

Ancient coverings adorned the walls with two intricately carved marble fireplaces strategically placed on both ends. Leaving the bags, Sam walked over to gaze at amazing views of the lake and expansive gardens. But, it was the large, king size, four poster bed, plush to the nines, that gained her attention.

"Think you will be comfortable? Look in here. I have a writing room I don't need. I prefer my study. You can use it for anything you desire."

She glanced in. It looked suitable enough for now until the cottage was ready. Her mind went to Abbey. She'd need to seek her out and get an update, then take a walk down and see the progress.

The room was silent as they both seemed preoccupied right now.

"I'm going to leave you to unpack. Tuck the bags in the armoire, they will fit. I'll send Abbey up in short order to get the rest of your things. Oh, that door leads to the bathroom."

Her eyes met his, steady and studying. Something was wrong.

"Does that hallway lead down a back stairway to your study?"

"Aye, it does. You should explore this side of the house. There is a lot of history."

"Sounds cool, will do. As soon as I finish I'm going to the stables and a ride."

He pulled her into his arms. "Sam, just for the rest of the day will you stick around the house, or, in the veranda area? Don't be stubborn about it. I need to make sure everything is in order outside before I leave. Will you do this for me?"

She kissed him, feeling the softness of those lips that could wreak havoc on mind and skin simultaneously.

"Okay, I will."

He grinned, easing her discomfort. "What, now? I don't have to go until the morning."

She laughed glancing around his body toward the large bed.

"So, we can christen this together tonight?"

"Indeed, madam, we can. I'll go see to Abbey. You get things done here. I want you well settled before I go. Come to my study when you are through." He kissed both her hands and walked out of the rooms.

She moved over to one of the large windows and wondered if he saw someone outside? Was that why he wanted her to move into his? Or, did he see something coming her way he could not tell her about now? Indeed, he was an enigma.

A light rap at the door preceded Abbey's arrival. Same gave her instructions as, bless her soul, someone must have told her in advance. For she arrived with a tray of biscuits and a hot pot of tea.

"Ah, Abbey, you are a gem. Thank you. I'll come and help you pack up the rest of my things."

"Oh no, mistress. I was advised to not trouble you with any of it. I will take care of it myself."

"Very well." she halted placing sugar and cream into her teacup, poured the aromatic blend and sipped, "Thank you. We can talk later about what's been going on."

As Abbey rushed out of the room, closing the door softly behind.

His bear claw porcelain tub was a glory to behold. It reminded her of the night he crept through her Exeter home, into her bathroom and took from her what he wanted. Her body felt the heat even now. Glancing up, she noticed Abbey had returned more than once. Where the hell was her mind? She knew. It had been lingering on Adam.

"This looks like all of it, right?"

"Yes, mistress it is. I'll finish unpacking it all for you."

"That's okay. By the way, I still plan on moving into the cottage. Have you been able to view their progress by any chance?"

"I have. It is coming along nicely. They have cleaned it all out, plugged all the holes and were fixing the roof yesterday. Today, they were going to whitewash the walls and clean the floors. Mr. Bruce thought it may be ready in another week or so. We need a good rain to make sure the roof does not leak at all."

"Wonderful! Let's not mention this to anyone just yet? Lord Griffin wanted me to move in here with him for reasons I can't explain. But it's more than what is obvious, I can assure you." She glanced at Abbey's blushed cheeks and bright eyes and nearly laughed out loud.

"But, as soon as it's all set, we will move. Do you still want to come? I promise to not work you hard and there will be plenty of time to yourself. Every night you can go back home to your parents."

"When will I start, as soon as we move? I think I need to say something to Mrs. Hoyt."

"Don't concern yourself with that. I'll take care of it. Now, go ahead and take the tray to the kitchens. We can discuss this more over the next few days." Sam nodded needing the conversation over. He'd be pissed she knew, but she was going to hold fast at moving in there. Both would eventually benefit from this decision.

Winding down the private staircase, she suddenly felt a bit odd. Hesitating, she glanced over at him before entering. He was penning a letter as she leaned on the corner of his gorgeously carved mahogany desk. Not speaking, she let him finish. He set the quill into the inkwell, shook the paper to dry, then folded it up, dropping wax onto it, sealing it with his family crest.

"These traditions have been taking place throughout time. I hope they never stop and I'm here long enough to witness more of them."

He found that thought unsettling. "You do belong here. There's no doubt in my mind about that."

Sam shrugged her shoulders. "I'm all settled. I don't want you to get angry with me, but tomorrow I am heading to see Father G and Mrs. Baker." She decided not to discuss the cottage right now. "I've missed them both."

"Let me suggest you do that in reverse order and absolutely. I think that would be good for you."

"So, we have until morning, right?" She moved resting down, straddling his hips. Her lips met with no resistance when pressed to his. "Correct."

She moved off as his hands let her go, undoing his trousers, sliding them down. Grabbing her back, close, his fingers moved her dress up into a heap.

"Ah, madam, no undergarments today. What is this?"

Seductively, she moved onto his lap and took him inside of her in one sweet, quick motion. He started to move but she stopped him.

"No, sit still."

As their eye's locked, it was felt by them both.

"What are you about?"

She kissed him long, hard, as the heat of her moistness seared his soul. She held him tight not allowing movement as deep within a wave of ecstasy flowed.

Moaning into his mouth, the kiss evolved into its own form of lovemaking. The pleasure spread through them as if they were one. He pulled her closer, harder against him until it swept them both into a dimension so beyond, they shook together.

His arms nearly crushed her as she sagged against his hard chest.

"Oh, my God, how is it we can do this?"

"I don't know." she could barely get out.

"You have me spellbound. Lord, I can't even imagine not being with you."

She kissed him deeply, craving more.

"I just wanted to make sure if any wenches were in your midst, you'd remember what you have back here." She grinned coyly.

"Oh, I hear that warning and understand, mistress. It is look, but not touch, right? Well, I remember when it was not apparent I was holding you in my arms back in Norway. So, in your reality you were kissing another man."

She stood so fast, much to his chagrin. "Yes." she smoothed her gown down producing quite a grin. "But you were always toying with me. You got what you deserved, Lord Griffin."

"What the hell am I going to do with you?"

"I expect you don't need a comment for you have no idea."

Laughter bellowed out as he slid his boots up on the corner of the desk.

"Really, Sam, could you think of yourself with anyone but me?"

As she swished her skirts away from the desk, he eyed every bit, shaking his head. The need for her again growing apparent. This woman had indeed bewitched him and he'd have it no other way. Shit, it took into his early fifties and her to do it.

"I'd be a fool to say it's not true." As a cold shiver suddenly doused the passion they had just shared. Was this a warning? What had the Tinker said then the Healer?

In a few quick strides, he was at her side, pulling her into his arms, claiming her lips with near brutal force.

"I was just talking to you and you were a thousand years away. What's up?"

Sam's hand moved up his trousers, over his enlarged manhood. Not uttering a word, rubbing up against the fabric, the other hand tugged his head down to awaiting parted lips. Like a thief in the night, she took everything he had left.

"Black magic woman, that's what you are."

"That's right and don't turn your back on me, ever."

He grinned. The knock at the door only separated their bodies, but not their souls.

"Sir, pardon the intrusion. But I have a letter for you." The butler handed him a sealed envelope, which he quickly opened, read and placed back in it. He opened the desk draw and slid it inside.

Sam did not bother to ask. If he wanted her to know she'd know. Period.

"Shall we go to dinner?" Switching gears, Adam took her hand, heading them out of the study toward the dining hall. "After we dine, I'm going to take you someplace special on the grounds you've not seen."

"I keep finding these secret places, so I can't wait. How much land do you actually own?"

"On the estate, over two hundred acres."

"Well then, it may take a long time to explore it all."

She stopped talking to eat. He would always know when she was truly hungry. She got quiet. As they finished he rose, laughing, while Sam, placed her linen napkin up beside her plate.

"Come, it's a bit of a walk. But, a fine night it is all the same."

As they journeyed through the woods, she absorbed how peaceful it was, then stopped, mesmerized.

"Oh my, who designed this?"

"Capability Brown years ago."

She was speechless. It was like stepping back and being transported to Rome; the Acropolis lit at night where she had once been when roaming around Athens.

"It's beautiful." All other words failed her.

"Well, remember this place. It will deliver you to a safe place when needed. Plus, there is a bonus near your cottage. But I'll let you discover that on your own if the shrubs and plants have not overtaken it."

That piqued her curiosity as she turned toward him and slid quite neatly into the fold of his arm. Warning signs interfered with this reflective moment. Apparent and unable to ignore it any longer, Sam knew something big was coming her way.

Chapter Fifteen

Running her hand over his still warm pillow, Sam kept her eyes closed knowing he was gone. After she rang for Abbey, she took out what would be worn today. Glancing out the large windows toward the gardens to a bright blue sky, a sigh escaped her lips. Today would have been an outstanding day for a cycle through the countryside. Instead, she'd settle for a jaunt to the village to see the good father, then she'd stop off at the cottage.

Abbey, knocked and waited.

"Come in."

Sliding open the door, she was quickly followed by two man servants carrying hot water.

"Mistress, do you want me to get you a breakfast tray?"

"Is there still food down in the kitchen? I know I rose a bit late today."

"Eat in the kitchen? Oh, mistress I don't know about that."

Sam smiled. "Abbey, it's fine. You can let cook know I'll be down as soon as I bathe. Can you take out the rest of my things? I'll be just a few minutes."

Dressed and prepared for the day, she left Abbey to drain the water and make up the bed. Humming down the stairs to the kitchen, she entered to a lively Mrs. Lilly, smiling.

"I could hear your jaunty tune all the way down the hall. I have a warmed plate of eggs and crumpets for you."

She slid up on a high chair and nodded eating at an unladylike pace. "Sorry, Mrs. Lilly, but I was famished. Would you happen to know where Mrs. Hoyt is?"

"Roaming the rooms making sure things are in order. You want me to pass her a message?"

"No, just wanted to say hello. I'm headed into the village to the Bakers. Do you need any orders placed? I'm happy to bring them with me."

"Mistress, I surely do. Let me get the paper for you. I'll just be a moment." She reached over with floured hands and wiped them off on her apron. "Let her know she can deliver these on Thursday. There is no rush at all."

Nodding, Sam dabbed her lips with the linen napkin, washed her dishes then placed them on the rack to dry. Mrs. Lilly shook her head and continued kneading the dough

Today, Sam took the main lane down to the village, preferring to be seen rather than take any chances on the back path to the church. She opened the side rectory door and found him immediately.

"Hello, Father Godwin."

He stepped back having filled the daily wine.

"Ah, Samantha, come in. I've missed you. I gather you've been busy."

She shook his hand. "I have. But you are indeed a face I've quite longed to see."

"Things have gone well, my child. I'm sure you are just tired from all your travels." He grinned. "Come and sit so we can have a nice long chat. I think a lot has changed for you since we last spoke."

They sat opposite each other. "It feels like a hundred years." Then she realized how that sounded and started laughing as he joined in. "I hope I'm here for a bit before I'm off again. I need some downtime."

"Don't get to settled, Sam, you do have some place to go. But it will be nice and warm place. You will be welcomed there."

“Why can’t people just come out and say, Sam, you are going to Ireland next. You will meet so and so and do this and that and then come home.”

He patted her gloved hand. Sounds too programmed for me. I think you would be bored knowing all that up front, right?”

“Maybe it would be just good to know how long I’ll be here before I leave.”

“You are really unsettled, aren’t you? Why is that?”

“Savoy. I don’t know why. But I feel like I need to find out what’s up with that man. Father, I’ve seen him in Scotland, here and Norway. I don’t know how to find out why he’s always around wherever it seems that I am.”

“So, to use some futuristic language, it is some recon you desire. Well, first you need to know his background and that can be tricky. You can’t just show up where he was actually born and start asking a whole batch of questions.”

“Well, I have to start someplace. He seems to know about me. I need to return the favor. Besides, with Lord Griffin away now appears like a good time to put idle hours to good use.”

“Seems to me he’d like you to hang about a bit longer, Sam, to rest up.”

She knew he was referring to her recent wounds, but all the same!

“What does everyone know about my business?” She grinned not expecting an answer.

“Why don’t you wait about for a few days. I’ll see what I can find out. I do have a few resources to tap into.”

She rose.

“Okay then have at it and trust I’ll run into you when the times right. I’m off to see Mrs. Baker and Anne. Then I think a spot of tea in the village is in order. Do you know where he is by the way?”

Pondering if indeed Savoy was dead back in Norway.

"Not exactly. But he's not here now. I think you will have a little bit of freedom, Sam. I don't always pay attention to his comings and goings. But I'll be more diligent in focusing on this for you."

She patted his shoulder,

"Father G, thank you. Any news, you know where to find me. Well, most of the time anyway."

She grinned, as she stood and closed the rectory door. The late summer day was warm and pleasant as she continued toward the bakery with passersby nodding a greeting. Smiling warmly, Sam knew this part of England, this era, was quickly becoming her home. Grudgingly, she silently admitted to liking the lovely estate and even the bloke who owned it.

Opening the shop door, she was quickly embraced by the short, stalky arms of Mrs. Baker.

"Where have you been, mistress? I've missed you in the last few weeks. Have you been away?"

"Indeed, I have. I smell the aroma of heaven in here. What is it?"

"A new pastry I've created with fresh berries, cream and other ingredients. I'll box a slice up for you to take back."

"Can you please make it a whole pie so I can share it with everyone? You may like to have several opinions if you are going to put it out in your shop window. Perhaps if it's as delectable as it smells, you will offer it at the Tea Room?"

"Me, branching out? I don't know about that."

"Why not? You have the shop. You could increase your revenue and if you are making them anyway, why not a few more?" Pondering that, Sam shifted gears.

"How is Anne? Is she about?"

"She just left to run errands. If you don't see her, I'll say hello for you." Tightly tying the string around the box, Sam slid a shilling on the counter. Mrs. Baker gave up long ago telling her not to pay.

"Oh, I nearly neglected to give you Mrs. Lilly's order. There is no rush. The next delivery date will be fine." She pressed it into her hand. "I'm off. I will be back in town soon. I'll let you know the polling results on your new creation."

"Mistress, wait. One more thing. I see clear sailing for the next few days, if you know what I mean."

Nodding, a bit more frustrated, she closed the shop door spewing out loud. "Okay, enough of this. It would be wrong of me to get pissed off at good, sound advice."

"You were fortunate it was just me looming about, Mistress Samantha, with that mouth of yours."

Smiling, Adam pulled her right into his arms nearly knocking the box down. The desire to place a hearty kiss on those lips was so very tempting, as she glanced around. No, this was not the time as she took his arm.

"I thought you were going to be gone for a while?"

"Plans change sometimes and I must say it was welcoming. For some reason, getting out of bed this morning was a bit of an issue."

Their eyes locked.

"I was going to the Tea Room. Perhaps that's no longer a good idea and we should return to your estate?"

Her body was on fire. She needed to get out of the public eye before everyone else could see it.

"Shall we take a different path along the meadow, or have you discovered it already?"

She grinned coyly. "Busted, but let's go that way anyway."

Strolling from town and down the path, he went ahead of her over a stile, then lifted her down by the waist.

On tiptoes, she let her boots touch slowly to the ground as their bodies touched, lips very close.

He took her gloved hand as they continued.

"I hear you have Father Godwin researching a matter for you."

She stopped, stomping a foot. "Bloody hell! How did you know that? I only left there thirty minutes ago! Were you that close to my heels?"

"Aye, you had left the kitchen and headed out when I came back. If we had cellphones, I'd have texted my arrival."

She smiled, truly glad he was here. As the trees grew thicker, he stepped in front of her blocking the path. Somehow the box was removed and set down as he pulled her roughly into his arms, lips taking total command of hers.

His hands cupped her buttocks, as Sam clutched his back feeling every bit of him against her. She unbuttoned his trousers as he lifted her onto him. Falling gently into the tall grass, a moan escaped their slightly parted lips.

"I don't know if I can let you go next time."

He tossed her onto her back. "Next time we go together."

He kissed her neck then trailed a heated blaze back to her lips as she felt him grow hard inside of her again. Arching, taking all of him, their bodies met and melded into one as the outside world faded around them both.

"Did you hear that?"

He stood, pulling her quickly up. "Yes. Be quiet. Quick. Grab the box and come back into the brush."

Crouching, she pressed her gloved hand to her mouth to stifle a sure laugh as his stern look nearly broke her down completely. They watched two riders off in the distance pass by them unnoticed.

"Damn, that was close, woman. Next time we'd better take a good look around first."

"As always, it's your fault. You grabbed me leaving me with no other choice but to succumb to your charms, Lord Griffin."

He chuckled. "Madam, your hat has come off." Picking it up and brushing the grass off, he placed it back on just at the correct angle. She tipped a shoulder in the cutest motion.

"If anyone sees us, they are going to know we've been up to something." He took the box in his hand. "Especially if this is all scrambled. Shall we make sure it's not?"

She untied the box and flipped open the cover. "Oh, this does look magnificent. Straight from a patisserie in Paris. Look."

He was tempted to pick a piece off but she closed the cover and tied it snugly.

"I brought this back for all of us to try. It is Mrs. Baker's latest concoction and I, for one, could have a piece right this very moment. So, let's hurry."

Deep into their own conversation, Mrs. Hoyt and Lilly's talk immediately halted eyeing the handsome pair.

"What have you there, mistress?"

"Something we can all share tonight after our dinner. Now no peeking until then."

She slid the box onto the counter. Sam went about business pouring hot water into a pot, grabbed everything else they needed and set it all on a large silver serving tray.

"Lord Griffin, I don't want to start gossip or worse than that a scandal." She glanced at both ladies faces, surprise clearly written on both. "But would you carry this tray to your study for me?"

"Bossy lass, isn't she?"

The two women went nose deep into conversation as soon as the door closed. But Sam did not care. That was fun! Sauntering down the halls she opened his study door and closed it, as he came through.

"Liked that, didn't you?"

"Yeah, I did."

"Just remember that I pay staff to do things like this because they like to work. Don't go taking all their tasks or it will leave them idle."

She shrugged. "After tea, can you take me on that grand tour inside? Remember, you promised a while ago and I think it is long overdue. Are there dark passages? Dungeons? Any ghosts?"

He laughed, taking the saucer and cup.

"Exactly what I was thinking. But we don't have a dungeon here, Sam. But, plenty of dark secret passages. Perhaps you will want to change into your jeans and more suitable shoes."

"Sounds smart. After we can both go up and change." She watched his eyes darken and knew they were on the same page. "Then you can show me and along the way, we can have a talk about my good friend, Major Victor Savoy."

Chapter Sixteen

Her hair was a tousled mess as they dressed, the glances toward each other were both intense and humorous at the same time.

"Good thing I did not know you in my younger days, Adam, we'd have twenty-five kids by now."

He broke out in laughter. "I suppose at some point I should do the right thing by you."

She shrugged her shoulders.

"That's the nice part of being slightly older, people are less interested in your private lives than the young scandalous ones."

"I can tell you the two clacking hens in the kitchen are enjoying keeping an eye on us."

"True, but they are sweet and harmless. Nothing like some of the so-called ladies in the surrounds and you know it."

"Bitches are more like it. That's the very reason why I kept the few dalliances I had to villages outside this area. You never know when one day, one of them is going to decide they had enough and speak up."

Hands on hips, she cocked a brow.

"What?"

"Oh, your mistress, right. So how many will I run into along my adventures? I wondered if that was why you gave up that large suite in Venice? Because you were ditching one."

He ignored that part. "Sam, that's possible. Do you think we could change the subject?"

"You brought it up, you know, but sure. I am ready. Where do we begin?"

"Right in this room." He stood inside the bathroom door. "In there, look."

"Are you kidding?"

He grinned, twisting an intricately fanciful knob at the bottom of a wall sconce. The wallpapered panel opened, producing a very nasty set of narrow, rickety stairs.

"Great, spider webs and who knows what else. Hang on a second, I'll get my cap."

Racing back with it firmly in place, hair tucked up inside, she walked down them gingerly not wanting to touch a bloody thing, catching up with him. When they reached the end, he felt for the release panel.

"You know you may have a bit of trouble if you ever needed this exit. The panel may be out of reach. Here, put your hand on mine, so you know how high it is."

She had to go on tiptoes but she could feel it and pressed against it, as the wall opened inside toward them. She gasped. They were down under the first floor in the wine cellar.

Creeping along through the eerie space, Sam wondered who kept this place up. Stopping for a second, she listened. There was no sound of water dribbling nor could she feel air coming through of any kind. A shudder passed up her spine, raising the hairs on the back of her neck as the flames of the closest lit lanterns danced about, nearly flickering off.

"Are there any spirits here, Adam?"

He patted her ass as he moved along to the opposite side.

"Do you really want to know how many, or just if there are any specifically where we are?"

Damn jerk was baiting her and she knew it.

"No, not really. Better I don't. But, what about evil ones?"

"One or two are a bit more spirited than the rest. I'm sure you can handle them. If you have outwitted Savoy and take passages. I've always thought they knew what we all are about anyway, leaving us to our devices."

Stopping, he leaned against one of the stone walls.

"Try and find this exit yourself."

Tugging on her baseball cap, she eyed it knowing where he was leaning it was not. Glancing at the large kegs she knew that would be too obvious by turning a knob. It had to be on the floor, or perhaps it was not that wall at all!

Sam moved back and glanced at the entire end of the room, the three walls, then moved left behind the kegs and saw one stone slightly discolored. The lighting was not helping and it was well planted, so larger frames would hardly notice it.

Pressing the corner panel, it opened.

"Excellent, I thought we may be here a while."

She grinned. "That was cool." As she vanished up ahead leaving him standing there alone. Moving quite a bit ahead he jogged to catch up remaining quiet as they approached the end of the dark corridor. Sam halted, placing a hand up to stop him from speaking, inhaled sharply then smiled.

Glancing above, little was in view. But, when she stretched out an arm, the roughness of the wood caused a slight wince. She had snagged a splinter. If the ceiling was this low, there had to be a release up there somewhere. As she felt further, her fingertips caught a latch. It opened automatically producing a few short steps up.

Once inside, she spun around like a little kid who had found the pie on the windowsill with no grownups in sight.

"The stables, how frigging bloody brilliant! You must have had such a grand time as a kid living here."

"I did. Now that's the best route because it gets you quite a distance away from the house and to a fast means of escape. Can you ride bareback?"

"Indeed, I can. Not well, but in a pinch I could do it. Let me make sure I've found them all. There's one from your study up to our suite, this one, but surely there are more?"

"There are a few others. One to the attic, one under the kitchen to a cave toward the river and one in the other side of the house where your rooms were."

"So, you've shown me the best one. How about giving me a clue where the one is under the kitchen. You go and wait where it exits and let's see how long before I find you."

He shook his head laughing. "Okay, chit, bet's on if you can be there in less than thirty minutes. How about I allow you to ask one thing of me that I will not refuse you. If it is after thirty. I do the asking."

"Damn, it's a deal. Tell me where it is."

She bolted from the stables with breakneck speed, running quite unladylike into the building, sliding to a stop as she passed the butler, and thought about what he had said. Turning down the hall of ancestors on the first floor, Sam stood in awe; there were so many different things she could try! Damn, caution had to be used here with this many valuable items.

Wait, she thought, hadn't he said, "Not all that glitters is gold?"

A large embossed fireplace struck her fancy. Staring into the eyes of the lion, intricately and quite beautifully engraved, she pushed simultaneously with both pointer fingers into his eyes. The trap door to the right slid open.

Feeling quite smug for withholding information from him, she removed her small pen light from her jeans pocket and switched it on. As she quickly walked, it was apparent the kitchen was receding as the clang of pots could be heard then faded away. Onward her progress went until the corridor became rougher, with water seeping onto the floor rising an inch or so up over the sole of her boots.

The eerie noise of things crawling about did not slow the pace. Further up, a pinhead of light started to grow bigger and brighter as she carefully picked up the pace. Stepping outside, glancing up to a darkening sky, she saw him leaning against a tree chewing on a blade of grass. Creeping over, she tapped his right shoulder while moving to his left.

He grabbed her up over his shoulder and swung her down into the grass moving on top.

"Damn, Sam, that was less than twenty minutes."

"Darn good, don't you think? So, let's see. What shall I ask of you? Do I have to make the request right this second? Or, can I bank it for when I decide exactly what I want."

"Woman, you are too smart for your own good." He swept her up on her feet as he grabbed her hand. "While we are here, let me show you one more thing. Then you can take me back the way you came out."

"Is that an old boat down there?"

"Yes, I won't even ask you if you know how to row. But, your toughest challenge may be pulling up the anchor. It's quite deep in this part of the river.".

"Hopefully, I won't have to do that. So, are you ready to go back? I need a bath, change of clothes and dinner. I am really hungry."

"Well, lead on then."

As they entered the cave, she pulled out the penlight and smiled, shrugging her shoulders as laughter vibrated around the tunnel.

"When did you even have time to grab that? Oh, I get it. When you went to retrieve your hat. Right."

"That's about it." They had reached the floor hall of ancestors. "There are some really handsome portraits of your family, in particular this one." She was standing looking up at one of him.

His hands wove around pulling her back against him, then settled his chin on top of her cap.

"That's my brother to the left, James, and in the smaller portrait is his wife, Anna, and their daughter, Catriona. You will meet them soon. Just before I met you in Venice, we were all in Ireland. My niece just married a bloke from there, but in essence he's a good sort."

"What a handsome family. Is he older or younger?"

"Two years' younger. That is why I am the grand owner of all this." She knew the aristocracy's diplomatic order. His brother would inherit all when Adam was no longer around. Then it would follow his niece.

"Isn't Catriona an Irish name? Does your family have roots there as well?"

He moved her to the center of the hall.

"Yes, my mother was Irish. My father a split between English and Welsh. That is them. They have been gone for a few years. The rooms you were in were my mother's; she passed away a few years after my father did and it's said that she still has a presence in there."

Sam turned into his arms staring up into his dark blue eyes.

"I know, she liked my lace and handkerchiefs. I did not know whose room it was, now that makes sense."

He kept his mouth shut. "Let's get cleaned up so we can eat. If we don't get a move on, Mrs. Lilly will leave us scraps as punishment for making her keep our food warm."

As they reached their rooms, Abbey, and a few other servants were hurrying their exit having left the hot water in the tub. She blushed, head bowed low, and rushed by them.

"Poor girl. Do you think she's pondering two people, unmarried and one tub?" Sam laughed, sliding out of her shoes, clothes quickly dropping down to the floor in a heap. A quick glance over her shoulder proved amusing, he was quite naked and closing in fast.

Sliding into one end, the hot water and coolness of the porcelain tub brought a sincere sigh of gratification out of her mouth. Submerging, she soaked her hair, put in cleanser and rinsed it out. Soaping up, she crawled over, sliding on top of his warm skin.

Kissing him was just as easy as breathing as he pulled away, sliding inside of her. He sat straight, eyes locking as she resisted his lips on purpose.

Sliding over him again and again, back arching, he gripped her strongly as water spilled over the tub onto the tile floor. As they climaxed together, it was only then she allowed his kiss.

It was powerful.

"You are getting cold. We had better get you dried off."

"It's not cold, Lord Griffin, of that I can assure you." She stood over him reaching for a warming towel on a rack placed in front of the fireplace as he kissed a breast.

Her warm smile drove his heart to skip a beat.

She dried off, wrapped her hair, then stepped out handing him one.

He caught up with her as she reached the dresser, spun her around playfully, hands roaming over hips while lowering his lips to claim hers once again.

Finally, they pulled away.

"I should have left you in my mother's suite. It's pretty clear that with you here, we may never leave this room, woman."

She smiled that special smile. When a woman is sure she has a man. But the truth was he had her too. Suddenly, the idea she was sharing his rooms under the presence of the entire household had her feeling a bit annoyed. What was the difference with her being in the tower, his mother's suite or here? The bottom line was clear, with her own admittance and acceptance, she had indeed become his mistress. But that would be less obvious when she moved into the cottage and paid rent.

Then things would be different. She'd not be so available as she was right now. Truth though, she liked being in close proximity to this man.

"Is that my imagination or can I actually smell our dinner from the kitchen? It can't be. It is nearly a mile between there and here."

She laughed. "I think that's my cue we need to go down. I am truly starving."

She had been quiet, mood changed. Even though she tried to mask it, he knew. It was not until the berry concoction from Mrs. Baker was finished that she perked up.

"I need to let her know how spectacular that was, don't you think?"

"Another one could come this way any time. She could make a fortune with those."

"I'm going to make sure that happens. I insist on arranging some to be present on the ladies' menu at the Tea Room. If I need to use your name to push this through, I will. I'm going to go see her tomorrow and get it moving along. I was thinking if they did not readily have the funds for multiple production, that this may just be a great idea to present to them the possibility of my being a partner. A silent one, of course. But I'll see what they think tomorrow."

"Tomorrow, you say? Well, that's not going to be possible."

She took his arm as they headed for his study, he was going to take a smoke out on the veranda.

"Why is that?"

"Tomorrow we leave for New Orleans in the United States of America."

"Oh, my goodness, I love New Orleans. I've had a lot of fun there in the past, well, the future. Ah, hell, you know what I mean. Have you been there before?"

"Not in a few years. We have a joint mission that's not completely clear yet."

Suddenly, she felt the need to get to the cottage before full darkness emerged. A quick little white lie was in order.

"I want to hear more about that, but I just remembered that I have something to do of importance. I'll see you in a bit."

Quickly, she disappeared out of sight just as he was forming a question. Soon, the gardens beyond swallowed her up as his brows furrowed. His cigar finished, he stomped it out, irritated, beneath a boot then picked it up and put it in the bucket.

Walking back in, he closed and locked the double wide French doors. Up in their rooms, he strode out to the balcony listening to night sounds. Still she had not returned. As the sky turned from red to orange and darkness took over, it was then he gave up, sitting down in one of the chairs. Finally, she came in through the hall door.

Her grin was mischievous. Unfortunately, any inquisition was to be left for later. There was something that needed to be addressed and it was now or never. Actually, he thought about it. Damn, he silently mouthed. It would have to be now or if it came up later, he was sure to be in big trouble.

She was undressing in the changing room when he finally spoke.

"Sam, when I was in New Orleans last, I had a mistress. I was there for quite a while. Anyway, I just want you to be aware in case she's still around."

"Is this your way of telling me you are going to reacquaint yourself with her, or just a warning in case she expects that of you?"

He knew this was not going to go as planned. It was the tone of the question that was not right.

"I have no plans to do either." To him that was a declaration that he would not. To her it was a declaration that he did not plan on it, but hell, it sure could happen.

"We all have pasts, but thanks for the warning. Do you think Savoy already knows we are headed there?"

"He seems to turn up wherever you are, so we had better assume he's going to be."

She yawned, crawling in bed beside him noticing he had turned down the gas lit lanterns.

"Are we going back or forward?"

"Back. By now, Sam, you should be able to see what will transpire." He fluffed up his own pillow placing one arm under his head. "Don't you?" He paused. But, not long enough for her to answer. "Anyway, I wanted to ask you where you went earlier. Care to share?"

Glancing over by the silence in the room, he quickly realized she was sound asleep.

Chapter Seventeen

Stretching like a panther, she slid from bed and pulled aside a heavy drape before he could reach for her.

"It's going be a lot warmer and sunnier there than it is here today, that's for sure." She let it fall back and slipped into a robe and slippers. With a messy mop, she went into the bathroom to get cleaned up.

She seemed all business this morning. Like she had something on her mind and it sure as hell was not him.

"We head out as soon as you are ready." He called toward the closed door.

"Uh huh."

He dressed and put together a few things. But basically, he knew where they were going, staying and they would be taken care of completely when arrived.

Suddenly she appeared out of the dressing room ready to go. He eyed her warily. When had she done that? Did she have time to put her clothes in there last night?

Pinning up her hair and taking the bag, she turned looking at him. "I'm set, shall we?"

He strode over as she opened the door. He followed as they went down a different hall toward the rear entrance. Once they were outside, he moved in front, walking backwards.

"Lord Griffin, I'm ready to get this going. I can now see a lot of very interesting things coming my way. Why are you deterring me?" Her voice was quite playful as he wondered where this shift of gear came from.

"So, you are getting visuals?"

"Yup, I sure am."

He moved in step beside her, as they descended the stairs of the ruin and back up, right onto deck of the

Angeline, owned by Captain Jean Lafitte. The schooner was in the throes of outrunning a British frigate, cutting sail at a quick pace through the choppy Atlantic. It was in a race, and winning, toward New Orleans.

Adam glanced down, presenting a smashing smile, and quickened his steps as he reached the first mate, clasping hands.

"Damn, you old, salty dog. I knew I'd see you again. But figured it would be in a rift over some bar wench, not here. Damn, how the hell are you?"

Adam glanced over his shoulder laughing as the cannon fire was having less results as the sleek schooner moved on.

"Bastard. You have always been a bastard Lord this or that, matters not to me." They both laughed.

Suddenly, he glanced around. Fuck. Where was she? Striding around up on deck, he took a good, long look.

She was nowhere to be seen. What the hell? This was unique. When they walked up the stairs together there had been only one exit. Strange, he did not have an option for two passages, but she must have. A good shove brought him around in a flash.

"Ah, Lafitte, seems as if you've avoided another issue with the British again. How are you, my old friend?"

"A little of this and that. It's good to have you on board. But, your arrival always means extra trouble for me. So, come clean. What's this all about?"

"Well, it's not entirely clear. But, it appears I have lost someone upon my arrival. You have not seen a handsome woman roaming on board, have you?"

"I assure you, handsome or not, if a woman was on the Angelina, someone would have accosted her onto her back by now and we'd know she was here."

He grinned, flashing a devilish smile. Was this why he could not see as much as normal and she woke this morning to what seemed like a clarity of vision? Shit, this was not good.

"You putting into 'Orleans?"

"*Oui*, should be in about an hour and then you and I, my friend, will go ashore and see what we can turn up before my mistress even knows I am about. Now, come below. For I've good Jamaican Rum to share."

***

Sam, on the other hand, was climbing up a set of rickety stairs outside an old inn. It had rained, she noticed glancing down. Street mud was adhering to her boots. Opening the door, she slid through.

"Yeah, I've been waiting on you. Come, get yourself over here and be quick about it. Close that damn door."

"Who are you?"

Sam stood with hands on hips, nearly falling over at the reflection staring back across the room in a framed floor glass. Dressed like a tavern wench, breasts barely contained under a fluff of lace, her grin expanded. There was but a breath between her and flesh expelling out in total freedom. Damn, this was getting better by the second.

"Molly's the name." She eyed her attire, nodding in approval. "I understand you need a bit of assistance. Specifically, how to fend for yourself. The crowds here about get pretty rowdy at times."

Sam felt an instant kinship to this woman. Eyeing her head to toe. No, she was more than just a bar wench. This person was her own special training operative. Oh, how funny, she thought, moving closer.

"Yeah, will be my first night in a tavern actually working. I need you to set me straight so I know the trouble before it finds me. As shit smells, it will."

"Well, sweetie, hike up that skirt and let's see what you got under there."

Eyebrows raised in surprise, Sam picked up the hem.

"Higher, honey, I know you are strapping."

Sam eyed her bag briefly knowing in there was a gun. A real one and a knife.

"That is not good for you. What you think is in that bag may not be and you and I both thought you would arrive with protection."

Glancing down, Sam was astonished; both upper thighs were indeed missing them. Molly tied a sheath encased with a knife high on the inside making sure it was secure.

"Open the bag."

Sam reached down and untied it.

"Damn it, Molly, I've never been anywhere and not had more than this."

"No shit. There must be other means you are to use, dear, if you get my drift." Inside her dress pocket, she produced a small corked glass alchemy bottle and slid it between Sam's breasts, tucking it down low.

"What's that for?"

"A magical blend of herbs and rum that will burn the eyes of those that think they got you. All you do is tell them you want to be on top, take it out, pop the cork and throw it right at their eyes. That will give you time to get away."

"Is everyone around here pirates and privateers?"

"There are a few that roam these parts, now and again, that aren't so bad. Take Lafitte and his salty crew. They can be a bit rough, but they always leave a hard coin or two for you to get by with." She winked.

"Issues with the girls?" Sam was having a hard time not cracking up laughing at her true southern belle, 'Orleans' accent.

"Watch out for Lucinda. She is quick to recognize and pretty to be sure. Oh, but wait until she catches a glimpse of you. The fur's going to fly."

Oh, a bit of territorial competition, eh? Well, Sam thought internally, she was up for it after their conversation last night, feeling the need to be independent and in charge.

"When they pinch your ass for the hundredth time, you may get a bit testy. But, remember your tips come from the likes of them and other things of importance. Don't let them follow you to the back taps, though, or you may get more bargained for. At times, the bar keep is too busy to notice if you need a bit of assistance."

"What if I have to stab one? Won't that evoke more trouble?" Her mirth was shared.

"Depends on who you stab. If it is a local grub, no one will care. But, if it's one of Lafitte's men, then you had better be prepared. You will get no support from anyone. Just keep to yourself in the main room or go back there with one of us."

She sat down on the corner of the bed.

"Here, drink this. It will warm you. Settle the nerves and prepare you for what's ahead." Swigging it down, she bit back a choke as it burned from throat to gut. Damn, it was not smooth but bloody potent.

"Here, have another."

The two tipped glasses and swigged down another two-finger shot.

"Whoa, no more of that or I won't be able to walk."

"Honey, you had betta get used to it. Sometimes, it is the only way to get by. Now, let's get that hair tied back so no bloke can grab it, because they will try. We need to get our asses down there, now."

The red ribbon matched the red in her itsy, bitsy dress and seemed laughable that a portion of her hair was pulled back and tied in a bow. A nice little ladies' bow, even though she was nearly naked. Oh, hell, she thought, pinching cheeks and putting some stain on her lips Molly handed her. She had always wanted to be a bar wench.

Check mark. Fantasy fulfilled.

Downstairs, she was quickly immersed into the ill lit, smoky tavern. This was a bar room brawl waiting to happen. Flashing some pearly whites, she exaggerated the swish of her hips and focused straight on a table overflowing with an unsavory lot. Sliding a boot up on the curve of the bench, she exposed a bit of leg.

"What have you, gents?"

"Well, hello, my sweet. Rum it will be. Damn, make it a round for all!" He beat a fist on top of the table as she took her large tray off toward the bar keep. He slid the tankards up onto it.

"Ah, another new one. Well, get your skirts a swaying about the room, we've money to make."

His toothless grin and the way he raked her over proved a point with Sam. Yeah, some men were just plain ole stupid.

Sliding the mugs in front of each, the language turned cantankerous as calloused, hardened, groping hands began getting more adventuresome.

"Now gents, give the new girl a chance. She won't come back if you keep touching her like that. She's the third one in a week."

Turning an appreciative nod to Molly, Sam's face suddenly froze.

It was Savoy.

"Be a love, honey, get me one of those."

Emotions ran through her so fast, she nearly lost her sight as her whole body turned stiff before moving on.

Composure, Samantha, she screamed inside her head. Calm the fuck down!

The barkeep slid a mug and a small cup.

"For you, drink up lass, you are doing well. Pay them all no mind."

The fiery liquid worked magic settling rattled nerves.

Collecting the money and pocketing it, Sam maneuvered through the crowded room, serving other tables when her gaze locked with piercing green eyes. Although shorter than Sam, she was pretty with flailing red hair. Yup, sure as the sun sets over Egypt, this was Lucinda.

A nod of agreement passed between them.

Lines were drawn. Sides acknowledged.

Turning, she wafted back toward the group to check on refills. Eyes narrowing briefly, she watched intently, listening while ducking into the shadows paying close attention to two men deep in conversation.

"The Angeline pulled into port a short time ago. My source tells me they are heading here now. We'd better drink up and go. If he lays eyes on me, he will know no good is about."

One waved Sam over. "Here you go, missy. Buy a new ribbon for your pretty hair."

"Why, thank you!"

Leaving the coinage up on the bar top, Sam knew something was amiss. My, how their language had changed when they thought no one was keen on hearing. But, it was apparent from the shine of their boots that they were not harbor riff-raff. Rather, spies, possibly officers under cover.

The room grew rowdy, filling with electricity as emotions ramped up. Everyone felt it. Every damn soul was drunk as a skunk as Molly stopped next to her.

"This is when you need to pay extra attention."

She nodded, staring down Savoy; the rum having its effect. In her eyes was a clear warning. *You fuck with me and I'll fuck with you.*

He grinned, tipped his hat and slugged back a tankard, slamming it down on the table.

"Wench! Get your ass over here now. Refills!"

Her grin was lethal as she leaned over him displaying every bit of her creamy flesh.

His eyes briefly raked her over.

"Seems like you've been neglecting us, woman. We need another round. You see it is like this. I was with a rather reckless woman a bit ago and she left me with a lump on me head. I need that rum to ease the pain."

She laughed.

"You got what you deserved, I'm sure!"

The bloke opposite grabbed her as she tugged out of his alcohol weakened grip just before he planted a foul breath kiss on her mouth. The man stood, weaving, then slid back onto the bench, his head hitting the wood, before he passed out.

Then the shit hit the fan.

"Griffin, did not see you there, man. Warning, my friend. This wench isn't for you tonight. Even though I'm drunk as hell, I can see Lucinda heading your way."

Sam was halfway to the bar when she heard the dialogue; she watched, as the redhead used every charm, claiming him long before her body got there. It was apparent the affect it had on him.

The bastard!

Over in the corner of the room, she saw a group of men, knowing now who he had come in with. Damn, that explained why they were separated upon arrival. He was with Captain Jean Lafitte, the infamous pirate of the high seas and true Governor of New Orleans in the eyes of the locals.

Using her wits, it was apparent the two that left were important. As to why they were all here, that centered around one lofty pirate. Hell, now all she had to do was find out what the heck that was.

As she swayed by Adam, who was disengaging his mistress from his arms, the whole tavern could not help but hear her tirade as he held her back.

"Two years and not a bloody word from you. Now, you just show up and what is this? No kiss? How dare you treat me like that? So, who is she? Surely you must have another woman? Are you thinking about bedding that new wench right under this roof? I will slit your throat before you..."

"Woman, shut your mouth."

He pulled her close, whispering into her ear.

"There may be time later. Right now, I am on official business and can't be detained. Even by your loveliness."

She smiled up into his eyes.

Sam, truly pissed off, moved behind a door with Molly in tow.

"You know him?"

That was the cold water in her face she needed.

"Nay, just thought I may have a go at him. Handsome as sin and probably as evil as the Devil by listening to Lucinda's tirade. But, I know it's her man. So, I'll keep my thoughts to myself. When is closing?"

"For us, soon. For the girls coming on shortly, it will be early morning. You are coming with me to the inn. I have two rooms and will grab you when it is time to leave. Go back out there and finish collecting from your area."

"Thanks, Molly."

Sam slid back out and at several tables had to just pick up the coin spewed about carelessly, collecting the bills. Bringing it up to the bar keep, she nodded no to one more shot. Reaching for a cloak to wrap around, Sam looked to where Savoy had been. He had since vacated and replaced by another. Where had he gone this time and why did he keep showing up where ever she was?

Answers were needed and fast. As they left through a side alley, Sam never looked back to see where Adam and his mistress were, or what they were doing. To ensure sanity, it was clear there was a purpose to them both being here. Until that was understood, she was going to damn well remain clear of that man. Heaven help him if her hands found their way toward his neck!

"We'll be there in ten minutes. You stay close to me. These streets are filled with unsavory types, especially now that Lafitte's men are back in the city."

Sam stopped and grabbed Molly's arm whispering, "Hey you are speaking differently now, what's up with that?"

"New Orleans is filled with those who look like aristocrats and are slum dogs. Then there are wenches like us working in the darkest corners, who are here to do a task other than serve ale and rum. I'm here to help you in the tavern and make sure whatever is needed is done expeditiously."

Sam grinned. "You know, I like this. You had me fooled. But you knew what I was all about all along. You are one of us too?"

She nodded. "Don't worry about your man. You did not see how he was watching every swish of your hips when you were working the room. Those eyes caressed every inch of your body. Between you and me, he sure did like you in this outfit."

"You have a way of making me feel a whole lot better, Molly."

"Well sit tight, honey and pay good attention because there's a lot coming your way over the next few days. Tomorrow, we have a day off. I'll take you around the city and lend some helpful suggestions."

"Will I be working the tavern again?"

"No, we will go over that soon. There are other plans for you that I think you will find quite exciting."

As they reached the inn, Sam was glad it was away from the rowdy, waterfront pubs and quite a bit nicer. As they climbed the steps, Molly stopped in front of her door. Sam's was three down.

"Sleep well, you will be safe here."

"Thanks, see you in the morning."

At the end of the hall, Sam found her door and inserted the key. As she turned the doorknob and automatically adjusted her eyes to the darkened room, suddenly there was a hand over her mouth. Stomping a boot as hard as possible, raising an elbow and landing a hard jab, she spun around, swiftly lifting her skirts and pulled out a knife.

"Samantha put that away. It's me."

Feeling quite smug, she smiled at how quickly she reacted. Lighting a few candles, she put the glass domes back over them. A few seconds was all that she needed feeling calmer. Then turned toward him.

His heated gaze swept her head to toe.

"You have to bring this one back when we leave here."

The back of his hand smoothed over her exploding breasts. Pulling his head down, Sam took complete control swiftly unbuttoning his trousers and had her hand surrounding him before he knew what hit.

He moaned into her mouth before lifting her to the bed, roughly removing her dress.

"You have to be gone before sunrise."

He started to question her, but the roaming of possessive hands halted his speech. Then he felt her warmth surround them both as it quickly spread. Had jealousy spurred this on?

He'd get to the root source and get rid of it for good. There were never going to be any secrets between them ever again. But, right now, it was only the two of them.

Chapter Eighteen

Sunrise streaked in through sparse curtains as she stretched. It was early and Molly had said they were not working. Today she would learn more about her story and what was to come next. Then her brow furrowed, recalling Savoy. Ironically, as their other meetings were dissected, Sam realized he did not seem to pose a threat. Laughing inside the meager surroundings of the room, it was apparent an analyzation of events had to occur. He needed to be figured out, especially after she had left him for dead and he had not tried to settle the score. At least, not yet.

"What's your story?" she posed to dead air as her hand smoothed over where Adam's head had been.

He grumbled when nudged to get up and out. Her smile grew. Sure, he knew she was a little jealous about Lucinda. But, that admission would never leave her lips, ever. Then again, he could barely speak as she took control of their lovemaking, turning it into quite a flurry last night.

The floor was cool to the touch beneath her feet as she washed and dressed just as there was a knock at the door. Peering, opening it up a crack, Sam smiled.

"Hello, come on in."

"You look sprite and spirited this morning. Have a good night's sleep, did you?"

"How did you know?"

"Not much gets by me, missy. Besides, yours was the last room. So, when I heard the boots hitting the planks, a whistle along with it, I knew. Was it the bloke from the tavern?"

"I can't tell a lie, it was. We are acquainted."

"Glad I was a few doors down then. You sent him along the way before daylight. Smart move."

"Much to his chagrin." she winked. "But he'll get over it soon enough."

"You are quite a confident woman, I'll say, and comfortable knowing about his past with Lucinda."

She was. "Yes, because two can play at this game and here I feel like I have the upper hand."

Molly, grinned patting her on the arm.

"Well, let's get going then. I truly think you are going to find today damn interesting. We must fetch ourselves a couple of nice evening gowns. The night after next we are serving drinks and smokes to some society blokes at a high stakes poker game. I daresay your gent and Lafitte will both be there."

The warm morning air greeted them as they stepped outside.

"I've been here before, Molly, at a different time. This city's vibrancy never fades. I just love it."

"Twenty-four-seven it sure does. That's why I call this place home. A while ago I was given the opportunity to make an important decision. If I wanted to return to my dark, dismal flat in London or remain here. Obviously, you know the results. This was an easy choice."

Sam leaned closer. "What period are you from?"

"Nineteen-fifty. A blast from the past. No joke, right? Here, it's thriving morning to night and I do have tucked away a gentleman friend that comes to visit time to time. Calling this my home suits me real fine."

"You said you had a choice; do those only come once?"

"Well, I've heard for most indeed they do. You may be the one that's different. I'm not sure. But when yours does, it will be at the right moment in your life. It always comes during a passage. So, take warning of this now. A decision will need to be made soon on where you really want to be."

"They said for me it was unusual. When I arrived from 2015, I had all my bags. The few who I've been allowed to discuss this with have no explanations."

Molly halted, steadying eyes into Sam's.

"Well, then, that does paint a different picture. From all my travels, I've not encountered any stories such as you have described. I don't know what to say. You are different. Whether that makes it harder or easier for you, well, time will tell. Ah, here we are at Madame Thereault's Dress Shop. What do you say to going in and spending some loot?"

Sam's mouth gaped open as they entered the establishment. The proprietress swished toward them, producing a large, inviting smile.

"Surprised, mistress, at the variety? Well, Monsieur Lafitte made me aware of your arrival. Ensuring I was up-to-date with the finest Parisian fashions available. He's such a love."

Sam smiled, "And a good friend he is to have by the looks of all your choices, madame. Do you mind if I poke around? Or, would proper etiquette dictate I sit as a gentile lady, point at what I desire, and one of your shop girls would assist?"

The three women broke out in laughter.

"Madame likes you. Tell me, Molly, where ever did you find her?"

"Oh, don't allow her to give any airs. She's just a comely tavern wench, new to town, quite unique in her ways of travel and in need of a few special gowns."

Madame nodded, grinning. "Why that's just excellent, ladies. I shall be at the counter taking care of papers. You have my girls' undivided attention with all the fittings. Any alterations will be done on premise and delivered to you in plenty of time for your special event." She winked, crinoline and silk swishing off.

"Oh, I like her. Molly, look at that periwinkle silk dress and all that lace. The hat, I must have that hat. If I needed an additional weapon I could remove it and poke out an eye. Oh, yes, this works for me!"

She never even gave her companion a chance to voice an opinion. Quickly waving over one of the girls, they hastily disappeared behind a curtain.

Nearly three hours later, boxes tidied up and set on the seat of a hired carriage, they ladies stopped and took stock.

Should we have kept the driver a bit longer? What if we buy more?" Molly was completely pulling her leg.

"I can't imagine needing anything else. I know I purchased more than necessary, but I could not resist."

"What the hell. Anyway, you won't be in the inn much longer. Our plans arc to movc out this afternoon to more suitable arrangements. I have an apartment for us right in the heart of the Quarter. There is another bonus, my dear, no one will know you have relocated. So, if a certain gent comes a calling, he will find a new resident in that room at the inn and much to pay for!"

Sam burst out laughing, raising a gloved hand to her mouth to stifle further response as passers eyed them both.

"Oh, my gosh, did you see the looks on those faces? Are we not to laugh in public here?" Sam, waved off a reply not caring. She was enjoying this way too much. "Is there a reason for all of this? Something I should be made aware of upfront by any chance?"

"Of course, you little chit. But we will let that all unravel in due time. Enough of that. Shall we go back and get our things? We can be settled and out exploring by lunch."

They hailed a carriage and were back at the inn, packed and met in the hallway minutes later.

"Tell me about this poker game. Surely, there is more at stake than money."

"First things first. Let me pry a moment. Exactly how old are you and why this lifestyle?"

"In my forties. I was married. But, he decided to swap me in for a younger model. I basically said screw it and chucked it all in favor of travel. I was vacationing in Venice when I met up with my gentleman friend and then found myself transplanted to his England. I've been around for three months. I did not actually choose it. It seems to have chosen me. It seems to come with pretty nice benefits, if you know what I mean."

Molly must have bobbed her head up and down four or five times before lending a thought.

"How are your resources?"

Sam knew she was referring to finances.

"Ironically, my bank account was magically deposited into a local bank in the village near his estates."

"Blimey, that is rather odd, I must say. You know I have an idea. If you are up to a bit of fun. There is a woman living down on the bayou that's a bit eerie, but reads a good palm. If you want to go and check it out, we can."

"Sounds like a voodoo priestess. But, I must admit I'm intrigued. Sure, why the hell not? Let's do it. May be cool to hear what her story is about all of this. It seems like I am always one step away from discovering something, then uprooted again in a different direction. Yeah, I'm up for that. Sounds like another adventure." She chuckled. "Can we go before the poker game?"

"Yes, I'll send the servant with a note to her this afternoon and what the reply is." She laughed. "He hates it when I do that, thinking the old crone is going to cast a spell on him every time."

"Well, we all have read stories about these women. I won't pretend I am not a bit nervous already. Does an orange and white poisonous snake dangle about her crinkled neck?"

"Sam, it's a dark place for sure. But, we don't have to go. There are others here in the Quarter who have that special gift. But take caution. Most are hoaxers only interested in taking money. It's up to you."

"Oh, no, I'm game. I admit all that voodoo talk would give any good Christian woman the creeps. Good thing I'm not one of those!"

Halting in front of a tall black iron fence, Molly inserted a large skeleton key, turned the lock, opened the door and waved Sam ahead. "Welcome to your new home, at least for a while. Shall we?"

Excitement weaved through her as they strolled in. Senses at full alert, she gasped at the inner courtyard. Tranquil and inviting as it was, the water babbling at the statuesque fountain was soothing to her ears as the sweet smell of blooming magnolias wafted through the air. It was delightful as cozy metal tables, chairs and beautiful tile work surrounding the entire inside walls.

"This is your permanent home?"

"Indeed, it is. Come on, our parcels have been left in our rooms. I have you on the opposite side of me." She led the way up an outside set of stairs and through double-wide French doors. "Our rooms open up to this corridor. Remember, even though we secure the gates at night, you need to make sure you lock your doors as well."

"I will. This is gorgeous. I may never want to leave."

She set her bags down, unwrapped the parcels and began hanging the new dresses.

"I'll leave you to it then. If you pull the cord over there next to your bed, a servant will come help with anything you need. As soon as you are through, lock the doors and come through the interior hall. Take a left down the stairs and another into the morning room. I will meet you there with tea and snacks. That should tide us over until supper."

"Molly, I can't thank you enough. This is just lovely."

"Honey, you are going to be real busy, real soon, so enjoy it."

With everything neatly packed away and her bags in the mahogany armoire, Sam pulled the drapes, clicked the locks and exited the room. The hallway was light, airy and decorated in soft pastels. She found the morning room quickly stepping aside as a handsomely dressed servant dashing out clutching an envelope tightly in his white knuckled hand.

Grinning, she entered the plush parlor. "Yeah, I just saw your man looking none too happy."

"He will get over it. I've sent him on this type of an errand a few times. He's always worried he will not return and no one will know how to find him." She laughed softly. "Hugh, has been with me since I bought this place and would do anything for me. This sets his teeth on edge. Come sit. I have goodies."

As they chatted away for the next hour, Hugh, reappeared knocking on the door then reentered the room.

"Madame Molly, that woman is spooky. I say it every time. She handed me a note before I could give her yours. Seems she expected your request in advance, creepy woman."

"Thank you. Would you please have the carriage brought along the rear? We will be leaving shortly."

Molly stood taking out a small pistol from the top desk drawer and put it in her reticule.

"You are all set, right?"

"Yes, I am. Oh, my goodness. My nerves are on edge. Cripes, she's going to know I'm scared like bloody hell before I even arrive! By the way, what did the note say?"

"She's expecting us, that's it. Shall we?"

They slid into the carriage as the driver closed the door hiding them from pedestrians. Both settled back on opposite seats against the plush leather. Several minutes ticked by in silence, each in their own thoughts, when the coach halted.

"The driver will wait here just in case it's dark when we get back. Come on, we have a boat to catch."

Sam eyed the rowboat curiously recalling a time not that long ago when she was sitting in one watching for whom she believed was Gunner. Her mind drifted to him. What was he doing now? Where was he? With Lafitte or back at the tavern with that wench?

As the oarsman slowly rowed them up river, the air transformed into thick and steamy. Sam's stomach lurched up to her throat. Glancing down in near horror, she watched a long, poisonous snake weave its way downstream. When a gator slid off the bank into the murky water toward them, she nearly passed out in earnest.

She could whack a man in the ribs, stab him and even hit one over the head leaving him lifeless and unconscious. But the thought of her being swallowed up by that snake or thrashed and chewed up by the alligator, had her biting a lower lip.

Emotions played heavily across Sam's features as she contemplated today's visit deep into the bayou of the infamous swamp witch.

As the boat slid up against the nutrient rich grassy bank, she woke up as if in a deep trance. The oarsman helped them ashore, tied the boat to an overhanging branch, then stepped under a tree and lit up a smoke.

She could tell he knew this drill well enough. It was time to wait.

Sam clutched Molly's arm tightly, nearly causing her to blurt out to ease up. Cats seemed to appear out of nowhere, not all black as Sam had imagined. Their throaty chatter sent ripples of concern up both their spines. Hissing, they dispersed in several directions, vanishing into the cover of thick brush. Sam swatted at a bug on her neck, flicking it to the ground, stomping it in a very unladylike manner, as sweat from the humidity grew on an upper lip. Face moist to the touch, she felt her unruly hair. It had now coiled into an ugly mess.

The solid old Cyprus door swung open, but no one was there. As they stood on the stoop, both mouth agape, a hand came out encased partially by a ruby red robe. But, it was the strong voice that surprised Sam the most. She had expected a creaky, frightening one.

"You," she pointed to Sam, "come in. Molly, you stay put on the porch."

Sam shook as Molly disengaged her grip, giving a bit of a shove.

"Go, Sam."

Walking into the room, looking around, her brows drew in as a frown formed. It was warmly lit with candles and sunlight. Suddenly, optimism filled the air.

"I surprised you, didn't I? But I admit, Samantha Arnesen, I wanted to see you in person and have been looking forward to meeting you for a long time. Here, sit across from me so I can read your eyes."

She slid onto a wooden chair, clasped hands as their eyes locked. They were the darkest unreadable orbs she had ever seen.

"Come now, dear, you need not fear me. I know more about you than you think. My sister, Anna, told me you would be coming to New Orleans. Not all your journey here is to assist Lafitte. Let me hold your right hand."

Shaking slightly, Sam held it out forcing confidence she did not feel at all right now. Then realization dawned. So, the Tinker and swamp priestess were sisters?

This whole situation just went from frightening to bizarre in zero to sixty.

The room went quiet as the old woman moved her fingertip over the lines, stopping, contemplating, when at last she finally began.

Chapter Nineteen

The door creaked open as Sam came out, face blanched. Molly rushed to her side grabbing her just before legs gave way. Apprehensively, Molly glanced up at the old woman as their eyes fastened on one another.

"She has a lot to digest." Was all that was said before she slipped back into the shadows and closed the door.

Silence prevailed on the walk back as Sam's hand clutched Molly's arm tightly.

Sam glanced up noticing Hugh was waiting, having heard their approach. She was grateful no words had been uttered along the walk, nor now. As they all got back into the boat, she drifted off in time hardly realizing until the boat was being pulled up on shore, that they had returned.

"When we get back do you want a tray sent up? Anything in particular?"

Sam stepped down from the carriage as the door was opened.

"No. Aren't we going out to that swanky place you were talking about? We have time to wash and change before, don't we?"

They entered the rear courtyard.

"It's unavoidable, Sam, I'm going to ask you questions. But, I can see that now is just not the time. When you are ready, meet me in the study. It is opposite the morning room. Bring a shawl. It will get cooler. I expect we will be out late tonight."

Sam nodded disappearing behind a potted palm frock. With a quick glance, she took the stairs at a run. Unlocking the door and closing it with a boot, she jumped onto the beds downy comfort. Damn, that experience was stranger than being with the tinker.

Would he believe what she had just been told?

Did she?

Pulling on the cord she rang for her handmaid. Who was smart enough to show up with two gents in tow carrying hot water. As they exited, she slid into the hot water. It was just enough to shock the senses and reboot an overloaded brain.

Now, a whole hell of a lot made sense. Even Adam. Having the next two days free was going to be a needed benefit. A focus on her purpose. Making it clearer. She rose as the maid toweled the water off. Wrapping up her hair, Sam slid into the newly purchased, illegally imported, silk stockings.

"Manny, there's nothing like a lady putting on a pair of these lovelies that alters a whole mood. Do you own any?"

"Oh, no, mistress, I surely do not!"

"Go into the top drawer and pick yourself out a set. When you go back to your room tonight, you put them on. Then you will know what I am talking about in earnest."

The maid stared at her with bulbous eyes.

"Mistress?"

Sam laughed. "I'm not crazy at all. Even though I am aware the whole household knows I went to see the old crone on the bayou today. Now, be a good girl and do as I say. Take a pair. If anyone questions you, send them to me. I will take care of it."

As she tied her boots, shawl handbag and gloves, a smugness took over watching the maid. Good, the girl was following instructions. It was a priceless moment for Sam,

"You have the night off. When we get back I will take care of my needs. Go and do something fun. You hear?"

She pulled the door closed leaving the maid to clean up. When she entered the study, Molly had two shot glasses out filled with amber liquid.

"If that's rum I may pass. It caused me havoc last night. That is for damn sure."

"Ah, Sam is back…" she patted the swooning seat beside her chair. "It's not. We get this from Lafitte on his ventures to Mexico. It's referred to as Tequila. Have you ever tried it amongst your journey's?"

Sam groaned. It was her modern world poison of choice. It along with a few beers, would probably land them in jail. Or enslaved on some rogue ship toward the southern Caribbean islands. Who the hell cared anyway. Tonight, was ladies' night out and they deserved it.

She took the crystal glass in hand and held it up.

"You are a novel woman, Sam, of that I am sure. Let us raise glasses at our successful day of shopping, making it out of the swamp and the laughs to follow. To good friends." They clunked glasses swigging back.

"Oh, that's smooth. How about another because I have one more toast."

"I'm game." Molly filled the glasses again. "The floor's yours, Samantha."

With a somber face, she raised it.

"Here's to the men we love, here's to the men that love us. If the men we love don't love us, fuck them all and drink to us."

Molly burst out laughing, glasses touching.

"You are going to have to repeat that a few times to me, so I can share that with a few of my acquaintances."

"Can do. But, no word of the source. Long ago I had two very close friends and we traveled together all the time. Back then, we certainly lived by that mantra!"

She grinned, nodding.

"The carriage is awaiting us. Shall we go? Ricardo's should be entertaining by now. Great New

Orleans music and a fine dinner are awaiting. Just be warned, this is not ball room dancing. Get prepared for grabbing hands. This place is barely one step up from last night. Keep your wits if you saunter off."

"After experiencing the tavern, I'm using all my senses. Which may be a bit dulled by both those shots. Oh, this will be fun. Damn fine Tequila, Molly. We'd better get out of here before I do one more and we settle in and get drunk."

Rising, they went outside.

"Will Lafitte or Griffin be there?"

"You are feeling spunky, aren't you? No, I don't think so. Word on the street was they had cargo to move. Your man was helping Lafitte. He has new contacts lined up. It appears the last two disappeared rather quickly. But you will like this one, Sam. I heard that a certain wench wanted to run along with them on this trip. To keep your man busy. But, Lafitte stepped in and said no damn woman would be on his ship without one for every man. Then I heard he asked if she was up to the task. I guess she decided not to pursue it further."

They both laughed.

"Okay, funny enough. But, I refrain from comment on that one. If he decides he needs to use her to gain an advantage that's important, then he should. So long as I am oblivious to it, I mean. Anyway, what happened to the double agents? Did they get away with it?"

"No, they set up cargo to be confiscated, arranged it to be sold and it was all bogus. Lafitte took them on a bit of a ride up the river and, well, they haven't been seen since."

She nodded, now understanding. "Good, I'd like a bit of time before I see him again."

"The crone, did she frighten you?"

"Actually, she opened up my eyes to a lot of things."

"I hope she told you he loves you. Even my eyes can see he does."

Sam smiled lowering her gaze, but would not say a word. Molly leaned forward as if she knew in the dark night exactly where they were.

"If we get separated, make sure you don't go outside with anyone. There's much amiss about this night. I can feel it. Stay alert"

"The old crone got to you too. Even though you did not sit with her, eh?"

"No, this is New Orleans; mischief flows through the streets just as much as voodoo magic. You will recognize the difference when we get in there."

As if on cue, the carriage halted and the footman helped them out. Molly parted with final instructions.

"Three a.m. no later. We will be right here."

Taking Sam by the arm, they strode inside. Sweeping her eyes around the room. A smile formed as she surveyed the gas lit lamps, dark mahogany tables, thickly padded wooden chairs and crisp linen. How bad could it be, she pondered, looking at the lovely fine china and tableware.

"Is this for real?" she whispered, as the *maitre d'* nodded to Molly. They followed him to a table neatly tucked into a cozy alcove. Perfect, here they could chat unabated by nosey neighbors with ears listening in.

"Sam, you can have Cuban, Creole, Spanish and island food. But try to avoid anything with a heavy wine sauce. Regrets will come later if you mix that with drinks." She winked.

"Where does the wine come from?"

"Lafitte would have to tell you. Next time you see him, you ask."

Giggling, Sam lowered her face leaning closer to Molly. "This is utterly too much enjoyment. Don't look now, but we are being watched. I wonder what's going through all those inquisitive minds?"

"Yes, no one here knows you were a tavern wench last night. Tonight, tongues will wag believing you to be an aristocrat having just arrived. A steamy socialite with a large pocketbook. Be diligent. There are snakes here as well as the in the bayou swamps."

"Shit, I recognize those two over there. I saw them last night in the tavern. Oh, damn. This gets worse. I see someone else I have had previous dealings with."

Tilting her head right, Molly glanced over.

"I've seen them as well and I know where and when. They were there last night. All of them. Are they following you Sam? Surely this is no coincidence."

"Savoy, I know him as Savoy. I've had a few run-ins with him. I need to find out what they are up to."

"You will have your chance tomorrow night. All three of them along with your gent, Lafitte, and many diplomats from New Orleans will be at the poker game."

"Perhaps. But I will have a word with him before then."

Their dinner arrived as they kept the conversation light and flowing. Their minds engaged in different ways.

Molly signed the bill as both rose placing the linen napkins on top of the table.

"Through that hallway by their table is the entrance to the nightclub. Most of the so-called ladies in this room are not allowed entry; it could prove scandalous. Truth be told, it's because their husbands go in there and send them home in carriages. Otherwise, they would not be able to truly enjoy themselves with their mistresses, or gents. Whatever the flavor is." She let that trail off.

"Oh, *risqué.* I say. Well? What are we waiting for?"

As they strode along she made eye contact with Savoy. A silent message passed between them. It was as if she was daring him to follow.

He enjoyed dares.

As the double wide door closed, they found a table close to the stage and small dance floor. Yeah, this was hardly Saturday night rocking the Casbah. It was seedy, dangerous and just where she wanted to be. This was the real beat of New Orleans after dark.

They ordered up drinks. Sam picked hers up, nodding to Molly as they scoped out the interior inhabitants. A quartet walked up on stage, picked up their instruments and began playing a whizzing jazz piece as Sam's hand was grabbed. Swinging around, she found her hands in the iron tight grip of none other.

Savoy.

Surely tonight he was going to put her to the test.

"Shall we wait for a slower one?"

"Nope, this suits me fine."

As that piece ended, a much slower one took its place as the floor suddenly teemed with pairs.

"So, mistress, what has you in New Orleans? Seems our paths keep crossing. Now a gent like me can't help but wonder why that may be?"

Would a double fist to the ribs or a knee to the balls be appropriate about now? Sam internally contemplated which as a lethal grin formed.

His eyes narrowed.

"Stop plotting to maim me. I think we need to come to a kind of truce. I mean not to detain you. But I am quite sure we need each other's help."

"Now, why would I believe you? I've escaped from you a time or two and more recently hit you pretty hard and left you to your own devices."

He grinned, a devilish one at that. It worked, softening her resolve a bit. Damn, he was an enigma!

"I've never tried to hurt you, mistress, it's been entirely one way."

She knew that was true.

"So, do we have a temporary one?"

She locked horns with him until the tune ended.

"Can I get back to you on that?"

He took her hand into the crook of his arm as he walked back toward the vacant table.

"Just where are the blokes you were with at dinner? Are they no longer here?"

"No, they had prior arrangements. But they will be at the game tomorrow night. I understand you will as well."

She leaned toward him. "How the hell do you know all of my plans? Do you have someone following me?"

"I think you already know the answer to that and are the one baiting me, Samantha."

"Fine, I'm not in the mood for any of your antics. If I decide to join forces with you, I will give you a nod tomorrow night when I see you. Are you sure they don't recognize me from the tavern?"

"No, it was dark and they were deep in conversation. I'm sure all dolled up like you are now, they would never think you were that tavern wench." He chuckled, grinning roguishly.

"Oh, shut up."

She released her hand from his arm and swished away without so much as a goodbye not seeing the smug look of satisfaction on his face.

She sat down, smiling. That had gone exactly as planned. Perhaps a bit too neat and tidy. Yes, she'd work with him. It was important to make him believe they were on the same page, so more information could be gathered. Plus, he was her ticket to the other two gents. Yup, she needed Savoy. Damn if his timing was not perfect.

"So, I think we've accomplished all our goals this night," Molly asked. "Do you agree? Shall we head out? It's near three."

Sam rose taking her cloak. A sly smile hovering across her lips.

Yes, I want to make sure I get plenty of sleep for our main event."

"Absolutely, it's going to be quite a dandy. These old bones can feel it. You get up tomorrow when you are ready. Make sure to keep to the courtyard just in case. We can dine at seven before leaving to go to the club and Sam, wear the periwinkle dress. It's quite grand. We all want you to stand out."

"Oh, Molly, after all of this ends will our paths cross again? I've really enjoyed getting to know you."

"Probably not, but you never know. Maybe a visit back to the crone is in order so we can be enlightened?"

"I'll pass." she grinned. "You can go. Wow, that was a quick ride back. Good, I'm beat and looking forward to that plush bed I can evaporate into."

"Sleep well, Sam."

"You too. Thank you again. For everything."

Nodding at the top of the stairs, they parted ways.

Chapter Twenty

Sauntering into the kitchen unannounced, Sam quickly realized the error of her ways. Indeed, it was not Ard Aulinn where roaming free as a bird was allowed and completely tolerated. There, the staff just turned an eye to her comings and goings.

"Mistress, did you ring for your maid and she not come?"

She plopped a cherry into her mouth.

"Oh, no, I was just strolling and thought I'd come in and see what I could wrestle up for a snack to take out in the courtyard."

The two cooks eyed her briefly.

"What would you like? We will have it brought to you."

It was clear the emphasis was on 'you.'

"Bread, cheese, fruit and meats will do. Nothing too fancy and a pot of tea please."

She nodded knowing a hasty retreat was in order. Quickly, she caught up with Molly, who was holding some paperwork and appeared headed toward the study.

"Ah, you made it. When I get in I'll ring for some food brought to you. Would you like it served here?"

"Well, here is the thing. I screwed up and went in there already. Now, I am properly chastised and put in my place." She giggled. "I now know where I do and don't belong."

"Serves you right for crossing that boundary. Even I don't go in there.

"Yes, I've been sternly disciplined by your staff."

Watching her disappear inside the study. Sam picked just the right spot to sit. Viewing the street and the hub of activity brought much needed diversion at a time when it was needed. The fountain's water cascaded over forming a pool and the sound was indeed soothing as a palm tree provided shade.

Placing her feet up on an opposite chair, she hastily removed them sitting ramrod straight. Damn, she thought, this was the land of pirates, voodoo and lusty men. Yet she felt she needed to be more prim and proper here than back in Victorian England.

Attentive on her approach, the servant brought a large tray of food.

"Thank you. I'll serve myself. I'll leave this here when I am through so you can take it back to the kitchen."

She smiled, hoping to relay an apology of sorts for having crossed that imaginary boundary earlier.

"Thank you, mistress. I appreciate that." The maid curtsied hurrying away.

Diving in completely famished, Sam stuffed her mouth while watching the comings and goings out on the busy street. It was enjoyable indeed being smack dab in the middle of the Quarter. Off in the distance, the air filled with the sounds of clarinets and horns. Yes. The city was wakening up from the previous night's slumber.

Stomach filled, happy, sipping on the hot tea, she decided the hell with it. Those boots went up on the opposite chair as she poured another cup.

Mentally, a picture formed on how tonight's events should unfold. Toying with it over and over, a plan formed. Sam felt confident it would work. There would only be one opportunity to fulfill this passage. On top of that, a big decision had to be made. There was no way out now.

Lips slimming into a firm line, eyes narrowing, determination rose as her spirit matched. Yes, now she understood what needed to be done.

Molly suddenly plopped down in one of the other chairs producing a green concoction.

"Want one of your own?"

"Is that the infamous mint julep? If so, I'll pass. One thing I never touch is colored drinks; they can make for a fun time until they wear off. Then its hell to pay in the head."

"Damn true. What's on your mind? You were deep within your own thoughts."

Sam leaned close. "I'll tell you more in the carriage tonight on our way to the game." She sat back in her chair. "I decided on the periwinkle dress. You were right. It is a good choice. What time do we leave?"

"We need to be there by nine. Basically, we hover all night around our dedicated tables, ensuring the servants keep the drinks filled. There will be a lot going on. Your focus is different than mine. Only you know what that is. Money will flow like the alcohol. Don't bc astonished at who arrives. A few familiar faces from the history books will be there."

"Can I make sure I'm assigned to the tables where Savoy and his cohorts will be seated?"

"Already taken care of."

Locking eyes with Molly, Sam raised a brow. "Will the mistress be there?"

She laughed. "Ah, the green monster does live in you. No, she will not. A more comfortable place for that wench is in the tavern. We'd not want her about on such an important night as this, now would we?"

"True. I do not see you in my future after tomorrow."

"Correct. I will miss you. It has been fun having you about."

Sam reached over and squeezed her hand. "There won't be time later so thank you for everything. Will you take care of my things left behind?"

"Yes, already have a place for them. Indulge me for a moment. I need to know something. Do you have everything in case later you find an unexpected situation has come about?"

Sam laughed. "I'm prepared. Do you think we should start to get ready? It's going to take the maid a few hours to finish my hair. Those Parisian hairdos are quite the rage, but I'm not going with that awful powder in it. Don't be startled when you see me."

Molly stood grinning. "And I'd expect you no other way than doing your own thing. Have at it no matter what. You will stand out in any room, especially tonight."

Reaching over, Sam hugged her tightly just before leaving to go up to her room. Swinging open the doors, she was greeted by the servant.

"Mistress, I have your bath ready, dress pressed. But, we'd better hurry. It will take quite a long time to wash, dry and curl your hair."

"Okay. I know it is a bit tardy of me. But, what is your name?"

"It is Sofia, mistress."

Taking the sponge and lathering it, Sam cleansed then handed it over so she could do her back and neck. "That's a pretty name. How old are you?"

"Twenty, mistress."

"Did you enjoy the stockings?"

She grinned raising the skirt up a few inches, producing one silk stockinged leg.

"Indeed. They are just like you said. Completely wonderful."

"Well, how about another little gift. I am leaving soon and won't be able to take everything with me. I want you to pick out a day dress along with petticoat. Write down where you live so I can have it boxed and sent. I can assure you no one will question how it was obtained. I will not accept no for an answer, Sofia. I insist."

"Oh, honestly? Well, all right then, I will! It will bother my two other sisters and shall be worth it. They will be quite jealous I received a gift!"

"Good, then it's settled. Now hand me that warm towel. I will dry off while you take care of the rest. I need to get this whole ordeal done with."

Sitting at the dressing table, Sam was amazed at what had to come next. "Mistress, we need to put your gown on now. It is time to do your hair."

Luscious yards of silk slid down over her shoulders settling in a voluptuous heap at her hips to feet. Sofia buttoned while Sam lowered the top so it rested above the shoulders. A puff filled with lavender pearl powder was the finishing touch. Oh, how she wished this could be taken along when it was time to go. Extravagant, yes, but for this night it was entirely worth it.

"Your skin glows like a full moon rising up over the river."

"It does. Why don't you take it tonight? I cannot chance it in my satchel. If for some reason it opens, it will make a bloody mess of the rest of my things. I can always buy another when I get resettled."

"Oh, I was going to say I can't take any more. You have already been so generous. But, I will take that."

Sam laughed sitting back down. For the next two hours, Sofia worked magic on her hair. It was piled high with sassy ringlets swaying and one unruly but delicious curl lying softly down her back. Slipping on the amethyst and diamond earrings, bracelet and ring she borrowed from Molly, Sam dabbed lavender rose oil onto the pulse points. Later, the groomsman would retrieve these gems and bring them back to her.

"Well, shall I do?"

Silk swirled as she marveled at the reflection shining back from the mahogany floor mirror.

"You are lovely, mistress. Here, take your gloves and shawl."

Sam set the gloves back down.

Sofia gasped.

"No worry tonight. I am going to set a new fashion trend. I want to show off my beautiful jewelry. The gloves can stay behind. I will not need them."

Placing the shawl over her shoulders, Sam swung wide the double balcony doors throwing over her shoulder,

"Please lock everything and do not forget to set out what you want. I've sent a note to the housekeeper what's left on the bed will be sent to your address. Write it out and leave it on top of everything. And Sofia, thank you."

Not awaiting a reply she closed the door. Lifting the hem up from the ground, she walked down the stairs and outside to where Molly was already sitting. A gloved hand reached out, extended, as *de ja vu* took over. It was a time recalled when Mrs. H did the same thing. That was then. In his England. Now, new business needed to be concluded.

A deep saturated smile lifted Sam's lips while clasping that hand. Climbing in and sitting comfortably, the door closed as the coachman drove the horses on.

"I can tell you are ready. Your gaze says it all. This will be our last chat, Sam, anything you want to ask before we get there? We only have about fifteen minutes."

"No, but I want to thank you for setting up my meeting with the crone. I know now who asked you to do that and why. I have more than one task that befalls me that's crucially important over the next twenty-four hours."

They clutched hands.

"You left your gloves on purpose, didn't you? Oh, dear girl, I'm going to miss you a lot! We'd really paint this town bright red if you were here longer."

"I think we can still do a bit of painting tonight, don't you?"

"Lass, I'm just along for the ride. It's your show completely."

As the carriage came to a halt, Sam was assisted down first. Glancing up at the three-storied antebellum home, she realized they had quickly reached the outer perimeter of the Quarter. Drapes were drawn, but light was creeping out from behind, as she lifted her dress up a bit and was escorted inside by a handsomely dressed attendant.

"Mistresses, welcome. Follow me and I'll show you your stations and who will be under your management this evening. We have a full house. It's the who's who of society and government. With an added tip for flare with a few, umm, privateers thrown in for good measure."

The adrenaline heightened throughout her system as she observed Molly being escorted by a very handsome gent; one whom she already had engaged in a lively conversation.

"Mistress Samantha, these four tables are under your care. A quick nod to either of your two attendants will bring them quickly to your side. They will be responsible for delivering drinks and smokes to your section."

"When do they start to arrive?"

The shawl slid off as he retrieved and took care of it.

"In about thirty minutes. Walk around and get yourself familiar. Should you need to have a few minutes to yourself at any time during the evening, just make eye contact with me and I'll send backup."

"Excellent. Is that water?"

"Yes. It will be filled when you need it. Remember, there is no eating on the floor. If you are hungry, we have small snacks in the back hallway away from normal traffic. You can help yourself." He nodded, heading off then stopped briefly to chat with the gent with Molly.

As the two ladies' eye's locked, Sam smiled. Very happy her friend was situated in the next group. Sipping on the cool water, it was settling against the increasing warmth of nerves pulsating through her stomach.

Refraining from anxiety was not easy. Especially as the two guys from the tavern stood at the entrance. Their eyes raked Sam's attire. Under normal circumstance, that would have pissed her off. But, it was a clear indication, and a good one, they had not recognized her at all.

Taking their order as they sat, she nodded passing it off to the servant nearly laughing at how fast he hurried to get their booze.

Suddenly, the room filled with electricity.

Swinging around, Sam knew well before the ruckus hit the infamous Lafitte had arrived. Entourage in tow. They dispersed to separate tables. As if dividing they could conquer more, save one.

Years ago, when planning a visit to the Jazz City, Sam had googled places of interest and discovered much about the sea fairing Captain Lafitte. Including some artistic renditions. He was that mirror image. Handsome and roguish as he sauntered toward her.

There was a tour of his haunts, so to speak, she had taken and enjoyed immensely. Funny how knowing about him then brought her closer to understanding how he operated now.

It all made sense.

But where that tour left off, he began.... She was trying in vain to suppress a giggle.

His eyes rested on the handsome lass, smiling devilishly all along his short walk to where she stood. A hand roughly grabbed an arm halting forward progress.

"Lafitte, don't even go there."

"Ah, my friend. She is the one you've been searching for. But, I could swear to the swamps witches she's the tavern wench."

His eyes gleamed raking over her attire so boldly. Yet, with a familiarity only a lover truly knew.

"Ah, damn."

Adam swatted him on the back moving toward his chair, a roguish smile hovering on his face.

Seated, Cuban cigars lit, drinks served, Sam had every intention on causing chaos tonight as she leaned just close enough to him, eyes tempting, taunting, then moved away.

"She must keep you busy, my friend."

"More than I can say."

Both men belted out in laughter as she moved over near Savoy's associates happy Adam and Lafitte's banter had not been overheard.

Here was a conversation she wanted to hear.

"He should be here shortly. Still, we need the room to fill up before taking the document."

"Agreed. But doing this under the nose of Lafitte? As I said time and again, I'm still not sure this is the right move. I think it's a bit too risky?"

"Not at all. Here we can maneuver with more freedom and less observation than if we were just out on the street in some dark alley or in one of the taverns. You know he has spies all over the city. Here he has no idea who we are. Look at him. Completely oblivious and relaxed. Just what we want."

"Well, we both know how he' has contacts all over. There is the proof. The governor just arrived and I can bet you he's not sitting at our table."

Sam had no clue what their names are, but needed little more from them. Moving away, she needed to make sure the timely arrival of the governor was met with satisfaction. The astute waiter already had his drink of preference set before him. At Lafitte's table. As she passed by, he glanced up, momentarily taking in her beauty then finished engaging the gents at the table at how pissed off his wife was she could not attend.

Sam grinned, weaving around the outside perimeter of tables glancing quickly at Adam. Damn the man! His eyes were burning the clothes off her back!

Turning toward another table, Savoy came into focus weaving through the now smoked infused room. Nodding at him as he passed, she escorted him towards his two tavern associates. Leaning down, Sam placed a bourbon on the rocks beside his right hand, lightly grazing it as their eyes locked briefly. She knew he understood.

Doors opened as several dealers came out opening fresh decks of cards at each of their tables. The night of gaming was officially under way. Hours they played. Voices grew louder as the alcohol flow increased like the water pounding over Niagara Falls.

But time was of the essence and quickly running out. Something had to happen soon. Finally, it was one of the two men she had been observing closely that got it rolling along.

“Jackson, I call.”

Eyes squinting, the other threw a silent dare out to the entire table.

"What’s it going to be.” He glanced over to his companion and grinned knowing he won this round.

“Someday I’ll spit on your grave. Mark my word on it, Lee.” There was a deafening pause at their table as he toyed with a choice. “Dammit, fine. I take the bait. I call.”

Simultaneously, both flipped over their cards. The others at the table having folded theirs over in defeat.

Jackson slapped the table forcing cards to fly. He quickly realized his friend had pulled a fast one. “Damn, you shithead. I was sure to have you dead to rights in a bluff and you threw one over on me. Good move, ass.”

Laughing, hitting both on the back, Savoy stood as the chair grated against the wooden floor.

“Deal me out of this round. I’ll return shortly.”

As Sam observed, smiling, Molly seemed to have a different plan for him. Hardly a klutz, she bumped into him slightly, the contents of a glass full with whisky landing on his suit jacket.

"Pardon me, sir, I do apologize. You," she pointed towards an attendant, "bring a warm cloth. Quickly now. I've spilled a drink on this gentleman. One up until now was having such great luck."

Savoy indulged humored by the move.

Molly nodded as Sam walked by stopping to look over a shoulder. Leaning in to pick up empties between Lafitte and Adam, a strong, yet familiar hand slid up a thigh. It halted when it was met by the strap engulfing a knife. Just as quick as that, he slid it back down.

Really? Had she felt that? Glancing at him with a twinkle in her eyes, Sam shifted out of reach and moved away.

Adam sat back watching, eyes roaming up Sam's delicious backside. What a surprise was in store for her later. Surely the lass had seen it too. What Molly had done? Picking up the refreshed drink, he refocused attention on Savoy, who had returned to his gaming table. Leaning slightly towards, he was trying to catch an earful of the conversation taking place with the men there. What he heard next was music to his ears.

"Did you decide not to leave it?" Jackson asked quietly.

Savoy threw him a quick glance. "No, I thought the incident of the drink being spilled on me may be a diversion." Pulling the chair in, Savoy swiftly moved the document into Jackson's hands. His job was now done. Well, almost.

"Deal me in," Savoy said, glancing quickly at Sam. "The night's winding down. It may be too late to recoup my losses. You gents seem to be damn lucky tonight."

Relief swept through Sam at Savoy's silent acknowledgement. But, now she was in a true dilemma at which cat to chase first?

Savoy? Lafitte? Adam? Jackson and Lee?

She needed all of them!

A bell rang signaling the gamers that the night's events had ended. Shortly, the room started to clear out as servants cleaned up tables. Lines of carriages formed outside as gentlemen shook hands and headed in that direction.

Sam was already following behind a group of them then noticed Molly's servant.

"Oh, hello. You are the mistress groomsman? Please make sure you place this in her hands right away." She handed him a small pouch containing the borrowed jewels.

"Indeed, I was advised earlier to expect it. I see her coming out now. Pardon me, mistress, but I must go."

Both ladies' hands shot up in the air in a wave as Sam turned weaving between departing carriages. Waiting briefly, one rolled up, halted, a hand extended as she laughed. This was becoming a habit!

She got into Lafitte's carriage and sat opposite him as his hand released hers.

"Here." she slid onto his lap an envelope. "You will want to look at this now."

He ripped it open, unfolding a large piece of parchment.

"How the bloody hell did you get this?"

"That's not important. We must get back to your encampment as fast as possible. Time is not on your side while we just sit here. I know for a fact that fast on your heels, the militia is following. They only have one mission. To kill all your men, loot all your bounty and confiscate the Angelina.

Someone from your crew, Lafitte, has turned traitor on you and only I know who it is. Well, rather how to sniff him out."

Chapter Twenty-One

Lafitte banged roughly on the inside carriage roof. The driver hastened with quick action as it jerked into movement, pitching and rolling. Holding tight to the seat, Sam felt like her teeth were going to crack and fall right out of her mouth. The reverberation was so intense.

"Where is Griffin?"

He grinned. "I sent him up ahead on his stead. I wish I had been advised about this before. He could have ridden with orders. Then again, the knowledge of who this traitor is lies inside your pretty head, mistress."

"Anyone new to your party or disgruntled lately?"

"Aye, a few. So, it will be interesting to discover exactly who it is."

He eyed her keenly. "You must have a plan?"

She grinned, growing fonder of this handsome rogue pirate.

"I do. Are you willing to trust me completely? The fate of all of you hangs in the balance."

He locked eyes, clasping gloveless hands.

"You are steady, lass. Either you are a conniving wench, or Griffin has you pegged right and I must believe in you both completely."

"I'm here to help you. I give you my word and life on it."

"Okay, all that's good and fine." He removed a flask of rum and handed it to her. "Let us seal this alignment by sharing a drink."

It was a welcome sight to her as she swigged back a gulp, handing it back a cough spurted out.

"Yeah, took a bit much."

He laughed. "That wench Lucinda could very well be involved in this Samantha. I hope you don't mind my addressing you so informally?"

She shook her head. "I think you are right. A visit to her will be in order when this is done. Too bad we may not be here to see her face when you walk into that tavern. I wager she's expecting news of a dead man."

His eyes bore into hers. "What's your connection to Savoy?"

She took the flask right out of his hand and took another sip. "Finding a renewed fondness for this fiery liquid."

"You don't have to answer me. But Griffin will demand answers. You won't be able to keep his intentions at bay that long."

She shrugged her shoulders. "How much further? I hope we are close. My teeth are rattling around inside my head with this quick pace."

He knew the rum had settled nicely into her system.

"Okay, back to the business at hand. Is your entire encampment easily seen from where the coach will stop? I need it to be. I must have a full view of all your men. Shit, what if the one I seek is not there? I had not thought of that."

His grin grew.

"All of them were posted here tonight. If any of their snarly asses are missing, then they are dead men anyway. How will you point him out?"

"You leave that up to me." As she finished a final swig and handed it back to him, the carriage came to an abrupt stop. Not looking back, Lafitte stepped out shutting the door tight. From this vantage point, she could see the area well. The roaring fire was an asset. Yes, this worked as she quickly reviewed the entire encampment.

It took her no time to zero in on him.

Yes, she was right. Hand on the handle to get out, the opposite door opened as in slid Savoy. The cool steel blade of a sharp knife was pressed to her throat. Sam was rendered temporarily motionless. Quite in shock.

“Get out and go easy, mistress. Or, I slice up your pretty face. Then no man will want you."

Sam slid slowly as he shoved her forward. They both came into full view of the gathering as fear lit her eyes. Adam came out of the shadows, gun pointed right between the brows of Savoy.

Now it came down to this, who wanted to die more?

Silently, Sam’s eyes beseeched him, begging no shot be taken at this range. Especially with the type of gun he held. It was old. The shot accuracy sucked and she knew it from reading stories about them.

Seconds ticked by.

Finally, he lowered it slightly. Eyes dark as the blackest pool.

Lafitte glared at him. “Savoy, what the bloody hell are you doing here? What’s your grief with this woman?”

The air filled with tension.

Weapons were drawn.

A bat swooping by was heard so deafening was the silence.

But no one budged an inch.

“I’m feeling might generous tonight, Lafitte. How about the girl lives if you drop the keys to the storage barn at your boots? I’m giving you a chance. Kick them toward me now.”

Lafitte eyed him as if he was an errant child.

“You think the lass means anything to me? She may to Griffin, but not me. It’s not my issue.”

The whole group laughed except one man. It was what Lafitte had been waiting for, but could hardly believe who it was.

“Vashon?” Was all he said, approaching at swords length. “You bastard. Why would you do this to your men? A traitor to us all?”

Vashon panicked and pulled his pistol aiming it directly at Lafitte.

"If I go, so do you, my arrogant, bastard friend. All these years and you treat me no better than the hands that swab the deck. Equal divides of the loot, my ass! I am your first mate. I should have claimed a higher reward!”

Glancing briefly at Sam, amazed she knew of this all, Lafitte stepped into the pistol, daring him to pull the trigger. Anger grew in Vashon’s eyes. Hatred. Pure hatred.

A finger pulled back on the trigger, cocking it.

Suddenly out of nowhere, fast as lightning, a knife grazed his hand as the weapon dropped to the ground. Quickly set upon by two mates, Vashon realized he was fucked.

All eyes were suddenly on her as Adam aimed to shoot Savoy.

“No!” Sam Screamed, arms expanding out to block his frame.

“Madam, explain yourself! Now!”

“Well.” Turning, Savoy reached down, grabbed the knife and handed it over. He and Sam exchanged broad smiles. His gun and knife now tucked back inside his belt.

“Because he’s my brother, that’s why.” Sam spoke loud, proudly, out to them all.

Lafitte stopped, standing still, watching this escapade unfold. This woman was much more than a chit to be reckoned with. Hell, more than any three men could handle. He glanced over at Griffin, face tied up in a knot, trying to figure this all out.

Lafitte broke out in laughter.

“Men, while they sort out their business let’s get the ship down river and out to open water. Looks like we need to find a new place right away! You three, do you need my carriage to take you to someplace safe, or seek passage on my ship?"

Adam lowered his pistol and in short strides was standing with Savoy and Sam.

"I don't know what the fuck is going on here, but there's a lot of explaining to do. If you are not a part of this," he jabbed a finger into Savoy's chest, "advise what needs to be done and be quick about it."

"Oh, the militia will be looking for me in a fiery hurry. Especially when they realize the locked barn is empty and the ship and Lafitte are nowhere to be found. I say we run like hell and board, they are preparing to ship off. I can explain the rest on the fly!"

Sam hoisted her skirts way above lady-like level and ran just as fast as they did, out of breath and smiling, just before the plank was tossed into the river.

The breeze picked up as the ship creaked, sails expanding moving it downriver. In the distance, the sound of hooves approaching was growing louder. In this darkness, they would not be able to locate the ship until they were at the opening of New Orleans harbor and well on their way out to sea. Once there, the fate of the first mate would swiftly be dealt with.

Sam marched over to Lafitte, smiling and held out one hand.

He grinned, a devilish one it was, then placed the flask in it.

I'll need it more than you. There's going to be a brawl and if I get damn good and drunk they won't be able to irritate me more than they have already."

He laughed pulling her up against him, kissed he fully on the lips, then released just as fast.

"Take it and keep it. My thanks to you, Mistress Samantha. Wait. Is there anything else I need to know before you all leave here?"

"Ah, yes there is. The two men setting this up with Vashon are with the British Militia. I do know their last names are Jackson and Lee. They were at the games earlier tonight sitting at Savoy's Table. I know you were keeping an eye on them. Make sure you become acquainted pretty soon."

As she turned to join her newly discovered brother and the man she loved, Adam's rough chest halted progress. He claimed her lips in a fierce kiss. Both breathless, he released Sam only when he felt he'd done just duty.

"Shall we head down the stairs now? It's time."

She glanced at them both and nodded, handing him the flask.

"Wait. Will we all end up back at the same place? Savoy, will you be there as well? We have a lot of things to discuss."

Adam looked down at her.

"Do you know something that I don't?"

"I'm not actually sure. The old crone told me my biggest decision was about to come and to pay attention to it. So now I'm actually nervous about leaving the ship."

Adam tried to reassure her, "We have to go, it's time. Either that or we pay the price and will all be stuck here. So, it's now or never, Sam."

She nodded, feeling with each step the anxiety mount as darkness suddenly engulfed her entire being. As her eye's fluttered, voices sounded in the distance.

But they were not familiar voices at all. Nor the accent.

It was Italian. Yes. That's what they were speaking. Furrowing her brows, a softer feminine voice penetrated her brain.

"Look, I think she's awaking. Her eyelids just moved."

Sam gingerly opened them.

Glancing in total dismay, growing sadness filled her heart. She was in a hospital room.

A hand lifted her head up offering a sip of water through a straw.

A straw! Damnit all to hell, she was in modern times.

“Oh, my, miss. We are so happy to have you back amongst us. It was a nasty fall you took at the *dei Frari*! Do you feel well enough to speak? To tell us your name? We did not find anything on you for identification.”

Sam tried to sit up but was refrained.

“No, you must rest. Can you tell us who you are?”

“Yes, Samantha Arnesen. How long have I been here?”

“Nearly ten days, dear. You had a nasty fall and have been in a coma since you were brought here by the good priest. Several days ago.”

Tears formed in her eyes. Oh, my God, she felt such horrible sadness. It had not been real. It had been a dream. A very awful, nasty one. Quite suddenly it overtook as she wept openly. Tears streaming down her cheeks.

“Oh, don’t cry.” The nurse was applying a cold compress to her warm forehead. “You are safe now and all is well. Is there anyone we can ring for you and tell them you are better?”

Sam shook her head no, not able to utter a word.

“How much longer do I need to stay? My home is in England. I’d like to go back there as soon as you say I am able.”

“I’ll let the doctor know you are awake right now. If you are okay with me leaving you? It is very important that you eat. We have had you on liquids for a long time. Without strength, the doctor will keep you.”

“Then bring me a pizza, spaghetti, I do not care. I am very hungry.”

She was not; the pit in her stomach was as large as a cantaloupe. Adam, Mrs. H, her newly found brother. It was all just a dream. She shook her head again, pushing the pillow higher.

Suddenly, she felt lifeless.

"Wait. Nurse, just so I know I am not nuts, it is 2015, right?"

She smiled back at Sam. "Yes, it is."

Thirty minutes later, she was eating a hearty meal when the doctor came in, took her vitals and evaluated her chart.

"If you can keep the food down and we remove the IV, I'll discharge you tomorrow night. But, all your tests need to come back clear."

Thankfully, they did.

The next afternoon, with money donated from an unknown source, Sam took the train from Venice to Paris, through the Eurostar Channel Tunnel to London. At last, she arrived back to her home in Exeter.

Sitting in her car, engine running, she started to laugh uncontrollably. Shaking her head to on one at all, she shifted the car through the gears and left the train station.

"Damn, that was one hell of a coma, that's for sure." She said loudly, flicking the car blinker on just before pulling into the driveway. Everything dropped onto the sofa while she took the stairs slowly, recalling how he had showed up in her bathroom and what followed.

"Stop it, Sam!" she yelled into the hallway. "He is not real, none of it was real!"

But just to punish herself more that night, she ran a bath, waited until the water promoted shriveling and shivers, before she toweled off, eyes pooling and climbed into bed.

It was a lonely bed. It was a lonely house. It was a lonely life.

Fluffing the pillows in frustration, she rose going room to room praying for some damn sign he had been there.

But found none.

Sliding back into bed, roughly pulling the covers up to her chin, she spent the whole night just staring out at the night sky.

Chapter Twenty-Two

Four days slid by as she moped about, hardly being able to get herself out of the cottage, except for the small enjoyment of cycling. Eyeing her laptop, she finally opened it up and noticed it was already on. How could that be? Surely having been gone for so long the battery would be dead by now?

Emails filled the screen. Most of little interest until one caught her eye. It was from ancestry.com. Suddenly, it dawned on her! Grabbing at a pile of paper on her desk, strewing them quickly, shoving them aside, one held high interest. It was from her parent's attorney. One she had reviewed a while ago then left forgotten.

Glancing toward the stairs, thoughts of the ruins haunted every thought. Feet hit the wooden floor.

Dressed, keys and bag in hand, she and the Spark sped off heading on the motorway toward Chester. It was getting late. Would she arrive at Adam's ancestral estate before it closed?

Pressing the accelerator down and watching closely for the police, hours later she was exiting off the byway toward *Ard Aulin.* The large National Trust sign showed their hours. The parking lot was empty. It was four-o'clock which meant thirty minutes to closing.

In the gift shop, she found an attendant.

"What time do the grounds close?"

"Half past four. I won't charge you if you want to roam until then. But, we lock the gates after that so make sure you are off the property."

Sam nodded heading around the familiar backside of the house and found the path she was looking for.

As the ruins loomed up ahead, suddenly her brisk pace turned into a steady run. There it was. Ivy had woven thickly as she pried enough apart until she could slip through the opening of the ruins.

As she descended, wave after wave of strong vibrations reverberated through her being. Even before she climbed up the other side, she knew it completely.

She was back!

Running, breathless, her lungs positively burning, Sam flung the kitchen door wide, stopped briefly with pure delight hugging both Mrs. H and Mrs. Lilly. Strange glances followed her backside as she disappeared from their sight down toward his study. She stopped in front of the door. Halting briefly, eyes filling with tears, it was then their voices could be heard.

Sliding the door open and stepping in, her eyes flew to his. Quickly the distance was closed between them as she launched into his arms, wrapped her legs around his waist and kissed him.

Minutes passed and neither cared.

A clearing of the throat could be heard as Sam pulled back reluctantly.

"Victor?" She slid her feet to the ground and slipped out of Adam's warm, strong arms to stand in front of her brother, clasping his hands.

"I thought you were lost to me." She turned as Adam stood next to her. "Both of you were lost to me forever."

"Samantha," Victor's voice quivered slightly so full of emotion, "we both thought the same of you. That had to be the big decision. When you arrived back in 2015 to Exeter, you had to discover whether it was real. Then make your choices. I am so happy to see you here." He grabbed her hand and hugged her tightly, then stepped aside.

"I want you to meet the rest of your family while you are at it. This is my wife, Melinda, and our two children Vincent and Louisa. She's got your middle name, sweet one."

Sam dropped down to her knees, throwing her arms wide as both seemed to feel how special she was.

"And how old are you two?"

"I'm five and my sister is three and we are going to have a brother or sister soon, Aunt Sam."

She reeled. Aunt Sam. Her heart swelled with love at hearing those words.

"You are? Well you are both going to have big responsibilities you know? Being an older brother and sister. Are you ready for that?"

She tickled them both, standing as their hands clutched hers. Walking over with them in tow, she spoke to Melinda.

"I'd hug you. But they are holding on so tight. I don't want to let them go."

Melinda reached in and hugged her.

"They seem to have the will of you both. Heaven help me with not knowing who this one will take after." She patted her protruding stomach.

Sam turned to Victor. "We have so much to catch up on. Where do you all live?"

He laughed, lifting his son into his arms as Adam lifted Louisa.

"Why don't we go eat and talk about it more there. I think now that you have returned so will our appetites."

He glanced at Adam, knowing he had not fared well since she disappeared.

"After we do, we will leave you two alone. Our place is close. I think some catching up is in order, but can wait a bit longer." He slapped Adam on the back. "We can reconvene tomorrow later in the morning, Sam. I wondered how long before it would take you to find out about me and our true past together."

"Well, Victor, you see that's the question I still have burning. It all started to dawn on me. But, there are still pieces of the puzzle I do not have. I acted quickly and drove here without reading what would explain more. Anyway, I will leave that up to you. One thing I want to know right now is how old I was when they gave you up?"

He grinned. "Three. They sent me to live with Aunt Irene, who you probably never met. She was Mom's sister, a renegade and well, just like you. If you know what I mean."

"So, this merry goose chase is about you both, right?" Adams arm was wrapped tightly around her shoulder.

"It involves a whole lot more than that, I can assure. Sam, this is just a beginning for you. One of which will hold many twists and turns."

"I suppose that will do for now. By looking at the kids' faces they are positively bored by our adult conversation. Right?"

"Well, I think so." Came Louisa's soft reply.

Sam laughed. "True we can do that pretty well. But, you may grow up and do that like us."

"Do I have to?"

Victor reached down to his daughter, flouncing a long braid and laughed with the others.

"We will see. You may have no choice."

As they finished their meal and a pie from town, Adam took the bull by the horns, standing and placing the napkin on his plate. Victor grinned, knowing his patience had evaporated and wanted nothing more than to have his sister alone.

At the door, they hugged. "I'll come by tomorrow afternoon and we can sit down and go over a few things, alright, Sam?"

"Yes, please do. I can't wait." He tugged on her hand once, then let it drift as they got into the awaiting carriage.

"I have to tell you the God's truth. That was one hell of a four days I just spent. And woman, I don't want to ever go through that again." He claimed her by the hand as they went in the large front doors.

"Times like this that make me wish your home was not so big, Lord Griffin. It will take us fifteen minutes to get to your chambers."

They both understood.

Finally, they arrived as he closed their bedroom door.

"It's our chambers and our home, not just mine, Sam." The blouse came up over her shoulders, plush breasts teaming over a silky French bra.

"Oh, I like this one."

Lifting his chin, their eyes locked. "No mind about that right now. I want to tell you three things in order of importance."

He stopped after unhooking her bra, sliding it off creamy shoulders.

"What, now?"

"Yes, now."

The shirt fell to floor as his britches followed suit.

"Go on." His voice was beyond gruff, he needed her and she knew it.

"Now don't get pissed off until you hear it all. First, this is your home. I don't have any clue where I will end up. But I know you will be a part of my life wherever I am. I decided if you ask me, I do not want to marry right now."

"What the hell?"

She held up a hand to silence him and for once he stopped. But, not without raising both eyebrows with a very stern look of disapproval.

"I like being your only mistress. It leaves no room for anyone else." She was smiling in that way that wound right around his heart. It was fruitless to balk at this right now. But, it would come up again, soon.

"Second, I'm going to be moving out. I paid for those renovations and I want to fully enjoy having you court me properly. As your continued mistress, of course, by visiting me at my own home. How much more convenient can I make it for you and still be happy if I am here on your lands, right?"

"Oh, now, wait a minute…"

"Thirdly, it's easy for the rest of the world to see this, but I need to make myself clear to you so you never have to think about it again. I am in love with you. Whether we marry someday or no day. I will always be with you until this world, of which I don't fully understand, dictates otherwise."

Pushing her backwards, they fell onto their large bed. "Is anything negotiable with you? It seems all the men you've blazed a trail with since you left Italy all have given me the same advice, love. That I will always have my hands full with you."

She grinned, never wanting to be anywhere without him and wondered what her future would bring. But, until more was disclosed, she was completely content for their relationship to be like it is.

"Well, what can I say, Lord Griffin, other than please, let's stop talking so we can make love properly. I've sorely missed you."

Her smile was slight, her eyes bright as he leaned down absorbing her further into his life, mind and body in a lovely, wonderful kiss.

"Oh." She pulled back attempting to add in one final thought. But this time he'd had enough of their chatter.

"No, Sam, no more until later. I love you. But, now we need this more than further conversation."

He moved inside of her as she wrapped her legs around his strong back and did indeed give him as he asked.

Chapter Twenty-Three

"Mr. Bruce, you and your son have done a magnificent job with all the renovations. I apologize for having been away for so long. It was unavoidable. All the same, I am so happy with the results." Handing him a velvet pouch brimming with sterling pounds. "I'll let you know if I see anything else I want done and thank you both again."

"Mistress, it's been our pleasure. We now have several positions lined up with great thanks to your recommendations in the village. We much appreciate you as well."

He tipped his cap to her as they finished loading up the carriage and headed down her dirt drive.

It was a great day. Sam was feeling on top of the world. The good people in the heavens had allowed her a bit of time off from passages. Perhaps to absorb it all.

Around the back, she followed a beautifully discovered path as it wove between roses, honeysuckle, lavender and foxglove all which would soon depart as fall gave leave to winter.

Moving toward the sounds of a babbling stream, she could hear a voice. It was faint, but with each forward step it gathered strength. Closing her eyes and raising her head upwards, Sam felt the warmth of the day against her skin and listened intently.

Interesting, she thought, continuing along the intricately designed stone path. Surely this was mother nature's creation. Reaching the other side, her smile grew. It was a short walk when she halted in front of a beautiful statue of the Egyptian Goddess, Isis. This gorgeous replica had been discovered during the renovations of the grounds and brought Sam much pleasure.

Who knew when or why this was placed here. No old documents had been discovered at the big house or at the cottage to lay claim to its history. But, she loved this area. Lately, she imagined hearing the wind carrying a delicate voice calling out her name to come here. Sit. Pay Attention.

Just beneath the base, a carved stone bench beckoned. It was here as Sam sat down, that a tremor started in her head and worked with mighty strength through to her toes. Gripping the cold sides, visions of places long ago played in her mind as she tried desperately to keep a balanced reality.

Then she heard her. A voice that was strong and commanding.

"You must listen to me. It is time. You are well prepared. Now, you must go."

Sam refused to open her eyes.

"He needs you more there than you are needed here. You must lay your past to rest and give him great peace. Otherwise, many will be destroyed if you do not move swiftly. Do not worry about what you leave behind. That which is yours will be, when you are ready to reclaim it."

Sam blinked, nodding, as she stood as if in a trance. Yet with each passing step back to the cottage, sensations of such a grand nature flourished throughout her being. Her soul was alive, spirit happy and mind reeling to a time so far back in her lives that she must have suppressed it for a purpose.

She could see visions of him. As clear as if it was a cloudless day in her mind's eye.

He was powerful, tall, rugged and handsome. With chiseled features and a strong will and heart. He was a warrior in the highest sense and had been her lover.

Bands of gold wrapped around his upper arms. His was a time steeped in the traditions of an ancient empire.

One so vast and superior, when it moved to the heavens and stars, all traits were scooped up by new races and religions.

Coming around the back of the cozy cottage, Sam spotted a note that had been placed by her maid on the table in the hall. Turning it over in her hand, she saw Adam's seal. Ripping it open, she read his print, smiling.

This was as the Gods would have it.

Perfect timing.

"Sam, I'm away for a while to Canada. I can't tell you when I will return. I see a trip coming for you. But not to where or for how long. If you depart before I return, send a note up so I can get it when I come back. Love, Adam."

She placed it back where it was left and journeyed up the stairs to change. Then returned to the kitchen and ate the food already prepared. Finished, dishes washed, dried and put away, she headed back to climb those stairs.

Then it started.

Eyes blurred as a lightness began, becoming so strong she felt like passing out.

At last at the top, moving as if in a dream, Sam reached for the bedroom door handle, turning it. As soon as she opened and walked in, it was clear.

She was no longer in England.

She was in Egypt. In a bar with a hell of a scene unfolding!

The End of the Beginning…

About Sandra Waine

Tucked away in small country home, Sandra Waine resides in Central New Hampshire with her cats, Irene and Marie. When not traveling and writing, she enjoys cycling, hiking and photography.

Social Media Links:

Facebook:
https://www.facebook.com/profile.php?id=100000000507104

Twitter: https://twitter.com/

Instagram: https://www.instagram.com/seattlewinenirvana/

Website: www.sandrawaine.com

Acknowledgements:

I wish to thank everyone throughout time for all the experiences I've had that have led me to this series. One person in particular I wish to thank is Laconia. My spiritual friend.

www.ingramcontent.com/pod-product-compliance
Lightning Source LLC
Chambersburg PA
CBHW051639260626
47170CB00004B/1247

* 9 7 8 1 6 2 5 2 6 5 0 9 8 *